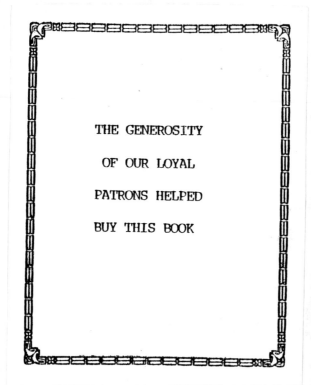

Nobody's Girl

A NOVEL BY *Antonya Nelson*

SCRIBNER PAPERBACK FICTION
Published by Simon & Schuster

SCRIBNER PAPERBACK FICTION
Simon & Schuster Inc.
Rockefeller Center
1230 Avenue of the Americas
New York, NY 10020

First Scribner Paperback Fiction edition 1999
SCRIBNER PAPERBACK FICTION and design are
trademarks of Simon & Schuster Inc.

Designed by Brooke Zimmer
Set in Monotype Baskerville
Manufactured in the United States of America

1 3 5 7 9 10 8 6 4 2

The Library of Congress has cataloged the Scribner edition as follows:
Nelson, Antonya.
Nobody's girl: a novel / by Antonya Nelson.
p.   cm.
I. Title.
PS3564.E428N6   1998
813'.54—dc21   97-34839
CIP

ISBN 0-684-83932-6
0-684-85207-1 (Pbk)

ACKNOWLEDGMENTS

Concerning this book, I'd like to thank the following people for their faith in it, good advice about it, and friendship during its writing:

Terry Boswell, Karen Brennan, Hamilton Cain, Emily Hammond, Ehud Havazelet, Laura Kasischke, Don Kurtz, Bonnie Nadell, Juliet Nelson, Jane Rosenman, Steven Schwartz, and, most especially, Robert Boswell.

Nobody's Girl

"She's fragile like a string of pearls,
She's nobody's girl . . ."

❧ *I*

"Miz Stone," the pregnant girl said in the way Birdy hated: here at Pinetop High, teachers came in either Missus or Miss. "Miz Stone," the pregnant girl repeated, her hand swaying forlornly, every part of her weary. "Why are all these stories and poems so de*pressing?*" As evidence, she now hefted the reader so that it fell splayed from her palm, a fat textbook covered with the bored graffiti of her predecessors, so heavy it appeared to be taxing her frail wrist just to hold it up. Outside, snow fell. Not the snow of November or December, which portended Christmas, nor the snow of January or February, which meant skiing, but the snow of March, that defeated, dreary, superfluous month no one could love.

Weather and room and subject matter were all gloomy. Birdy had smoked a joint over lunch break with her colleague Jesús Morales, and that, combined with the pregnant girl's question, the snow, and the body odor of twenty-three teenagers, made her feel hopeless for humanity. She ached for the girl anyway, so unprepared for what awaited her. Around the teachers' lounge, her plight had become a watershed: those who sympathized and those who judged. As the youngest teachers, Jesús and Birdy were inclined to identify with the students.

Birdy drew a big breath as if to blow out candles; her tongue still tasted dryly of pot. She explained to her senior lit class that, in the first place, the stories and poems weren't all depressing, and, in the second place, didn't tragic feelings linger longer? Would there be anything much to say about a happy day? Her students studied her, thinking of a thousand things to say about a happy day. A few of the girls thought she had nice clothes; the boys appreciated her long legs and long hair and the way she took jokes well. But they couldn't quite muster the enthusiasm she seemed to expect. Accustomed to Spanish pronunciation, they called novels "nobbles," reducing them to rabbit food. They all hopped to action in other classes, inspired by threats, eager to keep athletic eligibility, avidly cheating if necessary. But Ms. Birdy Stone, lover of sad literature, held no particular power; her class was good for relaxing. This afternoon she felt her kinship with her students develop a wrinkle, a space between her and them, an annoyance that was new to her. I'm getting old, she thought dejectedly. They'll all stay seventeen, year in, year out, but soon I'll be old enough to be their mother.

Everyone sat waiting for the bell, which wasn't a bell at all but a buzz like an oven timer. Inside the school it was unnaturally hot; they were done. The buzzer buzzed and they went away.

· · ·

ALL SMALL TOWNS are not alike. Having seen one, you had not seen them all. Everyone did not know everyone else's business, and the people were neither friendlier nor more genuine, the lifestyle not purer—just duller. Birdy Stone had lived for nineteen months in Pinetop, New Mexico, and still the old adages were being debunked.

She'd come from a big city, Chicago, and thought a high percentage of its inhabitants would fit right into Pinetop, far, far better than she did. She still tended to think of herself as temporarily installed here, not like a tourist but like a reporter on a story, a missionary on a mission, never mind that she could not name her cause. It seemed she was looking for something. She did not worry about the renewal of her teaching contract because its being terminated would finally give her a reason to pack up and flee. She was twenty-nine years old and unwilling to consider this place the backdrop for the rest of her life.

As an excuse for being a community, Pinetop had used mining and then timber industries. But that was over. Now those attendant structures hulked emptily on the hillsides as eyesores. Some nights they seemed to sneak closer, big boxes full of the void, square black windows and doors like holes punched in for a peek. The town had burned down twice in its one-hundred-year history, so there remained no interesting architecture, no quaint clapboard buildings or stately brick ones, nothing but the mountain of toxic mine tailings and the ravaged hillside where once there'd been a forest. A few towns away, the Apaches ran a gambling casino, and there was a large horse-racing trade in the vicinity, but neither of those lucrative businesses did much for Pinetop, although every Pinetop merchant sold T-shirts and postcards advertising both. Many of the locals seemed to think their town was about to be discovered by that most profitable of enterprises, tourism; little specialty shops popped up like flowers every spring—espresso bar, chocolate shoppe, Christmas ornament boutique—opening cheerfully with banners and bargains only to slowly wither over the summer and fall, the merchandise grown dusty, the clerk gloomy, the owner cynical, the crepe paper shabby and saggy, until the storefront stood desolate once more. Failure seemed its own thriving industry, like death.

On the highways leading in and out the national franchises lined up, jockeying for attention, pushed together like snap beads, the same eye-catching toy colors, red, yellow, blue, green. People in Pinetop considered it a coup when a fast-food chain selected their town for an outlet; they loved their Wendy's and their Jack in the Box and their Kentucky Fried. For the convenience of a drive-through window, they'd forsaken the downtown cafe, Dora's, in favor of McDonald's. Quaintness did not interest them. Charm was a little nothing you wore jingling on your wrist.

Plus, the wind blew. The mountains sat in such a way that a nearly constant wind howled through; pointed pine trees, those left standing, listed north-eastward as if yearning to give up and sail off, arrows into space. The gritty tailings, heaped in a barren yellow dune at the western end of town, flew overhead on particularly bad days, snicking against the window glass, thickening the air like flung salt, settling over the streets and yards and roofs. In the winter, it was snow that blanketed the ground, drifted against the east and north sides of houses, banked icy buttresses before windows and doors.

From the Windy City herself, Birdy should have been accustomed to the relentlessness. She'd hated the wind since she was a child, its cunning chill factor in the winter, its taunting tornadoes in the summer. But in Chicago you could huddle in doorways, escape into basements, dash between the high-rises, duck into steamy delis or crowded appliance shops. You could take solace in the fact that the wind swept away the litter and smog. The city fathers acknowledged its eminent domain; they heated the El stops and burrowed out parking lots underground; they called themselves Hog Butcher to the World, and girded their loins.

Here, people pretended the wind was not incessant. They walked out of their houses with tentative grips on their possessions, their hats and umbrellas and trash sacks. Their skirts flew up and their television antennas snapped, laundry defied the line. Both this year and last, everyone assured Birdy it was highly unusual, all this wind. They went around being astonished by it, exclaiming. She was suspicious of their wonder. She lived in a trailer, which rocked in the breeze like a bread box. Her neighbors owned aerodynamic A-frames, or peeling log cabins with portable carports lashed to them, or trailers such as her own, sitting atop concrete blocks and pink fiberglass bales, roofs dotted with old tires like sliced olives on saltines. It was not uncommon in Pinetop for houses to come rolling in on the highways—and, conversely, for automobiles to rest in fields among the flowers and cattle. Everywhere you looked there were signs reminding you not to dump: DO NOT DUMP, as if you might be tempted, otherwise, to unload all of your garbage, right here, right now. Birdy's street, she learned after the first winter, was situated where the prostitutes used to live in tiny shacks called cribs. The remaining cribs looked like fancy, albeit dilapidated, doghouses, a whole vacant row of them, six places, each no larger than a mattress. This was the side of town where people owned roosters and motorcycles; in the mornings, they crowed and roared. Property was marked by the use of cyclone fencing or scrawny chicken wire, or, most mysterious of all, plastic gallon milk jugs filled with colored water, set wobbling on the ground in rows like giant jelly beans, grotesque Easter eggs the same faded pastel shades, pink, aqua, lilac, daffodil. What trespass were they capable of discouraging? The backside of Main Street, Birdy's neighborhood was so close to where Mt. Ballard and Mt. Ajax met that it did not see sunshine for the months of December and January. Farther, a kind of stream ran through, making things chillier.

It probably had a name, this shivering water, but Birdy did not know it.

The other side of town was the sunny side, and that's where the reputable people had always lived on a gently sloping, brightly lit hillside. Their streets bisected the incline like bleachers, on each row rested the square facades of two-story bungalows, barrackslike, militantly overlooking the spectacle of Main Street, and, behind it, Birdy's squalid turf. Only the upstanding could keep their balance over there; the rest slid, as in a landfill, toward the bottom. Pinetop High was located in the bleachers, a 1950s yellow-brick building designed like a prison or mental institution: massive, functional, impenetrable as well as inescapable.

But Birdy had moved here in a fit of defiant self-pity, whimsical exile, so her grim living arrangement suited her. Of course her side of town was where the hookers and the poor foreign miners had lived. Of course her pipes would freeze and burst; of course her gas bill would skyrocket—her tin home leaked its heat like an old-fashioned pie cabinet. And in the humid late summer, the mosquitoes would descend along the riverbank to suck blood from whatever lived there.

"This town," Birdy would say to her friend, "it depresses me."

"Sadness," Jesús would agree, mildly, without emotion, the way their students said bummer. The symbol for grief, the shorthand recognition of others' pain.

Jesús had grown up in Pinetop. For a few weeks Birdy had

thought he was named Zeus. "Hey" was just a way of calling him. Affably, since he was homegrown. "Hey, Zeus." That's how naive she was concerning her new state and its culture. The Spanish language still scared her; she was convinced people were discussing her as they chattered with each other in it, going fast just to thwart her. At a critical juncture, Jesús had fled Pinetop for Albuquerque, which passed as the area's big city. There, he developed sophistication and a sense of humor, became gay without suffering trauma, then returned, having maintained good relations with his former teachers, his parents, his old friends. Birdy thought Jesús was nothing short of remarkable; she wished her family and hometown liked her as much as his liked him. The only snag in his life was his need to speed off to Albuquerque every few weeks to spend a weekend. There, he picked up men, visited clubs, wore women's clothes, ate pills like candy. Then he was back, in his saggy innocuous pants and big sweatshirt, perfectly jolly. He never quit smiling; was that his secret? It cheered you up just to see his shining, apple-cheeked face. In Pinetop, he joined the fan clubs advertised on cable television and waited for UPS to bring him esoteric old movies that the local video store did not stock. He smoked clove cigarettes and listened to Barbra Streisand on obsolete vinyl albums. Birdy relished his friendship; in a larger town, it wouldn't have been possible. In a larger town, he would be a member of a group that excluded her, a group two notches hipper than she, but here, in little Pinetop, they became pals.

"A mom called me," Birdy told Jesús one day when they were alone in the teachers' lounge.

"Not a mom!"

"Mark Anthony's mom."

"That Mark Anthony," Jesús said. "What a babe."

Besides his famous name, Birdy hadn't particularly noticed the boy, who sat dutifully in her Social Problems and

American Values section, a required senior class. The faculty called it Sock Probs and Am Vals, as if it concerned car engines, a course rotated among them; nobody enjoyed teaching it, too much reading was involved, and all of it dry, dry, dry. Birdy had caused a stir by introducing fiction texts to the curriculum, *Invisible Man*, *To Kill a Mockingbird*, *The Scarlet Letter*, those glum nobbles.

"What could she want?" Birdy fretted.

"You use the Lord's name in vain lately?"

"I think I might have said 'suck,' as in 'Your research essays suck.' " She hated conflict; she was prepared to confess to anything.

"You have a habit of blaspheming the American government."

"I know."

"You're in trouble, girl."

"A mom, a mom, a mom." Birdy laid her head on the lounge table.

"Don't you think Mark Anthony's a babe?" Jesús asked, laying his head down across from her so he could see her sideways. His eyebrows jumped, the way they did when Birdy seemed to be missing something obvious. He made a grin, which, up-ended, Birdy saw was a perfect rectangle, teeth like a package of peppermint Chiclets.

"I don't trust babes," Birdy told him.

"Interesting," he said.

Mrs. Pack, the school secretary, walked into the lounge then and regarded them suspiciously, as she always did, as if Jesús were still the student he'd once been—impish jailbait— and as if Birdy were the bad influence. They could not be up to anything good, with their faces on the tabletop. Other teachers called her by her first name, Edith, but Jesús and Birdy always said, "Good morning, Mrs. Pack" like brats.

This, Birdy decided, was the way she would stay young, by refusing to grow up.

Mrs. Pack told Birdy that her two o'clock appointment had just called to confirm.

"Wah!"

"Isadora Anthony," she added.

"Is she a good witch," Jesús asked, "or a bad one?"

Mrs. Pack pointedly did not answer, as if ignoring him might cure his irritating conduct. "I believe she said she was meeting with you, but our connection was bad. Is there weather?" All three of them looked toward the high windows, which revealed nothing certain.

"It's her phone," Birdy said. Yesterday there had been hissing on the line—cheap receiver, thick walls, or the simple interference of the infernal wind—then the woman had said, "Missus Stone?" in a long southern interrogative.

"*Miz* Stone," Birdy had answered, emphasizing it the way she hated her students to do, as if she were already an old maid.

Mrs. Anthony said, "Oh." More hissing. "Miz Stone? I was wondering if we could have a meeting? It's not about your class. It's another thing." She said "another" as if it were a girl's name, Anna Other. Birdy had agreed out of alarm, out of curiosity; now she invented a scenario in which Jesús and Mrs. Anthony's son Mark had become illicit lovers. Her heart thumped with the thrill of such a transgression—and someone else's transgression, not hers. Then she formulated her own sober response: despite the fact that Jesús was her friend and that Mark was a mature senior, Faculty Shalt Not Date Students. She suspected it would come between her and Jesús, when she had to draw the line, thereby ruining the only real fun she had in town. Wasn't that just like love? To throw a monkey wrench into a perfectly good friendship?

"It's been real," Jesús said as he left the lounge. "I'll never forget you, you loser, you."

"Scum," Birdy answered blandly, "freak," while Mrs. Pack recoiled.

Mark Anthony's mother had arranged to come to school during what was supposed to be Birdy's planning period, but which Birdy typically spent alone in the lounge, daydreaming over a bag of Fritos and a Fresca, feet on a stack of blue books. Mark must have been cloned from the father, she decided: his mother couldn't have looked any less like him, tiny where he was hulking, fair and henna-headed where he was swarthy. Her face was like a mouse's: tiny brown seed eyes, twitching little mouth, too-small teeth she seemed careful to keep hidden. It was as if someone had grabbed her features and made a fist, leaving them bunched together in the middle of her face. Her hair was thin and seemed spun, like sugar or glass, translucent. Her fingers clutched her green handbag like a squirreled nut against her chest. She looked at least as frightened as Birdy felt.

"Ms. Stone?" she said, peering into the empty room. "My Mark says you know about books?"

Birdy admitted she did. "I read a lot," she said cautiously. "All the time." As far as she could tell, she was the only Pinetop resident to take advantage of the bookmobile, which arrived in town every other Thursday and parked outside the Whitefront Bar, as if the drunks inside might be interested. Or maybe the driver drank. "You sure read a lot," he never failed to note from his springy driver's seat. "Yep," Birdy never failed to reply. Her last boyfriend, her former fiancé, back in Chicago, had accused her of lassitude, of cowardice, of letting novel characters do all her living for her. And why not? Birdy had asked him. Why the hell not? Let them do all the dying and fucking up for her, too. Vicarious tragedy, she told him, virtual woe: an idea whose time has come.

"I, too, am an avid reader," Mrs. Anthony confessed. "Spiritual guides," she added meaningfully. Birdy now felt sure she was going to be handed a Bible and some tract on the evils of literature. Who would have guessed that old lug Mark Anthony was actually paying attention, reporting on his required reading?

They sat by themselves in the teachers' lounge, a place like an ER waiting room, someone's tacky rejected couch and chairs, sputtering bitter-smelling coffee machine, whirring little refrigerator in desperate need of defrosting, windows providing some oblique white light. Smiley faces on the teachers' mailboxes. A metal case of books, the maroon leather-bound spines of former yearbooks, dozens of them, the only reading matter in the place—which apparent self-fascination seemed to Birdy incestuous, the narcissism of the pedestrian, as if those sitting in the lounge wanted only to look at photos of themselves, the building where they worked, the students they taught. Usually the lounge felt too cold to Birdy, although others did not seem bothered. She liked Mark's mother for looking cold, too; it gave them something in common. "Want some hot tea?" she asked her. "Shall I turn up the thermostat?"

But Mrs. Anthony had business on her mind, she wasn't concerned with her own discomfort. She said, "I'm writing a book, about my experience, and I thought you could help me."

Birdy's heart both rose—no lecture on immorality!—and fell; books were so big, and everybody thought they should be authoring one. Birdy's first college major had been creative writing, but even then she could tell she would have nothing fit to say; she'd been letting fictional characters provide her with drama for many years by that time. For the first semester she fruitlessly ransacked her past in search of something exciting to write about, marveling over the drivel her classmates offered up, their step-parents and pets and paramours. It embarrassed her, their naked and feeble obsessions, their trite dilemmas, their whiny and thinly veiled personae, their idiotic shallow fantasies. She sympathized with her professor, a burly alcoholic type who prohibited his students from writing about guitars, recreational drugs, and from the point of view of inanimate objects. What made people so confident their lives were worthy of a reading public?

Later, she'd become that professor's lover. One of the things he liked best about her was the fact that she didn't want to be a writer, just a reader. His reader, Birdy supposed, his poems all set in foreign countries, featuring exotic women, idiomatic cuisine and custom, consonant-mangling pronunciation. Tongue-tied, Birdy'd always felt, before him and his work.

Mrs. Anthony now pried open her handbag—a moss-colored leather contraption with a faux gold beetle as its catch—and produced a newspaper article, yellowed, laminated, stiffened like a dead leaf. After handing it to Birdy, she waited, watching with her seedy eyes.

There was no telling which newspaper had run the story, or when, as it had been tightly clipped without including masthead or date. PINETOP GIRL FALLS TO DEATH, the headline said. Birdy read as Mrs. Anthony unblinkingly watched. Apparently Mark had had an older sister, Teresa, whose body had been found in a ravine just outside town, beneath a very modest Anasazi cliff-dwelling site. Birdy had visited the ancient dwelling when she'd first moved to town, when she still had an outsider's touring enthusiasm for Pinetop, when the ramshackle modern junkiness of the place still beguiled her. You drove a few miles down the highway, parked in a sandy lot, then followed a path along the rocky rim of a mountain till a wide, lengthy opening appeared, like the mouth of a Muppet. Along the path ran a looping cable, some sort of measure toward safekeeping, although it seemed more likely that you'd trip over it than be caught by it. Pinetop's teenagers for many years had used the site as a party pit, having discovered the same advantages the Anasazi had in perching high above the valley, where they could watch for enemies, protected by the warm bulk of the soft sandstone mountain behind. In the main dwelling, the ceiling was crusty with black soot, its walls covered with twentieth-century petroglyphs: DUANE LOVES TRINA, ROXY IS FOXY, PUMAS RULE. On the counters of several local businesses rested pickle jars with slots knifed into their lids, hand-lettered signs soliciting donations for the cleanup of the ruins. Hopeless.

"Young Teresa C.S. Anthony" had been "a tender sixteen years of age"; there'd been no sign of what this article called "foul play," her death attributed to internal bleeding caused by a fall of five hundred feet onto rock. The article tactfully failed to mention the word "suicide," making do with "unfortunate accident." Birdy read with a growing anxiety, positive she was going to have to tell Mrs. Anthony what no doubt countless others had already told her: the girl, sad and sixteen, had thrown herself over the cliff, plain and heartbreakingly uncomplicated. There was no conspiracy, she would have to say, no one to blame. A teenager is a dangerous vessel, running around with your love in her careless, self-indulgent hands.

Toward Mrs. Anthony she felt a prickly kinship. "I'm very sorry about your daughter," she finally said to the woman. "My mother died last year and—" Mrs. Anthony reached into her handbag and plucked out another parchmentlike document without acknowledging Birdy's words; this meeting was not about Birdy.

The second article resembled the first—plastic-coated, yellowed, pimpled with tiny air bubbles, no indication of date or source—and was headed SECOND TRAGEDY IN LOCAL FAMILY. Birdy read with increasing dread, hoping suddenly that one of her colleagues—ideally, Jesús, but even the principal Hal Halfon would have been okay, or the retarded custodian, Mr. John, or sour Edith Pack, somebody—would come rescue her with inanities and chitchat. Her personality had a pushover aspect to it; the more she knew about the Anthonys, the more she was going to be involved. That was a reflex triggered by novel reading, she postulated, overidentifying with print characters, constructing wholecloth an accompanying landscape, gothic castle and English moor, beery barroom and cannery row—all based on the flimsiest of detail.

She sighed, scanning reluctantly the next installment. This story concerned the husband, Teresa's father, who'd been killed in a single-car accident two days after his daughter's death. He'd rolled on the highway down the mountain, on the road that ran between Pinetop and Albuquerque, the same one Jesús sped gaily down for his weekend furloughs, only a few hundred yards from the site of Teresa's plunge. The article mentioned two survivors, Isadora Anthony and her young son Mark.

Birdy turned over the laminated article as if to read the next chapter; on the back was an ad for rifles. The clip art figure selling them looked a good thirty years out of date. Yet, this was Pinetop; perhaps the same ad still ran in the *Pinetop Mountain Journal,* which came out once a week and included an anonymous phone-in column called "Speak Up!" that, in a year and a half of trying, Birdy had never been able to penetrate. She'd phone in every few months just to contribute her two cents: "Don't *speak* up," she'd say to the answering machine: "*shut* up!"

The third item Mrs. Anthony handed Birdy, what Birdy's mother would have wryly called the "coop de grass," was the family's photograph, taken a few months before the accidents, Mom and Dad, Brother and Sister, little Mark Anthony, all of six or eight years old, with his mischievous eyes turned toward his sister, as if the siblings shared a secret they kept from their parents. He wore cowboy boots and hat, a little silver six-shooter strapped to his hip; the sister smiled beguilingly at the photographer, sexy beyond her years. This picture, the quintessential nuclear family, posed before the ethereal blue backdrop of professional photo studios, plus the other two articles, Mrs. Anthony insisted that Birdy keep.

"I want you to help me write my story," she said, sitting properly, her knees pressed together beneath her purse as if restraining the need to pee. Was it primness? Simple cold? "I know what I want to say, but I can't do it, I don't know what should go where. I've tried and I've tried, but I can't; I never went to college. I thought since you teach all these books about terrible things, you could help."

Why are all the stories so de*pressing?* Birdy thought.

"I know there's a book in this," she added, when Birdy could think of no good enough excuse to say no. On a tangent, she was troubled that Mark had told his mother he only read books about terrible things. She hoped that wasn't what all the students thought, but knew they probably did. Ever since she'd moved to Pinetop, she'd been sending off her applications to other districts like bobbing forlorn messages in bottles: Help. Someday when the houses were on the move, she was just going to have to stand on the highway with her thumb in the air, hope to hitch a ride on one of those wide loads.

Meanwhile . . .

"Will you just say you'll think about it?" Mrs. Anthony pleaded. "Just take the stories and think about it?"

The only dead teenager Birdy had known was her sister Becca's first date, Corky Wilson. He had lived in Ohio, on the farm next door to Birdy's grandparents' farm, and he and Becca had had an ongoing summer flirtation from the time they were toddlers, finding each other fascinating while ignoring Birdy altogether, or, now and then, permitting her to tag along on their stumbles through the pastures or forays into town, abandoning her on strategic occasions just to watch her weep, relishing their own meanness, the hilarity of it. Finally, in ninth grade, Corky's and Becca's intimacy was to be confirmed by an official date. Corky, farmhand and tractor driver, had his license; Becca wore a new pair of jeans she could put on only by lying on a bed and inhaling mightily. At home, the grown-ups were sitting mesmerized before the television, watching as it was suggested that the President of the United States be impeached. "Impeached," Birdy had murmured all summer, in love with words even then. Becca and Corky planned to go see *There's a Girl in My Soup* at the Orpheum Theater—special permission had been telephoned to town, since it was R-rated.

But on his way across the acres dividing the two properties, Corky overturned his father's truck in a wide flooded ditch, trapping himself inside the cab, drowning in the muddy water that came spilling through his open window while the complacent cows stood by, munching. In her typical no-nonsense manner, Becca had later recounted the event as evidence of her quirky love life: on his way to fetch her, her first date had died. Hearing her tell this story in subsequent years, Birdy had always admired her sister's tone, her unsentimental view of the freak accident. What could Becca have done, after all? She'd liked him, but they weren't engaged. In any but rural Ohio summer neighborly circumstances, they wouldn't have dreamed of dating each other—from his merry boyhood Corky had grown conservative as an adolescent, his nature already showing the beginnings of reticence and solemnity: he'd thought the Democratic Party was framing Mr. Nixon, diverting the nation's attention from more menacing activities, while Becca continued in their childish ways, animated and cheeky, a giggling prankster. Had her own first date died in a ditch, Birdy imagined she would have taken up a different tone altogether in telling her tale, tragic and self-pitying, more apparently sensitive, and as explanation for many future travails.

Now Birdy knew about another dead teenager.

"I would have liked being confirmed," Birdy said to Jesús's mother.

It was the Saturday night after her meeting with Mrs. Anthony, and Birdy stood with Mrs. Morales waxing sentimental over her seven daughters' confirmation dresses. This was at the Morales house, where Jesús lived with his mother and Tía Blanca, his aunt. They lived on an avenue called Fort, and the place resembled one, heavy double doors opening on a ring of dark rooms, the courtyard they enclosed overgrown with black trees and shrubs and who knew what kind of eyeless nocturnal life forms. Nobody ever entered the courtyard.

Mrs. Morales had filled her home floor to ceiling with the wardrobes and toys of her children, as well as bric-a-brac, religious icons, and Americana, the Virgin of Guadalupe blessing an I'm A Pepper serving tray, photographs of her offspring enshrined everywhere, eleven others besides Jesús, most of them married and fertile, everyone modestly overweight, a legion of grandchildren with the same gleaming smiles, their school pictures affixed to a wide array of surfaces. She loved the colors of the U.S. flag, red, white, blue; it was the only aesthetic Birdy could decipher from the abundant evidence, collectibles both glass and plastic, valuable and total junk, culled from the antique stores and the garbage bins and her family's long thick history together. On the coffee table rested a hammer and a china bowl full of nails. Mrs. Morales brought home her treasures and applied them instantly to her walls. Collectors, Birdy had read in some college textbook, acquired physical matter to substitute for what they lacked in the spiritual department. But that didn't seem to be Mrs. Morales's problem; she seemed to have the knack for both.

"My family was atheist," Birdy confessed.

"*Pobrecita,*" sighed Mrs. Morales. "Is hard." But she wasn't entirely sympathetic, Birdy didn't think. She knew enough to know Birdy could have mended her ways, found her own spiritual track. Just the way Jesús had forsaken his.

While she and Tía Blanca attended Mass, Birdy and Jesús watched a movie on the giant television. What a TV. The screen was so big that if you didn't suspend disbelief, or at least blur your eyes, the picture broke down into dots like a Pointillist painting. Fortunately, Jesús was good enough to provide pot every week—otherwise, a person might find her forehead melded into the same shape as the curved surface of the television console. Birdy had always let boys buy the drugs. She considered it a masculine chore, like repairing cars, deciphering tax forms, brawling in barrooms.

Jesús, who fancied himself a future filmmaker, consumed actors or directors, one right.after the other until he had a deft, if eclectic, fluency. Together, he and Birdy had made their way through William Holden and Stanley Kubrick, Billy Wilder and Myrna Loy, Natalie Wood, Woody Allen, Martin Scorsese, Judy Holliday, Mastroianni, Fellini, Buñuel, and both Hepburns. Now Marlon Brando was a bank robber imprisoned in Mexico; he was also the movie's director, the megalomaniac. It was an unlikely scenario, and Jesús scoffed at the love interest, with her beaky nose and flat chest, her humorless martyrdom.

"She looks like Mary Jo Callahan," Birdy noted. Miss Callahan was the other English teacher at Pinetop High. She'd been Jesús's teacher way back when, and it was she who'd first tentatively suggested to him that he might be, well, *different* from the other boys. "Miss Callahan, after," Birdy went on.

"After what?"

"The makeover."

"Maybe," he said.

"A big makeover."

Across the barren desert the horses galloped, plumes of dust following them, the sky fizzing into a million silver dots before Birdy's eyes.

"Do you remember Teresa Anthony?" she asked Jesús, thinking of the newspaper articles and photograph waiting on her kitchen table at home. She'd agreed to tutor Mrs. Anthony for reasons of vanity: to think, the woman had sought her out, believed her to possess some expertise. But already the idea of this book was plaguing her like a class project, a due paper, a take-home exam. She wasn't so long out of college not to still have those nightmares.

"Sure I remember Teresa," Jesús said. He sucked on a joint the size of a forefinger that sizzled and popped, his plump brown cheeks going hollow with the effort, his eyes crossed. High, Birdy turned her attention from the dissembling TV screen to his face, focusing on his invisible beard. Did he wax, to obtain such smoothness?

He went on in the pinched voice of someone who's just inhaled two lungsful of moderately expensive smoke, "I just didn't realize that burning hunk of human funk was the brother." He looked at her sidelong, to see if she were shocked, then exhaled.

Jesús had been a stoner in high school, he explained, while Teresa Anthony had been one of the brains, a choir girl, too virtuous to have liked Jesús and his gang of sloths. Birdy imagined him hiding out in the parking lot the way the druggies did now, bad boys skipping class in their trucks and heaps, happy Jesús snickering with his friends, zooming on the weekends to the Anasazi party pit to get wasted while the little toy town of lights twinkled down below. From that height, you could watch the highway traffic, you could spot the police or your parents coming to bust you. Birdy wished she'd had a friend like Jesús at her high school. Instead, she'd caroused with perfect assholes, precisely the kind of boys her father predicted she would wind up with: witless, unkind, stupid, and stoned.

"In my head, Teresa is mixed up with this other girl," Jesús went on. "There was a flock of little cute girls who were friends with my sister Miti. Teresa was just this face in the fourth grade when I was in fifth, like my fan, filler, crowd-scene kid. She was there, but kind of not there, you know, part of my adoring audience?"

"Uh huh," Birdy said.

"Have you noticed how nobody who comes after you in school seems nearly as interesting as the ones who came before? I could tell you all about the girls a year ahead of me. Good old Zita Ingham, Ana Gutierrez, Laura Turchi, Vicki Taylor . . ." He sighed. "Those girls were gorgeous. I worshipped those girls."

"Mrs. Anthony says Teresa was gorgeous."

"No doubt," said Jesús. "But the rules say she was supposed to be watching me, not me watching her." He handed Birdy the roach, which looked like a roach: buggy, unsavory. She gingerly pinched her fingers and lips around the thing.

"She's pregnant," Jesús predicted of Marlon Brando's homely main squeeze. "Now Brando has a reason to reform. It'll be a moral imperative."

"This movie has everything," Birdy said. "Bandits, romance, Spanish, English, the desert, the ocean, moral imperative—"

"Karl Malden's nose."

"—and Karl Malden's nose." Brando broke out of both jail and handcuffs, shot the sheriff, and galloped out of town wearing a black hat. The credits rolled, the camera panned, and the music swelled, the ugly girl waving, tear-stricken, as Marlon Brando's masterful horse raced up the West Coast toward Oregon. Jesús sighed in utter satisfaction; Birdy said, "He's leaving because that girl is so hideous."

"If that were my film," Jesús told her, brandishing the remote at the screen, "Brando woulda died."

"Oh yeah? Why?"

"Because he had a heart of gold and a moral code. This world wasn't ready for him."

"I think the girl should have died." Birdy shook her head, clearing it as best she could. "At least Karl Malden got what he deserved."

"You'd think he would have had that nose fixed, all these years in front of a camera."

"You'd think."

Before Mrs. Morales and Tía Blanca came home, Birdy and Jesus had to scurry around using air freshener to cover one cloying odor with another, then activate the ceiling fan to whirl them together, and, finally, flush the contents of the ashtray down the toilet. *"Puercas afuera,"* Jesús muttered, quoting his mother: pigs outside.

"What is this?" Mrs. Morales would demand of her son's videos. She did not understand his taste in cinema. For the characters in *Who's Afraid of Virginia Woolf?* she'd had just one piece of advice: "Quitcher bitchin'."

She would join them for the second feature—she preferred modern millions-of-dollars adventures, blockbusters, big unlikely muscle men with their outlandish weapons, chesty sex kittens with their outrageous foul mouths. She found them amusing. Preposterousness tickled her, her faith in the unpreposterous was just that fervent. Tía Blanca, hunched and dour, would tie on an apron and head for the kitchen to fix plates of a spicy late dinner, *salsa cruda* she'd chopped herself, tortillas shaped on her own thighs, resigned to make sure everyone was happy before settling herself on her customary ottoman, not even a back support for her weary shoulders, nibbling on her own food, appalled at the bloodshed on the TV.

At first Birdy had thought Tía Blanca was Mrs. Morales's sister, her habit of addressing Mrs. Morales as "La Señora" due to some antiquated Mexican custom of sororital seniority, not unlike the landed gentry in British novels. They seemed like sisters, both stocky with cropped black hair, moving around the house and each other, companions of long-standing, the pigments of hatred and love blended to the colorless mud of dependence. Birdy supposed that her own sister would have preferred being called "La Señora" and permitted to sit around while Birdy waited on her. Fat chance. But it turned out that Tía Blanca was not a relative, but the housekeeper, thirty-five years an employee. She slept in a room off the kitchen, one whose walls were covered with religious imagery so dense it was like visiting a sacristy. She rose at dawn to brew coffee and roll cinnamon buns. The two women seemed as inseparable as a married couple, as symbiotically bound.

Birdy sometimes worried that Mrs. Morales and Tía Blanca thought she, Birdy, was reforming Jesús, persuading him that girls, after all, were the superior company. She hoped that wasn't the source of the women's friendliness. Alternately, she worried that they felt sorry for her, knowing that Birdy could never hope to claim his heart. She found herself thanking the two of them constantly—for the comfy couch and huge TV, for heat and food, for a place to go on a Saturday night, meanwhile making it clear she had a boatload of beaux waiting in the wings.

"*Gracias,*" Birdy said. Grassy ass, she always thought.

Tía Blanca shrugged; it wasn't her house, after all, she had no control over who came in. Mrs. Morales brushed off Birdy's appreciation. "*De nada, de nada.* I have a dozen children, what's one more?" It was this logic, Birdy supposed, that had led Jesús back here after college, reinstated in his old bedroom, reconstituted as his mother's last baby, heading off each morning to the same school his family had been sending children to for twenty some years. Jesús had done nothing . more than take the path of least resistance.

"*¿Como no?*" Jesús would have said. "*Por supuesto.*" Of

course. Why not? Who said you had to leave the nest, hoe your own row, come of age?

Tonight the second feature was set on a navy boat; the hero not only knew several useful martial arts but how to prepare a meal to feed a platoon of starving sailors.

Jesús grinned at his mother's wicked love of violence. "What did Father Sanchez say to you, to make you so bloodthirsty?" Tía Blanca shook her head, wounded as the pious always are by the levity of the irreverent. There were degrees of soul, and someone was always praying for yours, just one rung ahead of you. Jesús thought of Birdy as cold, and he would feel on her behalf, warm her with his forgiveness. Above him resided his mother, overlooking his nasty-ass homosexuality, and beyond her, up there on the spectral plain lived Tía Blanca, busy being charitable about this need for bloodshed every Saturday night. *Her* overseer must have lived at the church, forgiven Tía Blanca her choice of employers, and answered directly to his lord.

"He also *cooks!*" Señora Morales howled, about Steven Segal. She wiped her eyes, delighted beyond suppression. Even Tía Blanca, busy at her needlework, offered up a little smile at that.

It was still March and the snow still fell. The crocuses in Birdy's window box, misled by a few warm days, had popped up only to be buried, like hope. With her hair dryer, Birdy melted the snow and then covered the pathetic flowers with inverted Dairy Queen lids. Downtown, the ice-skating rink had melted to slush and then refrozen pockmarked and stewy. It seemed like it might never be anything but dirty March. The sun shone on her trailer for exactly six hours every day, from nine until three, as if launched late morning by Mt. Ballard into the waiting afternoon maw of Mt. Ajax. Of course, these were the hours she spent on the sunny side of town anyway, missing all the light and warmth at home. By the time she returned to her trailer after school, the sun had been cut off by this daily geologic conspiracy, her view nothing but the stony shoulders thrust up to cast her in cheerless shadow. It was hard to say why this seemed right and proper to Birdy, that two blocks away the sun shone—she could see a bright happy patch on the other side of town—but not on her.

EVER SINCE his mother's visit, Mark Anthony had become an object of curiosity to Birdy. In Sock Probs and Am Vals, she found herself seeking his placid face when she spoke before the class, his simple attentiveness as much as she could wish for. For his part, he seemed to be suddenly attuned to her, as well, as if attempting to aid his mother's cause. His was a distracted attention, one he seemed to have to remind himself to extend, suddenly alert at the tail end of a yawn.

Once she found him waiting in the parking lot after school, spinning a lasso at his feet. The circle spun before him and he watched it with a dreamy concentration, a faint unconscious smile that Birdy associated with thoughtfulness. He stepped inside the circle, spinning the rope a little wider, twisting his suddenly dexterous fingers. He could make it move up his body, or sideways in the air like a tunnel. His ability to do something this well impressed her. She noted, later, that his rope was stored in his belt loops, ever ready to be put to use.

Birdy wished she were developing a crush on one of her colleagues instead. It was funny how crushes came on—like the flu, like a speeding ticket, out of nowhere—how someone familiar and pigeonholed in the ordinary cubby could become, overnight, exotic, intriguing. The human animal liked to play these kinds of tricks on itself. One day he was generic, the next an idol. Soon, she thought, Mark would not be her student. She watched his pants pockets as he sauntered from the room, telling herself she did it for Jesús, knowing it was actually the result of her own deep boredom, of a desperate need to exercise her emotions. It just hadn't occurred to her before that she might do so with a student.

You wouldn't know by looking at him that Mark had suffered two tragedies that took out half of his family, and maybe that was part of his appeal. He seemed unfazed. True, the events were ten years distant, and he'd been a young boy. But he appeared to be a genuinely composed young man, untroubled by notoriety, unimpeded by the absence of a dad, unblemished by a bereaved mother's predictably overbearing, fearful love. He played pranks and made dumb jokes.

But there was that rope-turning, that absorbed concentration.

He had friends like himself: athletic, friendly, well-mannered, occasionally foolish, ordinarily bland. Birdy believed these were the people who glided over life as if on a long greased slide. Only by accident did they understand the knotty world below the elementary one they inhabited. Only if something dramatic disturbed the surface would they be permitted to glimpse what churned under there, in the vast and scary subterranean. She had to assume that Mark had depths; she seemed to want to uncover them.

Her own awareness of that world had percolated up slowly over the years, and she had absorbed it through literature. When she opened a book, she could still hear her mother's voice lifting the words from the page and setting them in the air, the two of them bundled on the couch while fiction began constructing its elaborate sets around them. To this day, Birdy tilted her head when she listened, as if her imagination worked best at a slant. She had particularly looked forward to the occasional interruption, the aside her mother might offer—that pig-headed Robinson Crusoe! Poor fool Joe Gargery with his "weal cutlets"! Her mother loved the dry commentators on the human condition, literature's Eeyores; nothing irked her more than a Pollyana. And she also loved the sighing fullness of a finished story, the sad twilight of decline and fall, the reluctant easing close of the covers. Birdy felt indebted to her mother, heard her voice as she read aloud to her students, was eager to promote the brief coherence a story gave the world, the coupling of humor and disaster, farce and carnage.

That was the real reason she taught, although she converted a disappointingly low number of students. Others would have to find their own way, and Mark Anthony was probably one of them. The deaths of his sister and father made Birdy think he possessed the key to what she thought of as the real world. He did not cling to the written word the way she did, but he had endured a loss, sustained some injury that must have scarred him in interesting ways. This scarring was not apparent; he gave no signals of a maturity beneath the boyish veneer. He initiated no trouble in class, although he wasn't opposed to the distraction trouble inspired. Until his mother had visited, he'd been only a member of Birdy's peanut gallery, the back row warm bodies, the necessary average C students who gave the bell curve its curve.

He was handsome, as Jesús had noted. His eyes were large and brown, ringed by lashes like a daisy, sweet eyes, and thick dark hair that often did not do what he seemed to want it to do. His smile was intended to make others join in, liberal with happiness. He had an inclusive friendliness that was not exactly charisma—more like generosity. He would not be a politician but a waiter, extending his good nature for the pleasure of others rather than for his own gain.

"He passes the ball," Jesús said, "to employ a sports metaphor. That's what makes him a good guy. And he is also fucking beautiful." The more often Birdy studied his beauty, the more enchanting beauty seemed. "A thing of beauty," she recalled, "was a joy forever." But wasn't that about a Greek urn?

She conducted some informal research into the Anthony family history. Given a subject about which to gossip, the other teachers warmed to her in a way they hadn't previously. They admired her sudden interest in their background, where before she'd had none. Before, she'd appeared to be somebody making a brief pit stop in their midst, someone they could not afford to invest in, someone they suspected of belittling traditional methods, soaking up local color and picturesqueness to trade later at their expense.

She thought they thought she thought she was better than them.

"Daylight Donuts?" Jesús asked one morning before the first bell.

Birdy quickly deposited the box of pastries on the lounge table, as if to disclaim its greasy contents. "Get 'em while they're hot," she said.

He crossed his forefingers in front of his face, then popped a sugared lump between his teeth. "These are bribes," he guessed, heading out of the room before his colleagues began arriving.

Birdy touched her nose. "Bingo."

The other teachers had already warmed to Birdy's inquiry, but Edith Pack remained suspicious. She'd been here longest; she knew some things. Now she circled the open bakery box like a trap, her coffee cup held over it like a radon detector; Birdy had not been known to provide treats before. "Help yourself," she said to the secretary. Tentatively, Edith Pack removed a raspberry-filled cruller and took a bite.

"I'm working with Mrs. Anthony on her book," Birdy began, "and I was wondering if you remembered Teresa?"

Mrs. Pack's eyeglasses, held by a strand of pearl-like beads, bobbed on her chest as she chewed. Birdy watched them instead of the woman's face. Mrs. Pack had a bosom big and cushy as bread dough. She should have been warm and maternal, but she wasn't. "Spoiled child," she finally pronounced. "Had her daddy and most the faculty wrapped 'round her little finger, most the men faculty, I should say, right, Miss Callahan?"

"Oh, now," said Principal—"Your pal, Hal!"—Halfon. He liked to think positively about both students and staff, see both sides of the story. He had been Pinetop High's principal for three years, but still considered himself new, a humble outsider with a lot to learn. He was too eager, in Birdy's opinion, too anxious to please everybody and disappoint no one. Too democratic, Christian, compromising, namby-pamby. Even his body was soft, his rump the wide clefted pillow of a woman's, his jowls loose, two breasts beneath his buttondown shirts. Anything having to do with the town's bygone times also delighted him, as he seemed to believe it a more compelling place than Birdy did; or maybe he thought he'd find the compelling part if he dug deep enough. He'd already begun writing a history of the defunct mine, chapters of which he occasionally read at convocation, as if knowing all about the town would ingratiate him with its natives.

Everyone thought he had a book to write, Birdy thought.

"I hate to see a child indulged," Edith Pack said.

"Do you have children?" Birdy asked, and Edith made a horrified face, setting down her half-eaten cruller.

"Teresa seemed more complicated than some other students," Miss Callahan ventured; Birdy had already assumed that most of the students in her classes led more complicated lives than Mary Jo Callahan did. Because she'd come to Pinetop eleven years ago with the identical intention as Birdy (to leave quickly), Mary Jo made Birdy profoundly depressed. Plus, she had a habit of staring at Birdy like a specimen. Usually, she avoided her.

"Of course," Mrs. Pack said, "most girls are spoiled, in my opinion, no one teaching them the consequences of their actions."

Birdy was tempted to ask Mrs. Pack if she thought Teresa deserved more than a violent death as a consequence. And to what action? Mrs. Pack might have been reconsidering the same thing, because she abruptly jumped to the topic of Mrs. Anthony. "After the accidents, Isadora went on the warpath about the tailings ponds. She said the mine debris was giving us cancer, and made such a stink that Silverado had to plant grass, remember, Hugh? Just ready to throw money away, might as well open a bag and toss dollar bills to the wind."

The music teacher, Hugh Gross, nodded, his lips white with powder. If you didn't know about the donuts, you might think he took lithium, which would maybe explain his awkwardness, the way his moods clicked quickly along like a slide show on his face. His many facial lines betrayed a host of strong expressions. "Those ponds did have a peculiar color," he said, frowning.

"Green?" Mrs. Pack cried. "You call green a peculiar color for water? The woman needed a hobby, pathetic thing. She just shouldn't have taken it out on the miners. Reported them to the ERA."

"EPA," Mr. Gross corrected.

"I believe Silverado was at one time under consideration as a Superfund site," said Principal Halfon. "It was rejected," he added quickly, when his secretary glowered at him.

"Just because she was miserable, she did not have to put all her worries into making other folks as miserable as herself.

Life handed her some lemons. She might have been making lemonade, that's all."

"The green did seem like it glowed," Mr. Gross insisted. "Teresa could sing," he went on, grinning abruptly at Birdy, employing his happy wrinkles, repeating what appeared to be the only thing he remembered about the girl. "Really, her range was extraordinary. I encouraged her to apply for a scholarship to my alma mater in Denton, Texas. They have a fabulous music school."

Birdy had already heard all about fabulous Denton, Texas.

"Did Teresa Anthony take your classes, Mr. Schweinbraten?" How Birdy loved saying Mr. Schweinbraten's name. He taught German and computers, and kept posting pathetic flyers about reinstating the chess club. Students liked to believe he was a Nazi, although they seemed a wee bit fuzzy on what a Nazi might be. When Mr. Schweinbraten spoke, he held his small hand at his mouth, fingertips all five together, as if he were pulling a string of words from between his teeth, chin bobbing forward as if he were gagging them up.

He had not known Teresa.

The lounge door banged open and there stood retarded Mr. John, the janitor, too late for the donuts, wearing his perennial khaki coveralls. He made his abiding hopeless query to the room at large: "Wouldja join me for a smoke?" Mr. John was not permitted to smoke without supervision. He'd had an accident one winter involving some insulation. Birdy had heard that he'd often shared a cigarette with Teresa Anthony's father in his idling car while he waited for her after school; overprotective, Mr. Anthony had insisted on driving her to and from Pinetop High like a bodyguard.

Guarding her body.

The wall clock minute hand jumped forward and the first

buzzer buzzed, startling the faculty into motion, cups and pens and clipboards clattering.

As the room emptied, Miss Callahan made a point of walking down the hall beside Birdy. She smelled of an overly feminine waxy deodorant.

In the allocation of peripheral duties, in the rounding out of the English teacher job description, Mary Jo had been awarded Theater, while Birdy received Yearbook. Ten years ago, Mary Jo was telling her, she had directed Teresa Anthony in *The Mikado.* "Her father objected to the costume. We had to sew up Yum Yum's slit." She drew her fingers up her own thigh. "She did have a nice voice, but she was willful." And, she confided, leaning a tad toward Birdy, bringing her deodorant odor with her while the students streamed past them, she also thought Teresa had been dating an older boy, a secret relationship that her parents had not known about.

"How'd *you* know about it?" Birdy asked. Mary Jo was not only the dreariest person Birdy had ever met, but also so ugly you could say practically anything to her. These aspects of character Birdy zealously wished not to rub off on her. Mary Jo was worse than plain—she might have aspired to homeliness—with her enormous nose and bad acne, a purple birthmark covering her chin and neck and who knew what else below her clothes, scrawny splotched limbs and dowager's hump. Coarse chin hairs. Plain, she might have been nearly invisible, camouflaged by it the way, say, functional furniture was, or innocuous office art. But her ugliness drew people's ire, Birdy couldn't guess why, and Mary Jo was a virtual doormat to her students, who nonetheless returned to see her after they'd graduated. Perhaps they came back in apology, ashamed at how badly they'd treated her, or with some misremembered sense of her significance in their lives. Birdy herself frequently felt ashamed; always angry on Mary Jo's behalf, she generally expressed it by being brusque or dismissive. Birdy's real fear was that she'd be here herself in eleven years, unmarried, whipped, smiling timidly in a corner, shoved against a locker, perfectly content to be an overlooked face in the crowd, shriveling away to a parched husk. She could not imagine any high school girl confiding in Mary Jo. "Why would Teresa tell you about an older boy?" Birdy demanded over the before-class ruckus.

"I saw her coming out of the Alpine Inn one night," Mary Jo said simply. "I asked her if she needed a ride, and she said she didn't, and then she begged me not to tell Mrs. Anthony." She smiled helplessly, as if Birdy were about to swing a fist into her jaw. Then Birdy could understand how Teresa, fifteen or sixteen years old, would have felt completely calm at being caught by Miss Callahan, utterly unthreatened, confident the woman wouldn't breathe a word.

"What were *you* doing at the motel?" Birdy almost asked, stopping herself just in time. Something about Mary Jo's total submissive hideousness made you want to trample her privacy as if it were your right. It was horrifying to consider what someone with less restraint might do to her.

"I wondered if she was a call girl," Mary Jo said as they reached her classroom door. Birdy was too surprised to answer—not so much because of the speculation, which would have been primary among Birdy's own pessimistic guesses, but because Mary Jo had come up with it. Mary Jo laughed lightly, as if she'd been making a joke.

"Miz Stone!" called out Mario Sanchez. "Looking *good*!" He did a pump and bump move with his fists and hips.

Birdy waved, wondering if her looking good to Mario was related to her standing beside Miss Callahan, who could never have been said to be looking good.

"Have a nice day," sighed Mary Jo, and turned into her classroom.

EVERYONE KNEW teachers got worn down and burned out, like shoes and lightbulbs. Like chewing gum, Birdy thought, like tires and politicians and coal miners, their collapse the result of too much use. The rest of the Pinetop faculty had already put in their time at the spring dance, so Birdy and Jesús acted as chaperones, as they had done last year. Only this year, when the students made their annual gawky invitations to dance, Birdy agreed, scandalizing everybody. Principal Hal frowned uneasily; all behavior reflected his administration. Birdy didn't care. Let him try to reprimand her in his puffy inoffensive way. Wearing his black suit, he resembled a penguin as he waddled and fussed around the food table, snacking endlessly.

She was aware of the girls watching her, of her black velvet kilt swinging at her thighs, of her long yellow hair that tonight might look lustrous instead of stringy, of Jesús grinning and waving from the punch bowl under the basketball rim, wearing his traditional tuxedo T-shirt. She could hear his laugh every once in a while when she circled in his direction, his terrific laugh, always ready to bubble out. He so wanted to have fun. He could find it almost anywhere. This year, like last year, the two of them showed up together chewing minty gum, slightly drunk as if teenagers themselves, a flask full of Cuervo Especial out in Jesús's VW beetle. Later, they'd steam up the windows, share a chaste good night peck on the cheek at Birdy's trailer, Jesús's infectious laugh gurgling away to keep them giddy. "Slug bug," he said whenever it was his turn to drive them somewhere, and socked Birdy on the arm. He wore a wonderful cologne—

nothing you could purchase at the Pinetop Rexall—which radiated from his body like aromatic vapor as he got hot.

She danced with other boys simply because she wanted to dance with Mark Anthony; intoxicated, she felt her attachment to him burgeoning over the course of the evening. She appreciated Mark's apparent attitude toward a school dance, enjoying himself without feeling too excited nor too bored. He was taking it as it came, living in the moment, hands modestly in his front pockets when he wasn't out on the floor. Maybe she had been waiting for someone to tell her whom to want, the way she had in her girlhood. Maybe Jesús had given her a good tip, or maybe she set her sights on Mark only because Jesús had expressed an interest in him first. But she recognized the romance virus as it made its way into her body. She was terribly susceptible. She simply had to have him, never mind what she might do with him once he was hers.

So there he stood with his friends, the accidental object of her unforeseen affection. He wore a vest over his usual school attire, a wool article that must have been his father's, dead Philip Anthony. It gave Mark a Gay Nineties appearance, a boost of a few years' maturity. Or maybe Birdy was just justifying her attraction. When she spun, she used him as her immovable object, the steady form that prevented seasickness. Him, and Jesús, and Principal Hal, and Luziana Rillos, the pregnant girl.

But Luziana didn't hold still long enough to be a good compass point. She'd come wearing a pretty baby doll dress that she filled gloriously, her swollen breasts pushed up like the corseted bosom of a sixteenth-century babe. To complement this, her big black army boots gave her the clunky sexiness of a rock star. Birdy had to admire her. Luziana didn't wait for boys to ask her to dance; she stalked up to them, indiscriminately, and pulled them to the floor, mere ballast

for her frenzied flapping. She danced by herself a few numbers, a rag doll, a round Mylar balloon with flimsy ribbon
limbs, held earthbound by her heavy boots; she extracted Mr.
John from the dark corner where he waited for the evening's
conclusion with his push broom, and made him stand before
her baffled while she gyrated around him. He beamed his
creamy retarded gaze at her, bumping his body up and down
like a toddler who hasn't yet coordinated vertical with hori-
zontal locomotion.

Jesús polka-ed Birdy from net to net, veering around the
clumsier forms on the floor, disregarding the thudding heartbeat thrum that constituted this band's rhythm. They were
called WarHead; they came from down south, near the Trin-
ity site. Their tight pants were made of burnished silver Naugahyde, every tendon, muscle, kneecap obscenely clear, and
they seemed extremely angry as they played.

"They think they're Iggy Pop," Jesús shouted in Birdy's
ear.

"I was wondering who they thought they were."

They passed the unfashionable girls who wouldn't dance,
and the cool girls who wouldn't. They passed the boys who
were probably responsible for spray painting all the empty
walls around town, marking territory like tomcats, and they
passed the yawning, burr-cut, bussed boys who were tired
from farm chores. They passed the two black students. They
passed Mark Anthony, whose social position seemed to be
that of chameleon. He could hang with just about anyone,
athlete, cholo, genius, or goof. Although the gym was deco-
rated and dark, you could still make out the icky ordinary
walls, the grubbiness of public education. "Ed-you-cation,"
spake Principal Hal, often, overenunciating like the far-flung
correspondent who can pronounce "Nicaragua" with native
marble-mouthedness. The chipped surface of everything, the
sad acidic odor of pubescent sweat, the posters applied

everywhere like Band-Aids, hopeless patches over the spilling or unseemly, their messages denying it all—BE ALL THAT YOU CAN BE! HOPE IS THE THING WITH WINGS! ¡SÍ, SE PUEDE!—while at the same time dumping responsibility in the laps of the students, abdicating like crazy.

Jesús spun Birdy, then pulled her close to say, "Why did the principal wear rubber bands on his wrists?"

Birdy caught a glimpse of Hal Halfon's arms as they whipped by. "I don't know," she told Jesús. "Why did the principal wear rubber bands on his wrists?"

"To keep his hands on," he said, throwing his head back to laugh.

It wasn't until WarHead's encore that Mark Anthony finally came to ask Birdy to dance. By then she was flushed with desire for him, with anticipation and dread, with tiredness and tequila. She wound her hair around itself and tied it into a knot behind her damp neck.

"Ms. Stone?" he said, and instead of offering his arm, motioned with his head.

The encore began like a car crash, sirens and radio noise, a woman's hysterical voice overwhelmed by amplified feedback, a needle dragging across an ancient record album. Mark was a terrible dancer; he lumbered and jerked, his big hands, when not stirring a circling loop of rope, turning like radar dishes on his wrists. The only improvement over Mr. John's style was Mark's expression, which was serious and charmed instead of simple. Birdy knew she danced well, even when flailing away at something as hopelessly undanceable as this.

Without pausing, WarHead's synthesizer careened grudgingly into a last slow song, the band understanding that the only way to leave a high school dance was with teenagers dry humping on the gymnasium floor. Mark's hands now ceased their aimless rotation and clamped onto Birdy in a perfectly respectful waltz position, one out in front of them, one on the small of her back. *The small,* she thought: it felt smaller than ever, under his palm. She could imagine his mother teaching him this, the two of them practicing, Mrs. Anthony's teased hair bobbing just under her son's nose. Accustomed to mocking the whole affair, Birdy was surprised by the abrupt dignity of the moment, as if she were suddenly in a Jane Austen novel instead of the ludicrous young-adult travesty she felt she usually inhabited.

"Propinquity," she murmured, one of her own, and Edith Wharton's, favorite words; always on the tongue, it felt alert and proper, like the call of a clever little bird.

She had not really been held for a long time, not since her last dreadful date here in Pinetop with the Wires Plus man, Ronny, who'd tried to force his way into her house after their second dinner together, his pretext having to do with her cable hookup. He seemed to have felt he'd spent enough money on her to merit a sleepover, as if the prostitutes still occupied her dark side of town. But having sex with him was so far from what Birdy wanted to do, she had laughed in his face. Since then, no dates, no hand holding, no kisses.

She'd told herself she was recovering from her breakup with her last boyfriend, but more than that, it seemed her mother's death had sapped some reservoir, leaving an echo where there ought to be a burble. There was breakup, and there was breakdown. She felt sometimes deeply confused, without time or charity to consider love, as if her internal organs had been wantonly rearranging themselves, tossing overboard a few of the less essential. Sometimes she just had to give herself a talking to, in the imperative mood.

"You look pretty," Mark said shyly. Along with the gentle way he held her, his nervousness also appealed to Birdy. He wasn't going to demand anything of her. Their conversation, while they danced, was an animated hollering into each other's ears, and stuck with the topic of his mother, of Birdy's agreement to help her, and of how much happier she seemed when she was writing about the family's troubles. That was how he put it: their troubles.

"It's good to air your feelings," Birdy shouted, astonished at the dullness of that insight, wondering if she actually believed it. If she aired her own feelings, for example, the whole town might ride her out on a rail after Her Pal Hal fired her.

But Mark nodded enthusiastically at her ear. His faint stubble gave her a chill down her neck.

She was tired from dancing so much and her feet ached, so it was nice to sag into a slow dance with a big boy. His large hands felt wonderful, like workgloves. She allowed herself to slip just slightly, to pretend not to know the result of her body's relaxing, so that his leg now barely brushed hers as they turned, so that her hip on occasion touched his, so that her cheek just once caught the bone of his chin. Another thrill ran through her, larger and with keener authority, like lightning, head to foot. He adjusted his hand that held hers; she imperceptibly tightened her grip. He smelled of wool, of fabric softener, of clean sweat. He moved his hand on her back not up or down, but simply around her, a squeeze. She wanted to lay her head against his shoulder and let him hold her the way the other couples danced, those shuffling fondlers, moving slower and slower, their eyes closed, their genitalia on fire. The gym was awash in suppressed moaning, she could sense it emanating from the long stretch of the vibrating floorboards, from the thickened air, pandemonium now localized in the hot spot of two touching bodies. Across the room, Luziana lay on a line of folding chairs, watching the floor with a dreamy look on her face. Mr. John stood once more with his push broom, patiently waiting to sweep the floor of cups and confetti. Birdy dared not look toward the punch bowl, not at Jesús, nor at Principal Hal, knew what she would see in each of their faces as they observed her, Jesús's bopping back and forth happily, Hal's now deeply concerned, his eyebrows a severe V. Faculty Shalt Never Slow Dance with Students.

Mark said in her ear, "I like to dance with you," the sibilant hiss making her knees threaten to give.

"Uh huh," she managed, mumbled into his tweedy collarbone. And just like that, she succumbed: to the illness and accident of her crush.

❧ 3

Whenever the phone rang in Birdy's trailer, she always jumped, expecting her father or sister on the other end. One of them, or the man she'd been engaged to, Reginald Leonardi. She'd treated Reginald badly, and when she heard the jangle of her telephone, she flushed with the notion he might someday demand her explanation, at the very least an apology. He was going to wake up and smell the coffee, sooner or later. She did not like to owe remorse. To Reg, she would have had to simply confess her confusion; it wasn't you, she rehearsed saying to him, it was me. But of course it was him; she'd found him insufficient, eventually, had envisioned somehow the boundaries of their relationship—as if bestowed with the all-important aerial view—and known that its limitations would not do, that her capacity for surprise and delight in him, her love for him, ended right over there. How could that sound like an acceptable thing to say to a person?

The unkindness had been in agreeing to marry him in the first place. She'd known the correct answer wasn't yes, but it wasn't no, either, and yes at least permitted her to mull her befuddlement for a while, a long stall that in the end made more of a mess than no ever would have. It was easier to agree than not, she thought, just the way it took fewer facial muscles to smile than frown. But even with the various loopholes of modern marriage—separation, divorce, infidelity—Birdy hadn't been able to go through with it. Reg's unhappy eyes still haunted her—if only he'd grown angry or vindictive, instead of simply submitting to his fate, head hanging, feeling it was his due.

Her family was another story. It was they, she felt, who owed the apology to her, maybe several. She relished the debt. She'd spoken to neither surviving member for nearly a year. The argument had to do with her father's new wife; he'd married after being a widower only three months. Ninety days! To Birdy, this suggested that he'd been plotting his next marriage, dreaming of a new wife while his first one lay dying. He'd betrayed Birdy's belief in her parents' happy marriage. He'd made her mother a fool.

"Just because you've blown your love life," her sister Becca had said, taking Reg's side just as Birdy had known she would, "doesn't mean Dad has to go celibate."

"What a fucking facile point," Birdy told her. "It's got nothing to do with me or my love life. It has to do with decency. They were married thirty-five years. He ought to show some respect. And don't tell me Mom would have wanted him to get married again. Don't you dare give me that tired old line."

Their mother had been bedridden for a year before her cancer finally claimed her; in her heart Birdy knew her father deserved a new wife—undoubtedly his down-to-earth first wife would, indeed, have been in favor of it. She had never been one to hold a grudge or wax nostalgic. He wasn't all that young or healthy himself; who knew how much time he had left to pursue happiness? But he'd not been much as a father, in Birdy's opinion, distant and, when not distant, simply disciplinarian, as if he were raising Thoroughbred horses or model prisoners, beasts about which strangers could make appraisals, appraisals which spoke of his prowess as a father, and nothing else. The sisters had grown up vaguely afraid of his temper, of displeasing him, cowering in the face of his sporadic rage like little pets. Now Birdy thought he ought to suffer more than he appeared to have at her mother's death. He ought to be taking stock of all he'd mishandled, reconcile his guilt, balance accounts in solitude. Instead, he had a wife who was only a few years older than Birdy, and two new infant twin sons—who'd come appallingly fast, you didn't want to do the math on it—roughly the same age as his younger grandson, Becca's second child. The family had been reconstituted, old members, new roles, expanded, improved, and seemed perfectly pleased with one another. Everyone back in Chicago was getting along swimmingly, without Birdy. And perhaps that was what spurred her, the knowledge that no one seemed to need her, that everyone appeared better off without both her and her mother. As if Birdy, too, had died, or ought to have the good grace to do so.

The fact that Birdy and her sister no longer spoke to each other would have broken her mother's heart, had she been alive to know it.

"And that's precisely the point," Birdy had told Jesús, attempting to be wry and merry. "She's not alive to know."

But Jesús had cried for her, setting down his martini to do so, pulling the olive pit from his mouth so he wouldn't choke. He cried more easily than she and more often. Did this make him further evolved, or less so? she wondered. Mature, or immature? Films often made him sad; the two of them at his mother's, Jesús snuffling unabashedly from the recliner while Birdy hardened herself against melodrama and mawkishness.

"Girl," he reproached her. "You're cold-blooded."

"Not really," she insisted. Someone was always telling her this, charging her with insensitivity. Her! The English teacher, the woman sniveling over John Keats, weeping for Willy Loman. She reassured herself that if she was worried about it, it couldn't be so. Isn't that what people's mothers told them?

Besides, she was too old to be pitied for having lost a mother. Young children, yes; fairy-tale princesses, yes; but grown-up women, no. Perhaps if she had babies of her own, this wouldn't plague her so. Perhaps that explained how Becca had so easily flourished after the funeral. To Becca, because of her children, their mother had become a grandmother—Becca had even taken to calling her Nana, the way her son did—and grandmothers were in a category permitted to die without overwhelming bereavement.

Grow up! Birdy commanded herself.

Her mother had died thinking Birdy would soon be married, a misconception that sometimes troubled Birdy, as if her mother had gone on her misty journey with the wrong road map. Maybe she would have been more contented, on her deathbed, thinking that Birdy wasn't going to marry Reg. She had always seemed slightly suspicious of his good nature, Birdy remembered, as if his sincerity and affability must mask something he was afraid to reveal. Birdy had more than once wished there were a way to update her mother, let her know that there had turned out to be nothing sinister beneath Reg's facade—in fact, nothing there at all. A desire to loaf around, to score cheap dope, to eat meals at other people's homes. "Bonus!" he would say enthusiastically, eyes gleaming hungrily, when receiving an invitation for dinner and drinks.

Her mother had thought Pinetop a hilarious topic, and understood the point of Birdy's anecdotes about it, rather than misconstruing them as criticism, or attaching herself to some spurious tangent, the way others did. Some had romantic notions about New Mexico, while others asked if a person had to get inoculated to go there, if the water was radioactive, if the coyotes and roadrunners dashed about, beeping and gnashing, foiling each other among the tumbleweeds. Her mother, however, appreciated a funny story, a good joke. She alone had seemed to understand the hybrid and evolving emotion Birdy felt toward the place, affection and impatience, pride and prejudice.

Because Birdy had moved west just a few months after learning of her mother's cancer, she often felt, in that first year, as if she were reporting on life's front as her mother languished in the rear guard. Her mother had not seemed to mind Birdy's moving away; she seemed, in fact, pleased by the vicarious escapade of it all, she who'd been no farther west than Iowa in her whole life. Birdy sent her the best of Southwestern kitsch, cactus jelly and rattlesnake eggs and, best of all, a square lollipop in which a whole scorpion was held in suspended animation. Over the phone her mother's voice crackled, "Thank you, honey," she said, and then attempted her famous laugh, which hurt Birdy's ear and heart. Its noise seemed shattering, as if that hard candy were being broken even then, as if her mother had crunched directly down upon that tiny erect stinger.

Of course it was Becca, the good daughter, who took care of necessary medical appointments and errands, hypodermics and colostomy bags. Becca, who'd resisted their mother's close attention, who preferred their father, did everything for the dying woman—and did it without undue drama. Birdy told herself Becca savored a project, expanded to include their mother on her list of people who needed her, enriched her vocabulary with tongue-twisting medical terminology. Meanwhile, Birdy had hoped she appeared settled down in New Mexico, at last, launched so that her mother wouldn't die fretting over the unfinished business of her younger daughter. She could only trust that she'd made the right decision in leaving, that it wasn't a flimsy excuse for cowardice, that it wasn't a result of squeamishness. She'd read a lot of literature about death, could summon plenty of images of sick rooms and bedpans, the contents of both. She dreaded Becca's updates on their mother's disease, her ease, perhaps even pleasure, at naming the body and its perishing parts.

So, along with the wish that her mother could keep apprised of her life now, there ran the parallel relief that she could not. There was much she would have worried about, much more, Birdy believed, than she would have found reassuring. Nothing was settled. She'd been launched, but it had been, maybe, a failure, a false alarm, a faltering earthbound dud.

Mrs. Anthony s instructions to her home were absurdly overdetailed, every protrusion in the landscape, whether man-made or natural, noted: billboard, county mile marker, haystack, potato-shaped hill, highway shrine to some dead driver. "Set your odometer when you pass Jerry's," Mrs. Anthony advised, "and at four point two you should be at the end of our road."

The house was a small adobe in the middle of a forlorn onion field. Too distant from Pinetop to be threatened by the two fires that had gutted the town, it had stood for more than one hundred years, and looked weary of holding itself up.

Adobe frequently appeared to Birdy as if it were melting, like a poorly thrown clay project, returning to the earth from which it had been pulled. There used to be trees surrounding the house, Mrs. Anthony explained over Ritz crackers, cocktail sausages, and bread-and-butter pickles, but their immense size had finally driven her mad; she'd made Marky cut them down.

"In a bad wind storm," she said, "they would crush the house." She held her small weathered hands up as if to keep the roof from collapsing. Birdy imagined she could hear the heavy *ooph* and slurp noises the mud structure would emit should a tree fall upon it. Mrs. Anthony, who wore an oddly formal tea-length dress, told Birdy that ever since her daughter's and husband's deaths, she took no chances with disaster. The pile of logs stacked outside the front door came from those loyal trees, cottonwoods that had been planted a few generations past by Mark's ancestors.

"Ancestors," Birdy said to herself, the word as alien as the concept. She was starting to feel as if she'd never had a family, as if she'd only begun conjuring herself when she moved to Pinetop. After her mother's death, she'd resolved to wash her hands of her family—who needed them? Her bossy sister and her double-crossing dad. She asked herself to look at it logically, empirically, like a behaviorist: did they not cause her more anguish than pleasure? And why invite such masochistic unhappiness? What sort of unnatural creature was she to keep yanking the chain that dispensed pain? So her past had disappeared when she drove away from Chicago, as if the city's receding skyline in the rearview mirror had been a literal shrinkage, toy buildings, tiny people, evaporating squeaky noise, all gone by the time she reached the Illinois border. Just Birdy in her car, Birdy in her mobile cage.

She'd returned that last time only to eulogize her mother, a task tarnished by suspicion: Birdy not only kept expecting her mother to appear—seeing her in other women's hairdos, in the skinny plume of someone's cigarette, catching a brief cackling laugh of a former friend—but also feeling accused by her surviving kin. She was jumpy and guilty and dumbfounded and sad. She had come home too late, and the glances of her family were unbearable, as if anyone could see how she would suffer, tsk tsk. She'd been a bad, bad girl, abandoning her mother, and she would surely pay. Then she understood fully the dissipation of her life there. And now it seemed she was still waiting for matter to accrue once more, as if the transferal, like something gone wrong on *Star Trek,* were incomplete, particles of her soul drifting willy-nilly in space.

The knowledge that Mark's family had lived in the same thick house for generations awed her. She sat at their oak kitchen table noting the solidity of everything around her: it would survive this, and the next, generation. The dark closeness of the place was cavelike and suggested forsaken human customs. Maybe babies had been born on the table; certainly something must have been slaughtered there, its surface pitted with grooves and scratches. Everything in the kitchen seemed designed for a monosyllabic hunting and gathering breed: the black cast-iron skillets hanging by descending size over the stove, the ancient Roper oven filling the wall and glowing blue with its perennial gas pilots, the lowslung gray enamel sink beside it scarred with the scrapes and nicks and burns and blows of axes and tongs and sabers, and the chopping block long enough to desiccate a full-grown deer. Birdy let her eyes rest on the electric toaster, where a bright, light-hearted needlepoint, toaster-shaped cozy cheerily declared that HOT TOAST MAKES THE BUTTER FLY! A butterfly spread its stitched yellow wings—it, at least, was an artifact from the twentieth century. This was where Mrs. Anthony toiled. If nothing else, the room was warm.

The rest of the home remained a mystery, concealed

beyond the kitchen like a private warren while Mrs. Anthony and Birdy discussed terms. Birdy wondered where Mark was, whether he was hiding from her and her prodigious affection for him.

Wouldn't he be amused by the way the bright box of Fruit Loops—briefly glanced in an open cupboard, surely his breakfast of choice—had made her chest spark?

"I can pay you eight dollars an hour," Mrs. Anthony said, stroking the fine fabric of her peach-colored dress. "I just want tutoring on authorship." She used *want* in the old-fashioned sense, as in *lack.* "After all," she said, "I am the authority."

"I'll read," Birdy said open-endedly, unclear about her role.

Mrs. A. nodded enthusiastically. "Yes, and make suggestions, and correct the rough spots. I have a feeling there may be some rough spots in the story."

"Okay." Birdy decided she would earmark her extra income for summer travel, treat herself to a hotel room far from Pinetop, among palm trees and swimming pools, a place where the wind never blew. Besides, it was a project of which her mother would have certainly approved.

Mrs. Anthony had been consulting various sources for hints on writing; her process, after trying several others, was to listen to a tape called *The Spontaneous Method of Inner Revelation* and do as it instructed. Birdy was handed this tape, and nothing more, as she left after their first meeting. Mrs. Anthony seemed troubled to part with it.

"I'll give it to Mark tomorrow, in class," Birdy promised, imagining their hands touching as she pressed the cassette into his.

Mrs. A. smiled in relief. "Thank you, Ms. Stone."

"Birdy," Birdy said.

"Is that short for Bridget?"

"No, for Ursula, but no one ever called me Ursula. That

was my father's idea, my mother named my older sister, Rebecca, so my father got to name me, and then my mother . . ." But Mrs. A. had meant politeness in asking, and was slowly shutting the thick door between them, pulling her wispy hem in, her smile rapidly fading as the crack shrunk, as if she were about to disappear herself under exposure to the outside world. The visit had apparently taxed her; her nervousness in hosting a guest betrayed the infrequency of the occasion. Whew, she must be saying, collapsed on the stone floor, fanning herself.

"Well, my mother just preferred Bird," Birdy said in her empty car. "And so do I. Thanks for asking. Shall I call you Isadora? Izzy?"

In her trailer, fortified with a mug of sour margarita, she played the tape. The cover showed a Vaselined-lens photo of the author/reader, whose bedroom eyes and big hair made Birdy deeply skeptical. After the hiss of empty tape, chimes played, angels *ahhh*ed, and the speaker began. Off into the tree-filled forest she sent the writer, her sexy, unnaturally slow voice instructing a painstakingly slow pace, attention to deep breathing and complete relaxation, to the noise of birds and tree leaves fluttering in the gentle breeze, those chimes and angels in the background like a chorus. Up ahead, after ten minutes of ponderous inhalation, emerged a peaceful flower-strewn meadow, and located in the center of the meadow was a flight of lovely stairs, winding upward. After laboriously climbing these—Birdy counted the steps, up, up, up, like Jack on his beanstalk, Rapunzel to her tower—the listener arrived in a beautiful room, furnished with whatever the listener found comforting, personal, the boudoir of your dreams, and then into this swell room floated a spirit, and when the spirit spoke, the writer was relaxed and confident and prepared to record what that spirit revealed. The news traveled from the ear to the pen—Birdy hoped with more alacrity than the journey from home to heaven; otherwise, the writer might just have dozed off. Either that, or hyperventilated.

Bored and mildly drunk, Birdy had begun chopping onions and celery and garlic while she listened, making a sloppy spaghetti sauce to pour over some noodles. Under the spell of this fairyland trance, Mrs. Anthony had been delivered of nearly one hundred pages already, her small hand guided by the spirit in the room at the top of a staircase located in an idyllic empty meadow of her mind. The tape ran scratchily through Birdy's machine, as if it had been put into service many, many times. The sexy voice counseled patience, implored self-indulgence, dripped forgiveness, and cautioned taking care when coming out of the relaxing meditation, as if the shock of being returned to the nontrance might send someone 'round the bend. Birdy rolled her eyes; she could only hope the real world might sometimes seem that startling.

She wondered what she herself would come up with, writing under this phlegmatic instruction. Since the tape seemed to encourage the outdoors, she supposed she might write about the sky, which, from her little bedroom window at night, often frightened her. Pinetop's altitude was seven thousand feet, which probably accounted for the proximity of things that had seemed, in Chicago, safely remote, fuzzy like infinity. Here, all the objects of the firmament appeared to exist exactly overhead, nearly within reach. The clouds blew silently and swiftly over, as if they might carry her in her bed far away, the world spinning irretrievably below her, Birdy hopelessly adrift. This tape seemed to endorse being adrift, as if the feeling were comforting instead of terrifying.

For Mrs. Anthony, it coaxed the chaotic random snapshot manner of memory. At their second meeting, Birdy read the garbled pages spun under this spell. They didn't need numbers because they weren't chronological anyway, they had no sense of cause and effect. You might read them in the way you read Tarot cards, endlessly shuffled and laid out for a prognosis. The story itself, Mrs. A. claimed, she had no difficulty with; it was coherence that thwarted her, the establishment of this fact and that speculation, the events themselves and her own recovery, which was paramount in her mind. She used the word constantly, that and *healing*. Recovery and healing—as if she'd broken her leg or undergone surgery. Ten years, Birdy kept thinking: time was supposed to take care of this business, bear away all things, heal all wounds. Mrs. Anthony had a problem with tone and emotional distance; Birdy cringed when she saw the note Mrs. Anthony had written to herself after Birdy had told her what she thought. *Sentiment = good,* it said, *sentimentality = bad.* True enough, but awfully blunt seeming, set down like a law.

At Birdy's suggestion, Mrs. Anthony was working on an outline for her magnum opus, drawing an elaborate schemata with a hundred subcategories, capital letters, Roman numerals, asterisks, and appendices. Like some true-crime television program, Mrs. Anthony depended on a sense of suspense to guide the reader through her various hypotheses. Jealousy, murder, revenge—the intercession of unforgiving destiny. She loved her outline. She had a pile of freewriting and a two-page prospectus: it was as if she'd completed the book itself, she was so pleased. This was what Birdy came to critique for their third meeting.

Who was the influence behind Isadora Anthony's desire to help mankind? she queried in the opening paragraph. *This type of person usually has someone significant in their life that leads them to a quest of service to others and Isadora Anthony is no exception. Her beloved daughter and late husband were two such type individuals.*

The story then leapt to the night of the first tragedy, the very early hours of July 5, 1984. Of course, it was storming. Of course, the lights had flickered out. When the police arrived at the Anthonys' front door, Mrs. Anthony had been tearing her hair out for what seemed like eternity. She greeted them with a candle and a feeling of doom in her heart. Lightning flashed behind the sheriff's menacing, six-foot-four stature. He laid the requisite hand on hers, as Mrs. Anthony collapsed, screaming as if there were no tomorrow, wracked by grief.

"I before e, except after c," Birdy said, of *greif*. Then she worked on defining cliché. Mrs. Anthony frowned; she thought these familiar phrases were what gave the writing sparkle.

"They give it the opposite of sparkle," Birdy said. "For example, when you say your hand was as cold as ice, I've heard that so many times it doesn't really mean anything anymore. The simile has lost its potency, do you see?"

Mrs. Anthony nodded uncertainly. She personally liked similes. In her revision, her fingers were frozen as solid as ten cherry popsicles. Birdy sighed, letting it stand. What she didn't mention was the peculiar way Mrs. Anthony slipped in and out of verb tense and point of view. It wasn't just that she randomly inhabited everyone's thoughts—telling her that her daughter was dead was by a long shot the hardest thing the sheriff had ever done in his twenty-odd years of law enforcement—or that the night was rendered simultaneously in the past, present, and past-perfect verb tenses, which resulted in a weirdly mythic tone to the series of events, or even that the vocabulary she used seemed to partake of some mystical jargon Birdy had never heard before. (What, for example, was a "life footprint"? Maybe it was a mangled cliché, akin to the tragedy's having "reeked haddock" in the Anthony household. "Fish'll do that," she muttered to herself.) No, the most disturbing part was that Mrs. Anthony occasionally cast herself in the third person. (Was Birdy fully qualified to remark on this? Was eight dollars an hour enough? Didn't competent therapists command at least a hundred dollars a pop?) This technique, too, replicated the effect of the true-crime television genre, as if Mrs. Anthony were scripting the process of interviewing herself, permitting herself to explain fully in her own words, then stepping back to narrate about herself only slightly more dispassionately, commenting on her wardrobe and wan expression. Mrs. Anthony with heavy heart woke her husband—Birdy kept picturing another woman in the house, a stand-in Mrs. Anthony playing the role of Mrs. Anthony. Sometimes she quoted herself; there were more exclamation points than periods.

And only then did it occur to Birdy that she ought to work on the larger problem of the truth, rather than the smaller one of style. After all, at school, the study of parts of speech had been allocated to Miss Callahan. Apparently, Birdy wasn't to be trusted. Miss Callahan, by virtue of her long unswerving rigid tenure at Pinetop High, had proven herself worthy, unflappable. Moreover, she did not desecrate conventional usage when she spoke, unlike Birdy, who scorned properness in favor of color, hyperbole, profanity. This was okay with Birdy; proper speech and its designated parts reminded her of other timeworn unforgiving rules, like math, where there was no leeway, no latitude. She felt herself too canny to be confined to parts of speech. Besides, students hated the stuff. Was there anything more deadening than diagramming sentences?

However, in the face of Mrs. Anthony's mess of a manuscript, Birdy felt grateful for rules to fall back on. Her red marks had the weight of all grammarians behind them.

After their third session, Birdy consulted Jesús once more. "What do you think happened to Teresa Anthony?" she asked him. He and the UPS man had just lugged into his mother's crowded house a huge box, a skiing machine for Jesús's tubby tummy; April, that cruel fellow, was upon them, and suddenly everyone was reminded that their bodies, like other pale tubers, would soon be uncovered, revealed to ridicule.

"Offed herself," he said instantly. "Teenage angst: I love it. Do you think we should read the instructions before or after we assemble?" He flapped the booklet.

"Mary Jo thinks Teresa Anthony was promiscuous," Birdy said. She couldn't remember exactly how Mary Jo had put it. "I never saw a place so fascinated by whores as Pinetop," she added, digressing. "Everyone is obsessed. If one more person tells me I live in the red-light district . . ."

"And I'll just work off these love handles while we watch cinema," Jesús said. "Could you hand me the screwdriver?"

Birdy gave him the tool. "Although if anyone ever visits me here, I guess I'll probably mention that fact first, too. 'That's my trailer, that's where the hookers lived.' "

"Prostitutes make everybody nervous," Jesús said. "They're like Madonna, women in control of their love things."

Birdy at first missed the reference; how, she wondered, could the virgin mother, her womb deployed by God, be considered in control of her love thing? "Oh, *that* Madonna," she said. "If Teresa was a whore, then her mother could be right about there being a murder."

"Who's she think killed her?"

Birdy shrugged. "I don't know. But I don't think she'd want to hear that her daughter was a whore, either."

"Who would?"

"Who would?" Birdy agreed, touching her own neck, remembering her own father's rage—"Whore!" he'd spat—when he discovered a hickey there. What a word, with the potency of a smack packed in its five simple letters. And all on account of a little harmless suction, trace red dots disappeared in a few days, the temporary tattoo of the round-heeled girl. Birdy felt a momentary pity for her teenage self. Poor girl, who loved to kiss, who loved lips on her neck.

She returned to the teenager under discussion, saying, "Mrs. Anthony's got an idea that there's a mystery, but she doesn't really want to solve it. She just wants somebody to admit that Teresa didn't kill herself. I think she thinks that if she writes it down and gets it published, then she'll be convinced, and that will be the official story. She doesn't actually want to find a murderer or anything, not to blame somebody specific. I guess," she added, not certain at all what Mrs. Anthony's motives were. The author of the book was as mysterious as her subject. A great deal of the text concerned her own journey from Georgia to Pinetop, a place that still seemed to menace her, where nothing had been easy on her, not the setting, not the characters. There was nothing of the South reflected in Pinetop, no gentility or gentleness in either weather or manners. On occasion, pain passed over her pinched features like a ripple of wind on an otherwise smooth pond. In those moments, Birdy knew she wished to be alone, closed behind her door with her private anguish. The fact that she dressed up for Birdy's visits didn't make things easier, either, Birdy the sole audience for Mrs. Anthony's extensive formal wardrobe. Birdy wondered where Mr. Anthony had taken his wife, to make use of such clothing.

"Is it a good story?" asked Jesús.

"No."

"Is it well-written?"

"No."

"She's hired you to fix it?"

"I don't know."

"To write it?"

"I don't think so."

"She just wants you to listen," he diagnosed. "That's not

so hard." He stood the two plastic ski machine parts together and unfolded an arm. "Is it?"

"No. And there *was* strangeness . . ." Birdy said. It was hard to cull the strangeness of the circumstances from the strangeness of its presentation in Mrs. Anthony's hands. She had an impassioned theory of a plot, either literal or spiritual: someone resentful of her husband's new promotion at the mill, or someone covetous of Teresa's good looks and talents, or some force omniscient and karmic, retribution beyond the conscious knowledge of any of the oh-so-mortal players. It could be Mrs. Anthony's punishment, these losses: like most everyone, she'd taken her loved ones "for granite." She leapt from theory to theory in her prose, in her own daily life, blaming living, breathing, unnamed people, then blaming nebulous destiny. It was a collage of prose, vignettes without linkage, a cross section of a grieving survivor's psychic muddle.

"She was a beautiful girl," Mrs. Anthony had pleaded. "You know that, you saw her picture. Wasn't she beautiful? You know how malicious high school girls can be to someone who's beautiful. Remember that prom queen in Texas who got acid thrown on her face? Remember that pretty ice-skater up in Portland? But maybe I wasn't meant to have a beautiful daughter." Birdy had agreed to the beauty, although Teresa didn't look so strikingly different from any other teenager. Luziana Rillos, the pregnant senior, for example, might perhaps be more attractive.

"Actually," Birdy told Jesús, "I'm afraid there was some sort of murder."

"Murder?" Jesús rose from his flurry of packing materials and NordicTrack decals to lay the back of his hand on Birdy's forehead. "Girl, you're the most paranoid person I ever met." Birdy's paranoia was, in Jesús's mind, like a party trick, something to trot out when other entertainments flagged. He would laugh while Birdy enumerated the crimes against her: her defective car muffler installed by the mechanic who hated her for doubting his ability to work on Saabs—just let the carbon monoxide flow!; her lousy classroom with ventilation straight from the greasy cafeteria kitchen provided by Edith Pack, who hated her for being young. "Who hates you this time?" he would want to know, ready to make sport.

"Just because she died doesn't mean there's a conspiracy," he said now. "You're just bored. Get that woman's son in bed and forget the murder thing."

"Your hand is hot," Birdy said, to hide her sudden flush. She'd thought so much about getting Mark Anthony in bed she was afraid it showed, her face readable as a mood ring. For some reason, Mark was never home when she visited his house. Either that, or he was keeping himself very quiet in the back rooms, like forbidden desire.

"Putting together this honey is an aerobic workout," Jesús was saying, to explain his hot hand. "Maybe I'll just take it apart and put it together every day."

"Really," she insisted. "I think there's a murder. I just think it might be more than Mrs. Anthony can handle."

Every week Mrs. Anthony bestowed something new on Birdy, first the tape, now a box full of materials, copies of the sheriff's reports, Teresa's grade cards of her last few years, Mr. Anthony's car keys and eyeglasses and insurance policy, the sad orange suede wallet Teresa had carried: more components of the collage, but no more coherence as a result. Just texture. In the report from the then-sheriff of Pinetop, the large-statured fellow who'd shown up at the Anthony house afterward, words had been crossed out with a row of typewritten Xs, and Os, words Birdy believed read *signs of struggle,* the three little G tails still showing beneath the line. Xs and Os, Birdy had thought, kisses and hugs. A strange mark had been noted on the girl's back, three concentric rings, a tiny bull's-eye target; the sheriff had drawn a little picture to illustrate. According to the report, the father had not been home when the sheriff had come to call—despite Mrs. Anthony's narrative claim that she had to wake him— but at a bar, behavior, Mrs. Anthony maintained when Birdy asked, that was out of keeping with his normal habit.

Either Mrs. Anthony wanted to hide the fact that her husband drank regularly, or he actually *was* behaving strangely, or she was merely confused about the events of the evening. At first, Birdy had thought Mr. Anthony had simply been visiting the scene of Teresa's death, had driven his car off in a terrible grieved miscalculation, eyes clouded with tears, road newly dangerous with recent catastrophe. Then she thought that the father was involved, had become blindly enraged with his daughter and pushed her from the cliff. It was a theory hatched in the gut, a dramatic exaggeration of the feelings of all fathers who could not reconcile their daughters' sexual awakening, a darker conjecture, unshakable once she had hit upon it.

Was she always looking for the negative, as her students claimed? Did she think her own father had wanted to do something like that to her? It wasn't really so far beyond the pale.

At the site a few days earlier, Birdy had parked above the cliff dwelling and then sat on the edge in the sand burrs, looking into the gorge. There might have once been a river down there; the Indians would have had the advantage of running water at their feet, a view of the surrounding countryside, protection from the wind, and fine morning sunlight. Since she had no sunlight herself, Birdy had grown to appreciate it more and more. Large birds circled overhead without moving their wings, riding the thermal air. If she knew anything about animals, she could identify these as buzzards or hawks or eagles or crows, and their presence could take on some tone, menacing or inspiring or annoying. As it was, they were only big birds, and she liked their lazy loops. In the distance, she could see snow-covered mountains, larger and balder than Ajax or Ballard, clouds foaming up behind them. The highway made a long sweeping curve here; plenty of opportunity to miss your turn, plenty of visibility for nefarious road-top activity. Mr. Anthony would have been able to wait until there was no traffic whatsoever.

It was his guilt that would have forced him to drive his own car over a few days later. He would join her, in the same place, fallen down the same steep incline to crash and burn at its bottom. Perhaps he felt he'd reached bottom already, being attracted to his daughter, repelled by the same attraction. Killing himself would be easy, by comparison. The events were sexual, Birdy felt, related to the forbidden, and that simmering shame had fueled Mrs. Anthony, bothered her for years, been a fiery force in the cavelike dwelling where she lived alone with her son as he arrived at his handsome manhood: she wanted it extinguished. She wanted the trees cut down so that there wouldn't be shade or shadow.

"Sadness," Jesús said benignly. He put his feet on his new skiing machine and promptly slid off the back. "Okay," he said, from his mother's living room floor. "Fuck fitness. I'll put the decals on my slug bug." Since he was not within Birdy's reach, he punched his own arm.

"Plus," Birdy said, "why did she wait ten years? What makes her need to write all the details on paper right now? What's the rush? I don't get the urgency." Because it *was* urgent. Birdy had been to the Anthony house three times now; whenever she returned, Mrs. A. had added to the pile of pages accumulating in the kitchen. She used a typewriter that looked like it belonged in a Kafka novel, round black keys that struck the page only as solidly as they'd been hit themselves, the letter *P* faint from a weak pinky, the letter *O* leaving tiny perforations on each onion-skinned page. Erasable bond, bearing the rolled impression of its cycle over the hard rubber wringer, a box full of it to match the box of mementos. She seemed to want to marry the two, fuse them into something lucid, an impossible mixed-media endeavor. After Birdy's initial editorial enthusiasm, she realized the hopelessness of the project, and wasn't doing much now as a tutor except reading. Maybe Jesús was right, that was all Mrs. Anthony had ever needed: a reader.

Maybe that was all anyone needed, Birdy thought, someone paying attention to your story, someone acceding to your declaration of primacy: I am the main character. This is about me. In that light, perhaps the chaos of the manuscript made sense. The point was, this was Mrs. Anthony's life, lumpy and disordered as it may have seemed, a mass of multicolored clay with sticks and razor blades and jewels adorning it. And every week she trotted out a costume to accompany it, silk jumpsuit, velvet gown, flowing red sateen skirt, hair whipped on her head like a heap of rare saffron.

"You really think I should go for Mark?" she asked weakly as Jesús put himself once again back on the skiing machine. Immediately, he fell again, this time sending a ski board into the wall, where it not only left a nick in the plaster but knocked off two blue and red pie tins his mother had nailed there, her grandchildren's smiling faces in the centers.

"If you like him. I personally think he's a big yes."

"He's a student."

Jesús shot his cuff and checked his watch. "Not for long. He's consenting—I saw you two at the dance—and you have the perfect alibi: research for his mother's book."

Birdy had already thought of all of this—and more—but it still upset her to have it spread like a blueprint before her by Jesús. How could she be entertaining ideas of seducing a student? It violated something primary and fundamental. It was the unwritten law of her profession—she was caretaker, beneficent warden, surrogate parent. To transgress was to fold her tent as a good teacher, to tumble into the league of the second rate, the sleazy. The needy.

She erected Mark's ignorance before her: he'd once asked her where he could find this Shakespeare play, holding out his notebook, where he'd written *A Fellow*. But evidence of his cloddishness kept getting wiped out by the memory of his arms around her at the dance. Her body was a slut, she decided, and she wasn't responsible. That thrill that ran again and again down the length of her spine was a renegade reflex, unrelated to gray matter. It was ridiculous; it was exciting; it was humiliating; it was incendiary.

"Mighty mighty," Jesús said.

"He's a *student*," she repeated. "I must be out of my mind." She conked her forehead with the heel of her palm. Moron, moron, she told herself.

"You just have six weeks till graduation," he consoled her. "Then you're legit."

"And he's also kind of dumb." But then Birdy recalled that spinning lasso, the intelligent way it spun for Mark.

"Who cares about his brains?" Jesús was back up on the skis, hands clenched around the ends of a jump-rope-like device. "At least he's got a hot bod."

TWO NIGHTS LATER, Birdy returned to the Anthonys' home. Mrs. Anthony had been inspired to her story by things besides *The Spontaneous Method* tape. *Your Past Lives* and *Write It and Be Free!* sat at her elbow as she worked. Their influence could be felt in her pages. From the simple details of her family's fatalities, she'd garnered the trappings of a metaphysical event. It had everything but a UFO. The most interesting aspect of the narrative, Birdy thought, was the description of Mrs. Anthony's Past Lives Therapy sessions, a route she'd undertaken the year following her daughter's and husband's deaths when her grief would not abate. Birdy wondered why she had seemed so surprised, early on, by the extent of her despair. What would a person expect? Her Past Lives therapist elicited an entire Egyptian history for Mrs. Anthony. Apparently she'd once been an intimate slave to a pharaoh, had birthed an illegitimate child for him, and was at present unable to deal with loss because she'd lost her ancient child, had it stolen away from her by the pharaoh's advisors, who'd beheaded the boy, saying that a bastard was bad for populace control. Her last thought, as a slave, her dying thought, had been of the unfairness. Hence, Mrs. Anthony explained in her book, her script in this life was that of living with a sense of unfairness. *This unfinished business,* she wrote, *is Isadora Anthony's present issue.*

Birdy sighed. Like the quaint, outdated belief in a bearded, benevolent God, other people's faith in the various quackeries of the times had to be accepted. Each of them contained some validity, she thought; other people's stories, their pain and victimization, were useful to study. Didn't she advocate reading literature, herself? But obviously Mrs. Anthony didn't want to think metaphorically about her past life. Her pharaoh story wasn't allegory; it was a literal existence, pitiful and poignant. She didn't want to engage in a dialogue about the compelling mythos behind it, the tinge of Jungian theory, the communal human bond—collective unconscious, schmunconscious! Instead, Mrs. Anthony attached herself to the most base and blasé of interpretations: she was a victim. She'd been one in Egypt, thousands of years ago; she was one still.

Karmically speaking, she'd written, she was due to be an oppressor soon.

So Birdy read what Mrs. Anthony had written with an eye on correcting grammar, on posing questions in the margins about details and adjectives, eradicating the third person whenever she cropped up, taking her own mental notes: why no autopsies? she wondered. Mrs. Anthony told her that her husband had forbade one on Teresa, and then she'd forbade one on him. "You wouldn't want your beloved cut up like a piece of meat, would you?" Mrs. Anthony demanded.

"My mother . . ." she started, but her listener wasn't listening. Birdy's sister had insisted on an autopsy of their mother; she wanted to know what sort of genetic prognosis lay waiting for her, what action she could take to reinforce herself. It was true, the procedure had disturbed Birdy. She could not override her horror with pragmatism, the way Becca seemed able to do. Becca, she realized, was really quite a lot more like their mother than Birdy was, straightforward and unsentimental. Perhaps that was why the two of them had not gotten along as well as Birdy and her mother. By this reckoning, Birdy ought to have been her father's favorite, but of course that wasn't the case either. Sure enough, life was not fair.

Was Teresa pregnant? Birdy wondered. Around her, Pinetop appeared more chilling and secretive, as if every house held an incestuous imbroglio behind its walls, and every teenager concealed a sickening scar.

The section she read tonight involved Teresa's shoes, which were missing at the site of her death. Barefoot, she'd gone from this world. Tonight, for the first time, Mark's presence in the house was audible. He padded in the hallway and bedrooms, avoiding the kitchen, but with his own stack of papers: college applications. Where his mother delighted in her productivity, in the sheer volume of her manuscript, Mark seemed tormented by the requirements of the state universities. His papers were ratty with his vexed ineptitude. Tonight, Birdy thought, he wanted her to know he was home. Soon she excused herself from the industrious Mrs. Anthony and the toasty kitchen, making her way to the bathroom and, afterward, as the ancient toilet chuckled behind her, to Mark's room at the end of the hall.

He lay on the bed wearing headphones, his shirt pulled up so that his flat stomach showed, hairless and perfect as a piece of Greek statuary. His eyes had been closed, his crossed feet twitching to the sound of the music in his head, but something about the air or floor alerted him to Birdy in his doorway. His eyes flew open. He grabbed at one of the ear jacks, pulling its tinny noise away from his head to ask her if his mother was all right.

Birdy admired his concern. He was a good boy. "How's the applying going?" she asked.

"I don't know," he said, sitting up, his white shirt falling over his skin, his feet plopping on the floor, where he turned one sideways and stepped on it with the other, as if to reduce their mass. "I hate writing essays about why I want to keep going to school. I don't think I *do* want to keep going to school." He scratched his sideburn, that place where masculinity kept popping up on his face, a perplexed gesture that Birdy had come to recognize from class. Her standing in his bedroom made him uneasy.

"I can help you," she said. "Show me your essay."

He shook his head as he agreed. That, too, was like him, contradictory, sending mixed signals. He'd held her at the dance, and then refused to make eye contact once they were back in Sock Probs and Am Vals the following Monday. Birdy had felt as flustered as she used to in high school, maybe more so. She'd sort of forgotten all the trickiness involved in romance; her recent boyfriends had been more mature, meaning more desperate. Poor Reg, the way he would push her against a wall or car, pelvis activated like a piston before his hands or mouth, as if he were on a meter with only a few minutes' time.

Mark's essay was appalling; Birdy felt she had to escape Pinetop High immediately, if this were what she was fostering. *I have no precocious notion,* he had written, *but I want to better my aspirations.*

She sat beside him on his bed and read the rest of his pathetic essay pleading and bleating that the University of New Mexico allow him in. She corrected his spelling and usage, the way she had his mother's, and then supplied a few replacement sentences about making contributions to society, about the wonders of a liberal education, about the diversity of a lively intellectual community. These phrases flowed from Birdy's jaded repertoire with appalling ease.

The two of them were sitting on a low sagging mattress, another ancestral hand-me-down, no doubt. Birdy could feel the absence of a few significant slats. The twelve years between them accordioned in her mind to a meaningless little gap. She tapped a word on the page as it rested on his knee, the paper warm. For a second, he hesitated, then laid his hand tentatively on hers, as if accidentally, testing her intentions. She caught her fingers around the tips of his, as if they might escape. His palm had a glossy callous, as if it had been painted with a fine coat of glue. It was a large thin hand with knobby knuckles and flat masculine nails; when it held a rope, it was beautiful, articulate, graceful. He watched his hand wrestle with Birdy's smaller one, then turned his gaze on her face, moving closer as if drawn by a thread to her lips. His eyes were so brown that the pupil blended with the iris, and his eyelashes were so crowded and thick that they stuck together like daisy petals, like the points of stars. He kissed her, tenderly, awkwardly, fearfully, as if he wanted to so badly it would kill him for her to discourage him. Birdy studied the doorway, expecting his mother any second. He was good at kissing, once he understood she would not refuse him. His lips had a slight dryness to them, chapped instead of spongy, plus, he didn't seem to feel the need to poke his tongue in her mouth right away, nor did he make an immediate grab at her breasts. He seemed to enjoy and be thankful for the simple pleasure of her lips on his, her hand on his hand, discreet body parts discovering one another, as if they had all the time in the world to do so, as if, now that she'd permitted this wild unthinkable thing, time had just as well simply stopped altogether. Birdy hoped her mouth didn't compare unfavorably with the mouths of less mature girls, ones without adult oral habits. She finally pulled away, flustered, blushing, cotton-tongued. She stood and crossed her arms, trapping her fingers under her own armpits like tricky widgets.

Mark smiled blissfully. "I'll walk you home," he said, standing. Even in his socks, he was a few inches taller than she.

She stepped back. "But I drove."

"Then I'll ride with you."

Birdy worried that a switch had been flipped inside him, releasing something singleminded and unyielding, that monstrous, primordial teenage hunger. He might be younger, his body language suggested, but he was also stronger than she.

"I have to finish with your mom," Birdy said feebly.

In an hour, when the full moon had risen and Mrs. Anthony's eyes were tired, Birdy said good-bye. Although he'd remained in his room after Birdy had left it, Mark appeared instantly at her side—he'd been listening, Birdy thought, the way she had for him—claiming he wanted a ride to a friend's house. His mother thanked Birdy for providing it, and Birdy felt ashamed, like the hustler who steals a wallet only to earn gratitude by giving it back unloaded.

They kissed in the car in Birdy's driveway. He moaned, involuntarily, so grateful. They both ducked their heads as the trailer's motion detector light went on, hurrying toward the door. Birdy felt drunk, reckless, notorious. On her couch, Mark experimented with other body parts and their attractions. He laughed uneasily when she brought out a condom packet from her bathroom, the bright light of that small room sending a beam of brilliance down the length of the tiny hall into the living room like a searchlight, where he waited with an erection inside his jeans.

"You don't wear underwear," Birdy noted.

"Uh uh."

"Why not?"

"Don't want my mom to wash it."

"Ah hah."

"You smell nice," he said. "Like Sweetarts."

That was the extent of their pillow talk. They made love on the floor in front of the couch, the cold linoleum beneath Birdy's knees as she lowered herself onto her student. Ten minutes later she padded down the hall for another condom. And fifteen minutes after that, she did it again. She loved youth, she decided, and she also loved that he could not spend the night, had no expectation of it, was as worried as she about scampering away.

"I'll drive you," she said.

"No, I want to walk."

"But it's four point two miles."

"I can do it easy," he assured her happily, ready to go move mountains, then promised, "I won't tell anyone," suddenly sincere and husky at her door, the fat moon behind him. He'd stepped down the two stairs, so his face was level with Birdy's.

Her eyes filled.

"That's good," she said, leaning forward to kiss his nose. "I won't either."

He sprinted down the street, making a basketball leap to swat at a tree branch.

Sweetarts, Birdy thought, as she closed the door.

❧ 4

Luziana Rillos's pregnancy blossomed with the spring; she wore sleeveless smocks and biking shorts, her skinny legs and arms sticking out of her inflated body like a voodoo doll. She had been of interest to Birdy before her pregnancy because she comported herself like a supermodel: lots of makeup, that 1960s raccoon-eyed look, dark hair straight and gleaming to her collar and then flipped out, like a bell, an inverted tulip. Though her eyes were brown, she wore contact lenses tinted Windex blue, which gave her dark face a curiously possessed look, two soulless holes like something from a demon movie. Tall and long-limbed, skinny and imperious, she walked leading with her bony hips, as if up on the big runway before the fashion editors and photographers. She didn't let being pregnant get in her way, comportment-wise. True, she couldn't flaunt her hipbones anymore—subsumed as they were—but she still sauntered in her loose style, swiveling her bloated tummy like another trendy statement, a medicine ball she was resigned to lug around for a few months.

Everyone stared, some, like Mr. John, more openly than was comfortable. Since his mental development was reputed to have stalled at twelve years, Mr. John's infatuation did not surprise Birdy. He was simply a boy in a man's anatomy, a sheep in wolf's clothing. He moved through the halls diligently spreading dirty ammonia water from locker to locker with a mophead the size and texture of a poodle. Luziana's lavish entrance or exit left him gape-mouthed, his duties forgotten. In the cafeteria he brought her extra chocolate milk, a gift Luziana had the graciousness to accept without humiliating him. Birdy admired Luziana's unself-consciousness. Either her pregnancy or some other experience had made her brash and careless about what people thought. So what if the retarded janitor adored her? So what if her navel had popped out like a gumball on her belly? She was destined for distant horizons, bigger fish to fry.

In class, she wedged herself sideways at her desk, one hand idly massaging the top of her abdomen. You just couldn't help gawking, so erotic was her appearance, so flagrant. The week before school ended, she remained in her seat after the rest of the class had plodded away, forcing Birdy to ask her how she was.

"I have hemorrhoids," Luziana said flatly. "That's how I am."

"Ugh," Birdy said, her lip curling involuntarily.

"Miz Stone? Will you do me a favor?"

Birdy's heart sank; not another favor.

"Will you come be my coach?"

"Your coach?" Birdy imagined posture drills, hair arranging, lip-lining and cheek-pinching, primping Luziana at a beauty pageant, Los Angeles, New York.

"For Lamaze and stuff? For when I go to the hospital? I don't think my friends can deal. They're all really immature. And the other teachers, the ladies, they like, think I'm a slut." Luziana was chewing Tums, the only student in class permitted to have candy.

"And the rest are men. You know?"

Birdy nodded. That left her, Birdy, Luziana's last resort.

The girl sighed. "The men probably think I'm a slut, too."

Lamaze had started a few weeks earlier. One of Luziana's little brothers had gone with her, but then stopped, the language too unappetizing. "He started thinking they thought he was the dad. I'm like, who cares what these old fat preggos think? They're all wearing house shoes, don't even get dressed to go out. But he's like, outta there. And I have to have a coach. My mom's dead," she added, without inflection. *Sadness,* Jesús would have said, just as uninflected.

Since Birdy's mom was dead, too, Birdy agreed to play coach, although she preferred thinking of herself as an older sister figure rather than mother. There was never mention of the baby's father; certainly Birdy wasn't going to bring it up. The high school boys all seemed intimidated by Luziana, her height and confidence frightening them. For all Birdy knew, Mr. John had sired the offspring, his Frankensteinian devotion thus accounted for.

Birdy's own experience with pregnancy was limited. She'd been pregnant for nine weeks once, nine years ago. Her boyfriend, the creative writing professor, had liked the idea of a baby. On his old face she'd seen pure elation, the wet sheen of his sentimental eyes. In class, he liked to be surly and brusque, but once you had him naked on a mattress he was as corny as they came. He knew his body could never cover its agedness the way his clothes or wit or poetry or retinue of young students could. These things had to be slowly stripped away, he'd made himself secure by their wrapping. But Birdy had worked her way in, bared him thoroughly. Her own body never pleased her more than when she saw it beside the professor's. Both of them liked to touch her, and for the brief time that she was pregnant, they seemed to both have good reason to caress her tender breasts. A fascinating brown stripe had begun emerging just below her navel, a darkening path through the nest of her pubic hair. Perhaps her poet had thought a baby would help keep him young. Perhaps he thought a baby would tie Birdy to him. She had known she could not keep their baby, had wandered whimsically through the early weeks, and then aborted it without ever entertaining a serious fantasy of doing otherwise. At that age, just the thought of maternity clothes had turned her stomach.

Now her poet was sixty-three—if he was still alive, which Birdy had no reason to suppose he wasn't; she'd never met anyone more dedicated to ensuring longevity, those rough bran muffins and nasty medicinal tea, those daily swims and runs and meditations and naps. Sixty-three and soon to retire from the university. Their baby would have been in third or fourth grade. Birdy would live in Champaign-Urbana in the midwestern frame house the poet had claimed was too big for him and his old cat. That cat, Godfrey, Birdy remembered. Godfrey the gray cat. She had aborted more than the infant, cleansed her whole life then with the arrogant assurance of a twenty-year-old, mature enough to decide for herself, young enough to be glib about her future entanglements. There would be plenty: other babies, other lovers, other landscapes, matches more fitting during times more fitting in a more fitting climate.

She'd been so sure, then, that life was about accumulation rather than loss.

Birdy wished she had something wise to impart to

Luziana, something about burning bridges or the spited face you left after cutting off your nose but she had the feeling the girl was way ahead of her.

BIRDY NOTICED that Mrs. Anthony's mouth was like her son's, flat along the top, flush and lippy on the bottom. A good mouth to kiss, she thought dreamily, to be kissed by. The woman wiped her hand nervously across her face a few times when she saw Birdy staring so intently at it.

"Here," she said, handing over a basket of correspondence she'd received in response to her losses, envelopes ten years old, the penmanship of other mothers and fathers and siblings and spouses who'd become bereft. Birdy's task was to compose a form letter, asking these survivors for permission to include their words in Mrs. Anthony's book, to reveal their names and hardships.

"There are so many," Birdy said. By and large, the writers simply recounted their own stories, most of them implying that what they'd suffered was worse than what Mrs. Anthony had suffered, occasionally actually telling Mrs. Anthony to count her blessings, thank her heavenly stars. One mother's son was in a coma from a motorcycle accident, and she let Mrs. Anthony know that the real godsend would have been his instantaneous death. His coma was three years old, ten years ago. "How can a person have so much bad happen to them, and still go on?" Mrs. Anthony asked, clearly anticipating no intelligent answer out of Birdy.

Holding the pile of letters, Birdy imagined the dozens of survivors whose tragedies she could delve into, the mother of the comatose boy, the girl—now a woman—who'd driven her family into the path of a semi truck, killing them all, her four-year-old brother, her ten-year-old sister, mom and dad and grandfather. There was always somebody in worse straits than your own, Birdy supposed. Was it comforting to know? Was that the prompt for writing to a total stranger? Did Mrs. Anthony actually feel lucky, as the vaguely scolding tone of some of these letters seemed to suggest she should? The girl driving the family had had her license only two days; they had been on their way home from church. Where was Vanna Dewberry now? And Miguel Angel? And Earnest Stubbs? And Mrs. Ricardo Ferrerez? Their names alone made Birdy sad; more than one had included the article they'd read that had prompted their reaching out, one story inspiring another, bad luck and sorrow, tag-team tragedy, as if Mrs. Anthony might want more copies of the news, or maybe they just wanted the clipping out of their houses. Some contained saint cards, prayers, pressed flowers, a recipe for Rob's Famous Lime Chile Chicken Soup. Many invoked good old Job, looking to locate God's methodology, He who'd chosen to exercise their heart muscles to the point of breaking.

"Did you ever write back to them?" asked Birdy.

"Of course," said Mrs. Anthony. "That was Mark's job, to write the thank-you cards. Teresa had taught him cursive, and he liked to practice. 'Thank you for your prayers. Sincerely yours, Mark Anthony.' We went through three boxes of stationery."

"That's a lot of sympathy," said Birdy, thinking that Mrs. Anthony had already sent her fellow sufferers a form letter, a generic empathetic gesture, hidden behind a child's endearing hand. She would have liked to see his handwriting, although she didn't like being reminded that when he was seven, learning cursive, she'd been nineteen, learning fellatio.

"People have great big hearts," said Mrs. Anthony. "That's why I'm putting together my book." She laid her palm proudly on her sheaf of pages; according to her, she did not "write," she "journaled," which, as a verb, seemed exactly like what it was: tunneling into one's own nasty navel with a pencil. "Others can benefit from my experience," she went on. "This is just a link in the chain of healing and recovery. Now, you need to get their permission to use their letters."

Birdy said, "Maybe you could use them anonymously. Just change some of the vocabulary so it wouldn't be plagiarism. I don't think you can copyright a narrative. Or a title," she added superfluously.

Mrs. Anthony frowned at her. "Why would I want to do that?"

"I mean I think you can tell their stories, in your own words."

"I don't want to use my own words, I want to use their words. That's why I'm asking you to send these people a release form. I want permission to print their stories and give their names."

"But maybe the point isn't how it's said, but what's being said. Maybe you don't want to bother these poor people . . ."

"I'm not bothering them. I'm letting them tell about the most devastating thing that ever happened to them."

Put that way, Birdy couldn't argue.

Mrs. Anthony went on, "I was thinking that each chapter could have a condolence letter at the beginning, centered, in italics. Like this one." She quoted from a letter: *"Don't forget that the number-one main ingredient is hours of prayer, bombarded for you with blessings by our loving family and anointed by Dr. Morris Casteneda of Morris Casteneda World Evangelism."* She paused to give Birdy a moment to appreciate the power of an unedited sentiment. "And then I'll mail them all free copies of the book, when it's published."

Birdy said she thought that would be very nice, wondering how far Mrs. Anthony's book fantasy extended. Did she see herself debating typeface with the printer? Speaking before Parents Without Partners? Was she practicing her own cursive writing, scrawling an autograph over and over like a physician with a prescription pad?

"You must have access to a Xerox machine," Mrs. Anthony said.

"Yep. Xerox *and* mimeo."

"Perfect. We'll need forty-two copies."

Birdy had to be reminded several times to carry out this chore. First typing the letter, then Xeroxing it, then applying stamps, and actually posting the things. She had some strange reluctance to hearing about more suffering, to be the one summoning tales of tragedies.

AT LAMAZE, under framed photographs of the men who'd reached grand Elkdom, Luziana rubbed her tummy like a magic lamp and hardly paid attention to the instructor, Birdy beside her jotting down notes—bloody show, mucus plug, Braxton Hicks, colostrum—and stifling nausea. She decided she was grateful not to be pregnant again herself; it sounded unbearable, and not just the nine-month siege on the body but all the rest as well, the wet howl of an infant, its fearsome squirming helplessness. They scared her, babies, more now than they had in her earlier life, back when she'd had enough moxie, enough blind confidence in her own infallibility, to support a dozen. You could drop them, or lose them, or even in the best of circumstances be certain to fuck them up.

On the Elks Club Lodge floor, leased for the purpose of Lamaze class by virtue of its padded carpet, Luziana lay as directed, her young head on her arm, her silky hair hanging beautifully, as if nothing could faze her youthful prettiness, her big tight belly brewing beneath her thin blouse. Birdy could see the elbows or knees of Luziana's child as it flung itself angrily around inside. Luziana seemed not to notice the uproar. She was bored with her pregnancy, as well as not very interested in how painful its outcome would be. She was a teenager; she lacked imagination about the future. Around her lay six other women with their coaches under the somber gazes of former Elk potentates—waxed mustaches and double chins—husbands not unlike Birdy's students, staring impassively, perhaps resentfully, at the instructor as she heaved and gesticulated, scratching their heads and avoiding one another's eyes. Never in a thousand years had they envisioned themselves in the Elks Club listening to some sprightly gal lecture them on the width of their wife's cervix. Mooning cars, yes; castrating cattle, sure thing; but clipping an umbilicus? No thanks. Neither Birdy nor Luziana had made friends among them.

"They probably think we're lezzies," Luziana claimed, giggling. "Let 'em." Her immediate desire was to go to Sonic after Lamaze and eat onion rings, watch her classmates drive in and out of the parking lot.

"My hand is sore," Birdy remarked after class, as they descended the Elks Club steps, flexing her right fingers.

"Look, you got a bump on your tall man from writing so much." Luziana shook her head; it just wasn't worth a callous, all that nonsense upstairs.

As usual, Birdy marveled at the rack of elk antlers sporting lightbulbs that hung over the club's entrance. It was, hands down, the most impressively tacky fixture she had ever seen, and she always wondered who in the world had dreamed up such a thing.

The evening was chilly but spring rites prevailed. Birdy drove to Sonic, then sat behind the steering wheel shivering, drinking a cherry limeade, waving at her students as they whirled through the lot, like a teenager herself, tracking the boys passing before them like ducks in a shooting gallery, looking longer as Mark Anthony went by riding shotgun in Mike Trujillo's pickup, the well-formed triangle his muscular shoulders made above the seat, his smooth neck with its one knob, his beautiful profile. Here, the music throbbed like an arrhythmic heartbeat, and his chin followed the pulse. She wondered if he was looking for her, if he were thinking about her hand gripped in his as they made love, which was what Birdy couldn't help thinking of. She had to admit that she, like Luziana, much preferred this milieu to Lamaze.

Luziana watched her watching Mark. "He's cute, huh?" she said.

Birdy fought down her lightheadedness, feigned nonchalance. "Who's his girlfriend?" she asked recklessly.

"Patty Arnett."

"What?"

Luziana studied her thoughtfully. "You like Mike?" she asked, smiling faintly. "I mean, *like* him?"

"Mike Trujillo? He's a student." Birdy composed herself, scoffing at the preposterous notion of her liking a student, especially Mike Trujillo in his monster truck, his tight Wrangler jeans that made him walk like a duck, can of snuff outlined in the rear pocket. *Merciful heavens,* her mother would have said sardonically, exhaling a braid of smoke.

"You're a beautiful blonde, Miz Stone, but the men in this town are the pits—I know, I've been scoping it out. All the good ones move away as soon as they can, and the losers stick around, the scum, the dribs."

"Dregs," Birdy corrected without thinking.

"Whatever."

Birdy named a few representative dregs. Mr. Wires Plus. The man who ran the Congoleum Floor Covering Showroom. Hugh Gross. Mr. John.

"Oh, Mr. John's okay," Luziana said lightly, resuming interest in her fries. The carhop brought out extra ketchup and dropped it through the open car window without saying a word, as if she were depositing the squishy packets in a trash can. "One time," Luziana said, "one time I got in a car crash, with my old boyfriend, and Mr. John really helped me out."

"How so?"

"This was a long time ago," Luziana said, "back when I was so dumb, my sophomore year, and I had this boyfriend Laszlo who crashed his car after a game. My leg was bleeding. If I wasn't such a bloated pig, I could show you the scar, but trust me it's down there." She jabbed her finger toward the dark space below where her feet rested. "Mr. John fixed me. We crashed into a pole in the parking lot, Laszlo was drunk—asshole Laszlo—'scuse me—they got him on a DWI later, he's one of those live-and-don't-learn type of guys—and anyway Mr. John brought out some SuperGlue and did my leg."

"With SuperGlue?"

"Sounds sick, huh? It worked really good. He was totally cool about it. Laszlo was freaking—here I am, bleeding on his seat—but Mr. John glued me up. That stuff stinks, boy. My dad thought I'd been sniffing, I smelled so bad. It's a funny scar, not like stitches, more like a leach. I'd show you, like I said, but I can't even see my own damn legs." Luziana suddenly swept aside her fry box, brushed away the ketchup packets, and kicked off her shoes, bending awkwardly to find them on the floorboard, then heaved them out the window onto the parking lot. She rolled the glass up. "I can't be a fashion victim anymore," she declared.

"Good." Birdy tried to imagine intentionally adhering her flesh with SuperGlue. Only a teenager or a retarded person would conceive of such a thing. How Mr. John must have enjoyed the proximity of Luziana's bare calf. She said, "He seems devoted to you."

"Who seems devoted to me?"

"Mr. John."

"Oh. I guess. He checks up on me. He takes care of our

sidewalk with the leaf blower. My brothers go out and call him names, but he doesn't care. I think it's kind of sweet. Do my feet stink?"

"Not at all," Birdy lied. "I've heard feet swell during pregnancy."

"Everything swells. There's not one part of me that isn't swollen. My shoe size went from a seven to an eight and a half. You shoulda seen my mama's feet, after the four of us. Sometimes she had to wear my dad's shoes. Sometimes his pants and shirts, too."

Thinking of her own mother, Birdy asked how Luziana's had died.

"Pneumonia," Luziana said. "Everybody at our house had it, and Mama, you know, nursed us all, making the soup, putting on the mustard plasters, steaming up the bathroom, being the saint. She forgot to look out for herself. We had to wait on the funeral till we all got better and the weather was nice. It was so cold they couldn't dig a hole at the cemetery. I wore her black dress," she added. "Same one I wear now, the one with the big see-through sleeves?" She stretched out her left arm so that her thin hand was near Birdy's nose, and pulled at imaginary cloth with the other slender hand. "My dad wanted to bury her in it, but I said, 'Hey, she don't care what she looks like, down there.' Not hell, but you know, underground. I'm sure she went to heaven, if there is one, taking care of all of us with pneumonia and all. I picked her out a red dress, polyester, no wrinkles, and I plucked her chin hairs. She would have wanted me to. She was very vain about her facial hair."

"My mother was cremated," Birdy said.

"Mr. John blows leaves off her grave," Luziana said, then slapped the seatback suddenly. "Here's Mike's stupid truck again." She twisted to follow the vehicle, her hair moving in a sleek curtain. Birdy didn't look this time, but the noise from the stereo seemed to rock her car, tremble around her like thunder rolling by. "Who's *she*?" Luziana asked, and before Birdy could think, she was struggling to get a glance. But of course there was nobody but Mike and Mark, the backs of their heads identical, military.

Luziana was grinning brattily. "Gotcha," she said, blowing imaginary smoke from her aimed finger.

Irked, Birdy explained that she knew Mark's mother, that was all.

"He's cute, too, but his family is weird. My dad used to work at the mill with his dad, before he died, and he said Mark's dad was a kiss-ass. Also, that sister, she used to be so mean. My mom slapped me on the face when I said I didn't care that she was dead. I was only six or something, what did I know about dead? But that's the way my mom was, slapping me around when she thought I wasn't nice. Is that a good positive role model, or what?"

This sounded like run-of-the-mill parental hypocrisy to Birdy, nothing very surprising. "How was she mean?" she asked. "Teresa, not your mom."

Through the windshield, Luziana exchanged a phony smile and crimped finger wave with one of her classmates, Barbie Rose. "Bitch," she muttered. "They're all dying to know who the father is," she went on as Barbie sauntered inside, ignoring Birdy's question. "And I'm not telling."

"Is it Mr. John?"

"Mr. John?" She scowled.

"Laszlo?"

"I told you I'm not telling."

"Why not?"

The girl looked at Birdy craftily. "No reason to tell—yet. Secrets are like money, Miz Stone, and it's better to save some than to spend it all at once."

"How was Teresa mean?" Birdy repeated.

"You know, bitchy like teenagers always are to little kids," Luziana said. "Like they never used to be seven years old themselves. That's one thing I promised myself—" she held up two fingers, scout's honor "—never be bitchy to little girls. Teenagers were always blabbing stuff to me and my friends they shouldn't of, like I remember Teresa once at church going on all about peeing blood and men sticking stuff inside her privates."

Carefully Birdy said, "Maybe she was abused. That sounds like some sort of terrible sexual abuse." Despite having believed Teresa the victim of a perverse passion she felt sickened by these concrete details.

"Miz Stone, you are so funny." Luziana laughed hard, holding her mounded abdomen. "She was just telling us about normal stuff, periods and sex. You crack me up, I feel like I'm going to pee my pants, it's so dangerous to laugh when you're pregnant. There are those damn boys again."

This time Birdy turned and watched them openly. She found Mark's face, and, astonishingly, he was staring at her. Instantly she felt her fist curled inside his, pit in peach, heart in rib cage. What did it mean to him, to have enclosed her hand as they made love? Around her, in the presence of this locked gaze, everything else in the cosmos fell momentarily away—greasy onion odor, pulsing music, green fluorescent tubes of the drive-in awning—a helpless orbiting moon pinned by gravity and reflected heat to its glowing sun.

AT SCHOOL, Birdy pulled Mark's file and studied it. Siblings (1) Sister, Teresa Christina Signaigo Anthony, DESEASED. The misspelling Birdy vaguely noted: deceased and diseased, together at last. And what a mouthful of a moniker. The parents hadn't felt compelled to load up the son, however. Just

Mark Anthony—maybe the Roman connotation could be assumed to carry the clout of additional names.

His SAT scores were embarrassingly low, but Jesús had told her she needed only to change his ethnicity from Caucasian to Hispanic and all would go well. With Wite-Out, in a moment when Mrs. Pack had tramped off to the lounge bathroom, Birdy fixed Mark's records—reeking haddock, in the words of his mother—telling herself she was sending him on to a better life, giving him chances he wouldn't have otherwise had.

Around the lounge, Birdy's colleagues treated her slightly differently, as if they appreciated her efforts on the students' behalf, first Mark Anthony, now Luziana Rillos. They thought Birdy was getting into the swing of Pinetop High at last. They congratulated themselves on having finally swayed her, broken her like a recalcitrant wild pony. When she asked for a CD-ROM for her classroom computer, Principal Hal put it at the top of the supplies request list.

But one of them, Mary Jo Callahan, bothered Birdy with her change in attitude. At first, she'd thought Mary Jo was just now coming out of her shy shell, initiating conversation by asking questions of Birdy, approaching her because she found her newly approachable. She had always liked to think that Mary Jo was intimidated by her comeliness. After a few weeks, however, Birdy realized that Mary Jo was not just being nice. She sincerely wanted to know about the Anthonys, in the nosy fashion of the snooping gossip. How could one person have so many unattractive traits? Birdy had supposed she felt permission to despise the woman in the way she did rats—just because of their unfortunate genetic ugliness, the greedy eyes and naked snaky tails. They couldn't help their appearance, but neither could she help her reaction. Not only physically repulsive, Mary Jo was now revealed as luridly curious, capable of insinuating volumes. The girl's death meant something to her, and it was with a strange hunger that she listened to what Birdy said.

As a result, Birdy tried hard to say very little.

"How's the book coming along?" Mary Jo would ask each week.

"Just fine," Birdy would say. She resorted to naming the page count, if Mary Jo pressed. "Nearly two hundred," she might reply, as if the book's accumulating pages, their sheer weight, would signify closure, as if there were a score to achieve, a record to break. What would it be? Three hundred pages? Five hundred? Mary Jo always nodded eagerly.

"Great!" she would say, then zero in on a specific. "Did they ever find Teresa's shoes?" she might ask.

"Never did," Birdy would reply, lips firmly sealed against saying more. Yet she always did say more, filling Mary Jo in against her will. She felt the uncomfortable desire to brag, to prove herself more knowledgeable, to continue to separate herself from Mary Jo's situation by stating the facts, by squelching the same rumors she privately entertained. She was helpless against her own nature to one-up the woman. Since they were both English teachers, people might classify them together, start thinking of them as two peas in a pod. Birdy dreaded the day some student or parent mistook her for Miss Callahan.

For her part, Mary Jo continued to supply small details that intrigued Birdy, withheld tidbits dispensed like candy or medication. "Teresa's dad had a gambling habit," she told Birdy one day over lunch. Mary Jo was one of those people who brought Tupperware containers of last night's dinner to the office, microwaving it and leaving a ghastly oily odor floating about. "Some people thought maybe he killed himself because he owed money at the track."

"Really?"

Mary Jo nodded. The birthmarked skin had less give than normal skin, and it went taut purple as her head moved. Birdy checked her gag reflex, embarrassed by her body's immature impulse.

Mary Jo went on, "Ask his wife if she had to pay somebody in Ruidoso a lot of money, afterward. Maybe she got an insurance check, for his life, and paid with that?"

"Maybe," Birdy said. She refrained from telling Mary Jo that Mr. Anthony's recent promotion had doubled his insurance coverage. Although the mill had predicted its own demise, they'd promoted him with the assumption that he would direct the skeleton crew the company left when it closed its doors. His was, perhaps, the most secure job in town. This fact had fueled Mrs. Anthony's belief in some resentment from a coworker, revenge. She used it as evidence, in Chapter 5, Part 1, of conspiracy. Of course, with doubled life insurance, Mrs. Anthony herself, beneficiary, had some incentive for murder. It seemed farfetched, to Birdy, though she knew Mary Jo would find it totally plausible. Her vicarious enthusiasm for the sordid made Birdy temper her own inclination toward the same.

Maybe Mary Jo stationed herself outside the Alpine Inn every night, waiting for the viceful to reveal themselves. Maybe that's how she'd caught poor Teresa Anthony. Maybe she planned to catch Birdy, up to no good with Mark.

Birdy hated to have to do it, but she said to Mary Jo, "I never heard about a gambling problem before." Like his questionable overprotectiveness of Teresa, Mr. A.'s gambling was not something Mrs. A. had mentioned.

Mary Jo backed down instantly; she was such a coward, such a toady, a 'fraidy crab scrambling back into its shell. "That was just what some people were saying, that he liked the horses and got in over his head. Could be a complete fabrication." She finished her foul-smelling casserole and excused herself. Along with her Tupperware leftovers, she also carried toothbrush, toothpaste, floss, and mouthwash with her. As if dental hygiene would save her.

Still, the topic of the Anthonys was better than the usual lounge fare. Conversation routinely went one of two equally stultifying ways. There was either small talk—diets, vacations, sales, lottery tickets, student rabble rousers—or a vague hypothetical discourse about The Ideal World, the preamble of which was always "They should . . ." or "We ought to . . ." Often this was prompted by an outrageous phone call in the "Speak Up!" column. "Those teachers at the high school sure aren't doing their job keeping gang members off the streets at night. Just want to say what are our taxes doing, anyway, with no homework?" There'd be a stir in the lounge, a proposal to write a letter or petition. Sometimes The Ideal World was heralded in by some altercation with parents, those necessary evils, people who generally lumped teachers categorically as the group represented by bumper sticker wisdom: they couldn't *do*, and so they *taught*.

In the lounge, opposing "theys" prevailed: they should straighten up or we ought to carry weapons! They should pay us more or we ought to go on strike! In The Ideal World, the community at large would mend their ways, kiss the feet of the brave educators who headed off to Pinetop High every morning, but mostly it was the students who would metamorphose: teenagers would never pierce body parts or swill alcohol or smoke in bathrooms or make improper displays of affection in the halls or do what the other teachers called "sassing back" and "smarting off." Having been a sass-back and smart-off from way back herself, Birdy couldn't in good conscience join in; she preferred believing she didn't believe in The Ideal World. Discipline was one of its cornerstones. So was Punishment. Students would be the bright-eyed, well-bred, flawlessly mannered automatons that made instruction simple. The children were sheep, the faculty their shepherds. Or, worse, the children were prisoners, the faculty their keepers.

What Birdy disliked most was the futility of this sort of discussion, the way it wasted time and words and space in the brain, the sort-of moral high road its proponents seemed to think masked the sheer whininess of it. Even if their ambitions had been more interesting, nothing would come of them—too many idea men, no grunts. Everyone's Ideal World required vast sums of money and manpower, an agreement to a standard, a bill of rights and a king. It was as foolish and naive as a hippie commune, the Biodome, an Aryan Nation, a balanced budget, a happy ending. Whenever her colleagues broached The Ideal World, Birdy sneaked away.

The real trouble, she realized as she eased quietly out one afternoon, was that if she began participating in the discussion, she would be counted among the adults. That was just about the last thing she had in mind. She'd chosen teaching teenagers because she could remember being one. I believe in youth, she told herself. Youth rules.

❧ 5

Each person has four major aspects of being. Physical, spiritual, mental, and emotional. Now the body communicates with itself through pulses from the brain (please think of them as teeny trains) chugging along in the nerve system like a divinely inspired railway to get the message across. What happens if these pathways are distorted or even blocked? Misalignment!—a terrible derailing that affects the way we think, the way we perceived our life and our situations around us. We are basically laying with our wheels spinning, unable to respond until we have created a mountain from a molehill or an elephant from a mosquito, as they say in Switzerland.

One Wednesday night, while sitting with Mrs. Anthony in her kitchen, reading the latest installment of her writing, the lights suddenly went off. Birdy had been thinking she could not bear any more of this rot: past lives made her impatient, fate made her wish for an Old Testament God who might smite the hell out of everyone; and if she came across just one more objective correlative for Mrs. A.'s lost, wounded, misrouted, annihilated soul she thought she'd scream. Air refused to circulate; impending weather felt like PMS. Mrs. Anthony sat beside her, silent and stoic in a starched coral-colored linen suit, waiting for Birdy to complain about her prose. Birdy twitched: tension, anxiety, apprehension.

She took it all back when the lights suddenly went out. How she hated the dark, much more than she hated Mrs. Anthony's book.

Mrs. Anthony gasped audibly; Birdy, city girl, moviegoer, instantly suspected bandits, rapists, hooligans such as only rural New Mexico would produce. Her heart banged; their weapons would be chainsaws and shotguns and blunt shovels, the implements she saw every day racked in the windows of their pickup trucks. Mark was not home, which further supported her fear that bad guys stalked the little house. The nearest neighbor would not hear their screams for help; the blackness was thick as tar.

From out of it, Mrs. Anthony's voice said, "We have an emergency generator. It'll come on soon." Birdy heard her chair scrape on the stone floor, then the click of the gas stove as first one burner and then another was lighted. The blue rings of flame made Mrs. Anthony's features shadowy, ancient looking as rock cliffs. "Tea?" she offered from the glowing clefted gloom of her own face.

Birdy accepted.

"There must be a storm down the canyon," Mrs. Anthony said. "This happens all the time." Even with this explanation, she look worried.

Before the water boiled, the lights popped back on, a trifle dimmer than before. Both women sighed. Their shared fear, and its abatement, seemed to open a more intimate space between them, their relieved breathing synchronized, as if they'd narrowly avoided disaster. Mrs. Anthony poured the steaming water over a tea bag and said hesitantly to Birdy, "I wonder if you could give me your opinion about Mark's social life?"

Birdy said she'd try.

"I'm worried that he's not dating anyone these days. He used to have a girlfriend, last fall, and he's always been a sociable young man . . ." She trailed off thoughtfully, filling her own cup and then standing with the kettle in her oven-mitted hand, steam wisping around her face. "I was thinking maybe bringing up Teresa all the time was upsetting him. He doesn't say anything, but I wonder all the same. If I'm upsetting him."

Birdy stirred sugar in her tea, her heart, which had calmed with the return of light now beating maniacally once more, her forehead sweating. Was the woman hinting at something? Had Mark let something slip about the puzzling love affair they seemed to be perpetrating? Was that why he wasn't home tonight, mysteriously truant so that his mother could accuse his seductress? Extinguish the lights and then douse her in scalding water, hide her parboiled flesh under the floorboards? Why were they drinking hot tea on a hot night? She knew it had no taste, but was arsenic also uncloudy as it dissolved? Or was Birdy dripping sweat for some other reason?

Or was Mrs. Anthony genuinely concerned? Afraid her son was withdrawing into his adolescence, that La Brea tar pit of despair. It was hard to know what she knew; as her book attested, her instincts for the truth fluctuated wildly, some reliable, some utterly un.

"I don't get around town much anymore," Mrs. Anthony went on, pinching her pleats with her rough fingers. "You know, Mark does our shopping and such, so I wondered if you could think of any girls he might want to ask out? A nice girl, from his class?" She smiled falteringly, her lips like earthworms, Birdy thought, two of them wriggling on her face. Maybe this expression meant embarrassment; maybe it was sly.

It was on the tip of Birdy's tongue to endorse her own candidacy as a nice girl from Mark's class. She cleared her throat. "I'll think about it," she promised.

"Thank you, Ms. Stone." That was that. Under the dim lights, they continued with the authoring and editing, the hunting and pecking, the scritch and scratch.

A nice girl. The phrase skulked around in Birdy's brain, asserting itself at inopportune moments, mocking her. Nice girls made everyone nervous, just like whores. Nice girls made your inner animal cringe, retreat with its tail between its legs. Nice girls made the sex of regular not-nice girls a schizophrenic business.

And she was having sex often, daily almost, Mark's amorous fixation big and insurmountable. If Mrs. A. were worried about her boy's sexual preferences, she might have been relieved to find out he was 100 percent hetero inclined. He began by removing his shoes and leaving them just inside the storm door. Then he would give Birdy a giant hug, enfolding her in the manner of a straitjacket, and murmur his hello into her hair. There was always his lasso to unwind from his belt loops. When Birdy had run out of condoms, he looked panicked at the prospect of his having to supply them. She had let him dangle there like a fish, fascinated by her hold on his fortune, then let him off the hook. "I'll get some," she said, and he'd shuddered with relief.

Ditto the day he inquired about Jesús. "Everyone thinks you and Mr. Morales are dating," he'd said.

"Me and Jesús? Jesús and I?"

He'd looked away, shy to expose his jealous uncertainty. Again, Birdy let him squirm, let him think her wildly bisexual, full of carnal secrets—carnal pockets, she'd thought: who knew what went where?

"Jesús is totally gay," she finally said.

"He is?"

"Uh huh."

Mark leaned back in the manner of conqueror, naked chest puffed, legs crossed casually at the calf.

"Were you worried?" Birdy asked him.

"No," he lied.

He was grateful for every small variation or trick Birdy concocted, unworldly in a touching way. He'd not understood the beauty of the ear, before Birdy, nor the thrill of his own nipples between her teeth. She traced rings around his testicles just to ponder his rigid pleasure; she sandwiched his fingers in her warm oiled palms and pulled at the tips just to hear him moan. It was enough to make her feel criminal, like a pedophile.

What had he been used to? The shocking thought came to Birdy: he'd been virginal until he met her. Could it be? Lounge lore held that all of Pinetop High was "sexually active," a phrase that always brought to Birdy's mind the hopping wind-up penis you could find in certain tacky gift shops. According to her colleagues, she taught in a buzzing swarm of licentiousness. Intimate as she and Mark were, there seemed no room to ask such a question of him. Plus, she had to admit, she did not want to know.

After their second evening together, he'd claimed to love Birdy.

"You don't love me," she'd assured him. "You just think you do."

"What's the difference?" he asked, sincerely curious.

Birdy couldn't say; it'd been a long time since she was a virgin. Because he loved her, she worked to put some distance in her own feelings. He was overeager, too simple, they had nothing in common but a few of the deadly sins, primarily lust. When she thought of him, it was not his intellect but his body that came to mind. All she wanted to do was fondle him, that wasn't love, etc. The circuitous route he wore to her trailer door, whether from schoolyard or basketball court or rec center or bowling alley, the half hour he could spare between one extracurricular ball game and another, between picking up mail or shopping for groceries or paying the gas bill, unnerved Birdy. He fit her in his busy life like a necessity, like a habit. He devoted serious attention to their sex, as if in training for marriage, despite the fact that he was only seventeen years old.

"Do you like me to do this?" he would ask, rolling Birdy's shoulders with his big palms.

"I do like that," Birdy said. The older it got, the more her body treasured such celebration. And he was so pleasingly modest about his talents. He seemed to feel sure she'd had better lovers, more experienced hands upon her. He worked hard to do her justice, to give her what he felt she deserved. Being worshipped was awfully addictive. Still, when word came that UNM had accepted him provisionally for the fall, Birdy was relieved. Making love every day was difficult; a person chafed. She did not want to be responsible for his unhappiness, the way she was for his predecessors'. As usual in romance, leverage kept shifting. Was he guileless and smitten, really truly? Or was he perpetrating some elaborate practical joke, Birdy the subject of a senior class prank? Back and forth she went, paranoid and infatuated, uncertain and overadulated. She found herself pretending to have other destinations after school so that she wouldn't have to meet Mark at her trailer, constructing a busy nonexistent social life with nonexistent Pinetopians—meetings, drinks, meals. She found herself crouching on the dusty floor of her own living room, the way she had way back when, in grade school, during tornado drills, not answering Mark's raps on her door.

She found herself driving to the cliff dwelling and looking over the roadside where half of his family had died.

Sometimes she thought of jumping off, the way the girl had, feet bare, wind rushing over her, the dazzling illusion of flight just before the smash. Other times she thought of driving off, the way Teresa's father had, taking that less courageous route. Birdy didn't hold his method against him; his adult being was heavier than Teresa's adolescent one, and he would have had to summon greater resources to carry through. Birdy would not wear her seat belt; she would have drunk a great deal of tequila first, to cushion whatever pain might be involved just before dying. Because even then—maybe especially then—it seemed a person ought to be spared, ought to be indulged a little purgatorial nothingness in which to contemplate the end. There'd been no autopsy when Mr. Anthony died, but the sheriff's report had speculated that he'd been drinking, had stated for certain that he'd worn no seat belt. Grief-stricken, or suicidal, or both. Birdy did not have to work hard to empathize; she had often enough felt suicide's dazzling appeal as a quick-fix solution. She especially liked to imagine her own father and sister as they regretted her death, as they raked themselves over the coals for not having kept better track of her. Why, why hadn't they read the signs? Why hadn't they saved her?

Save me, she prayed, beamed into the empty sky above her, waiting for interception.

When she saw a shooting star, she thought the childish thought: someone has died. Then it occurred to her that dying had become the only event that would shift the status quo with her family. It was as if she were waiting for death, so that she could change, as if she were wishing for it. Either she would die, or one of them would. Then the relationship would be clear and simple once more; then she—or her survivors—would know how to feel. Didn't she know just precisely how she felt about her dead mother?

In her dreams, her mother often returned, wearing her nightgown. Birdy had no instinct except to hold onto her like a child, Mama, Mama, prevent her from leaving again, her form vanishing as Birdy reached around, nothing remaining but the empty embrace of her own arms patting her own back, tangled in the cool silken nightie, Birdy desiring the physical contact when it was the most basic thing denied her. Nothing complicated in that. Funny how the loss continued to wound, to stun, to send Birdy spiraling. Some nasty talent her sleeping mind had, making her forget her mother was dead so that the news seemed eternally fresh, a sharp blade dragged over her heart. Perhaps Mrs. Anthony dreamed the same dream, reaching for Teresa only to have her evaporate, elude her grasp by falling over that cliff again and again, night after night.

Mrs. Anthony's story reminded Birdy of tragic Demeter, the original martyred mom, chasing after the suddenly sexualized Persephone. She, too, had to believe her daughter had been abducted by the dark powers of the underworld rather than legitimately seduced by its attractive king. A mother wouldn't want to believe her girl would go willingly. A mother would prefer to have her girl seized away into the black jaws of hell. Maybe Mrs. Anthony's obsession could be seen as Demeter's grief, her persistent attention to her daughter's fate. Her own guilt. Her not loving the girl enough, her love not being enough, unable, as it was, to prevent her from being lured away. But a mother could never compete with a suitor, could she? A suitor was so unlike, so intriguingly other, hard and dark and moody and boisterous to complement, to fill, all the inverse features. How could it compare with a mother's love, that force field as strong and familiar as an extra layer of skin, shrink-wrapped 'round a person so imperceptibly, so comfortably she might not miss it, might barely notice it, until it was flayed, peeled away to reveal the raw, unprepared thing beneath?

But if Mrs. A. were Demeter, where was her Persephone during the paroled leaves from hell? Where was the compensatory spring and summer, when the daughter lifted from the underworld to bring life back to earth?

The problem with life, Birdy concluded, was that it often did not feel obligated to play by the rules of literature.

JESÚS TOOK Birdy to Albuquerque one Saturday to shop. Birdy had not told him outright about her affair with Mark, but she assumed he'd guessed. He seemed just slightly miffed, his smile just one fraction smaller than before, something withheld like a secret or judgment. She hoped that Mark Anthony hadn't been blabbing at school about Jesús's homosexuality, and, if he were blabbing, that he wasn't naming his source. But maybe what Birdy read on Jesús's face was her own shame, manifesting itself in other people's countenances. She would shop, she decided, for a graduation gift for Mark. If Jesús asked, she would tell him all about her romance.

It felt good to travel at high speed down the mountain, to leave her ugly home and foul habit behind, to lose herself in the vibrating hum of the slug bug, to watch the rural landscape fly away on either side, become urban, cluttered, polluted. Traffic—how she craved it! At the mall, she soaked up the clamor, anonymous and giddy. Pinetop residents tended to look weather-beaten and poor, unlike these city folk, with their even suntans and machine-made muscles and clever haircuts and clean pressed clothes. At the mall, the lid was on and the contents were beautiful, climate-controlled, animated by soothing music and the hygienic flow of recycled fountain water, unlike Pinetop where something had blown apart long ago and never been properly righted, the colors leached gray, exposed like an exhumed coffin.

And look at all the other *men* in the world. In the state. In the county. There were men everywhere, in groups and alone, intellects and athletes, grown-up men, with real pasts, with developed senses of humor and aesthetics, living in their own apartments and paying their own rents, living in their own houses and paying their own mortgages, cooking for themselves or ordering out, men with cars and bank accounts and careers and credit cards and degrees from institutions of higher education. Men wandering around the mall on a Saturday, buying athletic shoes and Swiss Army knives and compact discs and computer paraphernalia, as well as gifts for their girlfriends and wives, fingering the underwear at Victoria's Secret not because they planned to jack off in it but to have it wrapped up for a lover. How had she lost sight of the largeness, the variety, the vast menu of options? Why was she sleeping with a matriculating high school senior? Why was she letting herself go limp over some small-fry, dumb-bell, ball-playing boy? Was she out of her cotton-picking, dag-blamed, fucking mind?

Depressed, she ordered a Chicago-style Polish sausage at a kiosk in the food court, dressing it just the way she liked, relish, onions, mustard. "If the pickles were neon green, it would be just like at the Loop," she told Jesús, who ate a cinnamon roll the size of his face.

"The Loop," he said several times, liking the sound.

"Before I came here," Birdy said, as if responding to some challenge from her friend, "I had a fiancé. I was going to get married."

"Hooray for you," Jesús said.

"But I dumped him, virtually at the altar," Birdy said.

"I believe it."

"What do you mean, you believe it?"

He shrugged. "I believe you could dump your fiancé at the altar. That's all."

"I should have done it sooner, it's true, but it was not a mistake. Before him, I dated one of my professors, a poet. He would have asked me to marry him, but I dumped him, too. I'm always dumping people."

"We call that the old preemptive strike," Jesús said.

"No, I just told you, they would have married me. But I would have made them miserable, poor guys. They're both better off without me. You probably think I'm cold, but that's my story, and I'm sticking to it."

"And now they both hate you, right?"

"Right."

He smiled. "I don't care who you dumped, or why, Bird," he said, looking out over the mall people. He'd said hardly anything all day. "I don't care who you love, either. Trust me." He turned to her and put his warm hand on her shoulder.

She blinked at him. He was her height, dressed today in a Mexican wedding shirt, shorts, and clogs. He hadn't taken his sunglasses off yet. "I'm sleeping with Mark Anthony," she blurted, and was immediately relieved to have confessed it while, simultaneously, awaiting her punishment.

"It's about time you told," he said calmly.

"You knew?"

His expression said, Please—give me some credit. Maybe this explained his recent aloofness: he'd expected her confidence.

"Do other people know?" She thought of Luziana, blowing on her finger as she'd pinpointed Birdy's secret.

"Who cares?" Jesús said imperiously. A slew of strangers,

milling among the bright wares, seemed to support his careless disregard of public opinion. The throngs broke fluidly on either side of Jesús and Birdy, then rejoined, water making its way around a couple of piffling stones.

"But does anybody know?"

"You're the soul of discretion, Bird, a regular poker face, Ms. Chill. No one but me has been watching." They threw away their trash, headed toward the unexplored south wing.

"But you could have told me."

"*You* don't tell *me* things." Birdy wondered if this was a product of their peculiar friendship. She'd had close male friends before, and known all about their romantic peccadilloes; same with female friends and theirs. But somehow she and Jesús had not made their way to the subject of his love life. The closest they'd come was hers.

"I'll tell you this," he said now. "Nobody's proposed marriage." He took off his sunglasses and for an instant, Birdy saw his lonely love life in his hungover weary eyes. Laughter had carved its lines around them like a dirty trick, and late nights had left bruisy bags beneath. Did he have no amorous entanglement, no place to stake his heart? Although she'd felt a kinship with him since meeting him—a common impishness—this was the first time Birdy felt serious entry into his person and its dilemma. How could she complain about her life, when Jesús had no one to love at all? This was the way her mother had used to make Birdy feel lucky, by pointing out the unlucky, the starving in India, the crippled and hungry and homeless in Chicago's own streets. Lucky, and undeserving, at once.

"Is there somebod—" she began.

"Our Pal Hal has a policy like the military," Jesús said. " 'Don't ask, don't tell.' My mother's thinking that's fine by her, too."

"What about your brothers and sisters?"

"I'm their baby brother. What can they do? Besides, they've got Miti to pray for. She married a skinhead."

"I'm sorry."

He shrugged, grinning abruptly as a bickering couple passed, the woman attempting to wrestle a receipt from her husband as he waved it overhead. "It's for me to know, for you to find out," he taunted.

"Whattya gonna do?" Jesús said. "Don't worry, I don't hate you." He put his arm around her shoulders and pulled her off balance.

"You don't?" she squeaked.

"Nobody hates you, you paranoid freak you." He steered her into the eclectic gift shop.

"But don't you think dating a student is kind of desperate? Kind of a Humbert Humbert thing?"

"Why are you so worried about how it looks? Time is short, sugar. If you love him, you love him."

"Love him?" she scoffed, picking up a hat that held two beer cans like headlights, intricate tubing winding to the mouth.

"Buy this for him." Jesús lifted a picture frame from a glass shelf, flipping its button. A woman's voice said, "Record your own personal message for your own special someone."

"Show," said Jesús, presenting the frame beside his cheek like a television product, "and tell." The woman repeated her message. Jesús said, "Put your nude self behind the glass."

Freed of her secret, Birdy seemed capable of spending money once more, magnanimous with what had been stashed away. She bought Jesús a box of chocolate-covered insects, herself silk underwear and Wonder Bra, and, for Mark, music discs. In the parking lot, Jesús undid his lumpy shirt to show her the talking frame he'd pilfered. "You're bad," she exclaimed.

"What'd you lift?" he asked.

"Only a ring." She showed him a silver band, perfect for his pinkie. They slapped hands as they exchanged stolen goods.

In the frame, she put her (not-nude) photograph. On it, she entered her message: I'm thinking of you.

COMMENCEMENT made Birdy's eyes well up, as ceremonies often did. Why? she wondered, pretending a gnat had flown up her nose, honking dispassionately. She knew it was all hogwash. But the uniforms of ritual touched her, the exposed socks, the shined shoes, the pomaded heads of the boys. And, on the girls, the thick waxy lipstick, the big barrettes and bows, the angled imprint of curling irons on their clean hair. Luziana promenaded hugely in her robe, flashing her long fingers and their pretty nails, onstage at last before the paparazzi, and then there was somber Mark in his, like a judge, like a condor. He looked more mannish than boyish, wearing cap and gown. On his sweet Adam's apple rode the knot of a skyblue necktie. Hugh Gross stood perfectly erect before a microphone, his hands clasped, spatulate fingers interlacing one another as if to throttle themselves. He sang "Climb Every Mountain," quavering his way through it with a great deal of operatic feeling, "Till . . . you . . . find . . . your . . . dream . . ."

"He always sings it," Jesús informed her. "Every year, just as regular as a bowel movement." She'd never been to the ceremony before, although Hal Halfon had strongly urged all his teachers to attend. Last summer, Birdy had already left for her vacation in California by this time; by this time, she was supposed to be baking on a beach or cooling in a cavernous movie theater or eating at an ethnic food establishment other than Mexican. For the past few summers she'd gone with Reginald, her betrothed, the perennial graduate student, the master of slumming, a philosophy that had seen them through three summers as itinerant guests of various friends and relations on the West Coast. In the winter, he lived in a broken-down school bus in the driveway of a friend in Austin. Only when they were breaking up, last summer, had the routine seemed humiliating, arguing in whispers behind closed doors, making up as the guest bed bumped rhythmically against the wall, chagrined over breakfast one way or another.

So Birdy had not seen Pinetop in June or July, and in August, she had driven her car into town only hours before the first bell of the first day of class. Convocation assembly had always seemed penance enough.

The auditorium was full and hot; parents chatted, children squabbled, babies cried. People wore headgear: berets and fedoras and straw hats and of course cowboy hats, tengallon or regular, black or white. Feathers, flowers. The women's faces plastered terra cotta with unaccustomed makeup, perfumes and aftershaves hanging pungent and gaseous in the air. Birdy looked for Mrs. Anthony, who certainly must have left her house for this day. She sat alone, near the back of the auditorium, near the exit. Her translucent puff of hair made her nervous face appear to be floating. Here was an occasion for her dressy wardrobe, but, although she looked as dapper as ever, clearly the woman didn't take pleasure in the opportunity to receive compliments about her fashion sense. Her expression was fixed on the podium in the front of the room, and though Birdy waved broadly, she drew no response. Perhaps Mrs. A. was afraid to let loose of her purse. Staying in her seat might seem tied to holding absolutely still, poised for emergency. Perhaps Mrs. A. wished to keep their association a secret. Birdy knew coming here represented a difficult chore for the woman. She didn't often venture out of her adobe home in the onion field. The last time she'd sat in the high school auditorium could very possibly have been ten years earlier, when Teresa appeared in *The Mikado*. Maybe the audience reminded her of that event, too, the girls on stage not unlike her girl who had also once stood there, costumed, adored.

Principal Hal nattered on about ed-you-cation for a long time before introducing the valedictorian, who wore a sparkling diamond nose stud. "Hey fellow Pinetoppers!" she began. Birdy glanced around absently, feeling sweat trickle from her bra to her navel, pooling there. At the end of her row sat Mr. John, wearing a suit and wingtips, his face flushed and his hairline damp. He was tipped forward on his tailbone, his brow resting on the seatback in front of him. The child who occupied the chair in front of him had complained loudly to his mother: "He's breathing down my neck!" Mr. John was snorting like an enraged bull, his red hands gripping his knees. Something was bringing him to a boil. Maybe the valedictorian was one of the kids who taunted him. Maybe wearing anything but his khaki jumpsuit made him want to kill someone. Or maybe Luziana's inevitable leave-taking from Pinetop High was breaking his heart.

"Look at him," Birdy whispered to Jesús. "Let's talk cardiac arrest."

"He came here in ninth grade, and never left," Jesús whispered back. "He's been to about twenty graduations, and never graduated."

"Always a bridesmaid," Birdy murmured. Mr. John turned his head abruptly, as if he'd heard her, and scowled in her direction. Birdy leaned back, hidden behind Jesús's massive chest. The twenty graduates received their scrolls and Hugh Gross sang a song in German that only the Schweinbratens would appreciate, and the event was ended.

After the ceremony, the graduates threw their mortarboards like Frisbees and the atmosphere thickened with closure as the black hats fell on the audience, glossy squares trailing their gold tassels and plastic 1994 tokens. The windows let in the weak smell of summer. Flashbulbs kept bursting. For most, this marked the end of formal instruction. Fourteen of the twenty kids did not plan on college; the other six, including Mark, would move down the mountain, three bound for UNM, and three for community colleges, one with an acronym that sounded like *enema*. These were the typical ratios; Birdy's appearance two years ago in their midst had not made a dent in the numbers. On her way west, she'd pictured herself as a tough marine type, storming a class full of blockheads and deadbeats and ne'er-do-wells, drawing forth their innate potential, uncovering their dormant enthusiasms and true, creative selves, capitalizing on her own charismatic powers of persuasion, fashioning a league of loyal devotees, an army of converts to the cause of art, a regular feel-good movie of the week.

But she knew better, now. They'd won. She would see the new graduates around town, clerking at the grocery store or driving heavy orange road machinery for the state, gold tassel and token dangling from the rearview mirror along with fuzzy dice and baby shoes. What good were all her sad books going to do them then? She could only hope they'd fit one in now and then, in between dating and work, marriage and supper, primetime and bedtime, children and middle age, illness and ennui, reckoning and death. Wasn't that why ritual troubled her, the way it forced life's tumblers to twirl toward oblivion, pulling along all the people?

That evening Mark drank Everclear at the Alpine Inn with the rest of the seniors, then stumbled to Birdy's trailer after midnight.

"Lightweight," she said, holding him while he threw up in her soup pot.

"Purple punch," he said. "Grape Expectations."

"Yes, I can see." She then led him to her bed for a nap, his drunken clumsiness tipping the house like a canoe. Unconscious, his form stirred her in contradictory ways. On the one hand, he looked beautiful, an angel, "My angel," she murmured, touched by his flawless vulnerability, by his unscathed skin, unslack, unravaged by time, by his lips releasing a steady clean stream of air. Birdy knelt beside the bed and stroked his jawline with the very tips of her fingers, hovering on the faint stubble, not wanting to disturb his pristine beauty. His innocent overindulgence, his utter ignorance concerning hangovers, his very stunning kind overtures toward her.

"You're so sweet," he told Birdy, "I could eat you up!" He didn't even have a concept of what he might have meant, *double entendre* probably stood for an ice cream concoction, in his mind. "Why do you like me, anyway?"

On the other hand, he could not hold his liquor, and he'd come to her not like a lover but like a miscreant youth—even drunk and sick, he'd wanted to have sex, his hard-on like a buoy in the churning ocean, a thing made grotesque by his treating it like a kinky toy he'd unearthed at a magic shop, a toxic toadstool he wished Birdy to taste. Birdy had pushed him before her to the bathroom, where she'd splashed him mercilessly and made him brush his teeth, using a washcloth dipped in paste instead of her own brush, scrubbing the violet stain from his teeth and rubbery lips. In her bedroom, she unlaced his shoes roughly and removed his sodden necktie for him before permitting him to collapse on the bed.

"I love you, Ms. Stone," he'd declared a few times, laughing. "Now I have a diploma."

"But alas, no brain," she said, recalling the lovable scarecrow who'd shared a similar problem.

Asleep, his aspect turned angelic. It was an evening that dramatized her dilemma concerning him. He was a beautiful goof, a divine disaster, that could become a fatal flaw, that pesky Achilles' heel.

Mark spent the whole of that night with her, slurredly

assuring her before he fell asleep that his mother would understand his tardiness, since he'd graduated. Birdy nudged her rump against his, used his warm body the way the settlers had used hot bricks. A half-empty bed, even in June, was a little chilly.

But she should have known Mrs. Anthony would panic. Of course she would assume the worst of her son's not coming home. Of course she would involve the police and the football coach and a battery of Mark's dingbatty friends. When Birdy's phone rang at five A.M., she assumed it would be her own sister, telling her their father had died, or vice versa. In a flash, she was repentant, sorry, reformed. "Please, please, please," she muttered, discovering, in the unstrung instant before lifting the phone receiver, that she did not want them dead: she loved them, flawed as they were. Instead, it was Mrs. Anthony on the other end, wondering in her soft southern accent if Birdy had any idea where Mark might be?

"I haven't seen him since yesterday afternoon," Birdy said croakily, heartbeat slowing, watching Mark come to slowly on the bed. His black gown was spread on her desk, his necktie on the chair post. The scene was debauched and disreputable. Mrs. Anthony's phone fizzled as if its line had been partially snipped, as if Mrs. Anthony were being carried away in a tornado. Birdy cleared her throat, attempting to tether the woman with insipid reassurance. "He's fine, I'm sure he's fine. It's graduation, after all, and the kids always stay up all night on graduation." She recalled her own high school graduation, the Ford Falcon she'd been a passenger in stopping at an intersection deep in downtown Chicago and all four doors swinging open, four heads popping out, a group vomit. At the time, it had seemed unbearably hilarious; now, Birdy looked back with queasiness. Her past seemed fragile to her, one continuous averted disaster.

"You can imagine my terror," Mrs. Anthony said. The

phone sizzled and snapped as if it might spark Birdy's ear for lying into it.

Birdy's hands were shaking when she hung up, and she felt as if she'd been the one to overindulge the night before. Mark was already getting dressed, pulling clothing on halfway, then reaching for another garment, constructing his story for his mother, moving his lips as he moved himself from place to place during the previous night. He didn't even look hungover. And he had another erection poking from his ill-attended dress pants, one Birdy wouldn't do anything about. She was annoyed at the proximity of discovery, ashamed of her lapse in restraint. His neediness exhausted her, his and his mother's. Her own, she supposed, it, too, was taking a toll.

"You have any eggs?" he asked as he tied the thin laces of his smudged dress shoes. No doubt they had once been his father's shoes.

"Go home," she said, cinching her bathrobe. "You don't have time to eat. Your mother's out of her mind with worry."

"I'm hungry."

"She'll feed you. Here." She handed him his gift, her picture in its stolen frame. "Don't show your mom," she added, as it seemed possible he was just that uninformed.

He saluted, then slapped Birdy's bottom when he left, a gesture that stunned her. Stunned her, and, oddly, pleased her. It was as if graduation had been more than symbolically transfigurative. There was some new mild smirk on his face as he tucked his gift beneath his armpit, tossed his black gown over his shoulder, and began his long four-point-two-mile walk home.

❧ 6

"**S**omebody mentioned a gambling debt," Birdy said delicately at the pitted kitchen table. Isadora Anthony bristled.

"Absolutely not." Her lips pursed as if anointed by a lime.

"Did your husband go to the track?"

"He didn't believe in gambling."

"A religious thing?"

"No. He was just careful with his money."

A tightwad, Birdy thought.

"Who told you he gambled?"

"I can't remember," Birdy said, wondering why she would bother to protect Mary Jo Callahan. That led her to wonder why Miss Callahan was not the tutor on this project. Why hadn't Mrs. Anthony asked her? Wouldn't Mary Jo have been the more sound choice? She'd actually known Teresa, been in town when the girl died, and, furthermore, taught the parts of speech. Why had Miss Callahan been rejected?

Maybe Mrs. Anthony didn't like Mary Jo any better than Birdy did, and for all the same reasons.

Or maybe—more likely—Mrs. Anthony thought she could pull the wool over Birdy's eyes. Maybe Birdy was supposed to be a sucker. This evening, for example, she was reading the expert opinion of an "authority on body language" who had gone through a pile of photographs with Mrs. Anthony, noting what various townspeople were unconsciously communicating. These were mostly grainy pictures from the *Pinetop Journal,* of banquets or parades or car accidents or weddings. There was not one of a single Anthony family member. Instead, they featured clubs and gatherings, a few local celebrities, like the owner of the Silverado Mining Company (his hands, plunged deep into his suit pockets, indicated a "perverse libido"), and the mayor (scared of his wife), and a bungling embezzler who'd forged the signature of her tenant pensioner on the very day he died (the body language expert claimed he could have seen that scandal coming just based on the plaid jacket the landlady wore, not to mention the ostentatious earrings; she was very insecure). Misappropriation of funds had reminded Birdy of the gambling tip about Mr. Anthony, and now Mrs. A. denied it.

So in the interest of independent journalism, she decided to investigate the story more aggressively, from the outside instead of the inside. She felt vaguely furtive about this, as if she were going behind the woman's back, but the time had come. She'd read three hundred and two pages of manuscript by now and her own mind seemed to have become as muddled as Mrs. A.'s, as uncertain about what the story's point was. She needed a second opinion.

In the blessed air-conditioning of the *Pinetop Journal* office, she asked to see copies of the newspaper for the year 1984.

She expected to be led to a cavernous dusty lair in the bowels of the building, yellowed papers stacked to the ceiling, cobwebs and bats hanging from musty wooden shelves, but, instead, was handed a roll of film and shown to the new microfiche machine in a sunny alcove on the first floor.

"Got ourselves a pretty little gadget," the woman ushering her across the hall declared. "State of the art."

"Uh huh," Birdy answered.

The woman spent a great deal of time training Birdy how to insert the film in the plastic spindles and over the glass slide, even though she didn't plan to look at any but the 1984 edition. "Thank you," Birdy told her several times, to make her go away. From high windows in the little room, the sun blazed, its glare so bright that she couldn't read the scrolling images very well. She leaned close as if spying on the machine's guts, hands cupped to either side of her face, her hair charged by static electricity and drawn to the opalescent screen.

Not much had changed in ten years; real estate prices seemed identical, issues of interest were hunting permits and the elk lottery, mining cleanup, highway maintenance, the welcoming of new businesses and the farewells to those that had folded, and the debate as to how obsequious the locals wanted to make themselves in the name of attracting tourists. (Restoring a broken patch of downtown sidewalk was seen by some as bowing to the demands of pansy outsiders.) Then, as now, the town seemed divided into curmudgeons and opportunists, the hick and the slick. The underlying assumption— that there was something so inherently interesting, so worthwhile about Pinetop that you ought to pinpoint it as the hub of your vacation plans—fascinated Birdy. The town's sole claim to fame was the meager cliff dwelling and its booty. After you'd seen that and filled your tank with gas, it would be time to get back on the road.

The sheriff's reports for 1984 included cattle rustling and snowmobile theft, the death and mortuary viewing of some- one named Leopard ("Leopard entered eternal life Friday afternoon," it said), drunken driving and fighting, mischief in the forms of broken windows and raided gardens and snatched laundry, bear spottings, wild dog packs. Deputies had actually shot and killed several members of the dog packs, which had been menacing small children who were on their way to school. Outlying areas, within the purview of the sheriff's beat, were named Spudpatch and Disappointment Creek, where a bull had been rustled and a refrigerator stolen, respectively.

Maybe Birdy lived on Disappointment Creek. It would figure.

The article about Teresa ran three days after the Fourth of July. Forty-five miles away, the Mescalero tribe had initiated pull-tab bingo that same week. Set on the bottom of the page and in the context of the other week's news, the article seemed smaller than it had before to Birdy, who retained the same clipped item at home, crisp and singular, luminous in its laminated state, Teresa's school photo running alongside it. Perhaps Mrs. Anthony's frustration had sprung from a simi- lar sense: her girl was becoming lost to her, a blip on the screen of human history, diminished in a coiled bit of trans- parent filament, a forgotten member of the mortal tribe.

There was Mark's name, the surviving brother, age seven. Just last night, that same boy had been pleased to have Birdy straddle his lap, make a saddle of his body, and ride him. He'd clung to her neck and whispered his love. And later he'd slipped out her backdoor into the evening. Seeing his name made Birdy miss him suddenly and acutely, as if it were he who'd disappeared over a cliff, as if she might not get to fin- ish whatever business they'd begun.

Birdy fanned herself and spun the microfiche handle. She noted that the weather, that week ten years ago, was dry—so dry there were forest fire warnings, emphatic notices about cigarette butts—totally contradicting Mrs. A.'s dark-and-stormy-night bit.

She continued rolling the flimsy membrane forward, using one hand to shade the screen, until she found the second article, a week later. Mr. Anthony occupied the second page instead of the front, and was not accompanied by a photograph. This time, reading about his accident, Birdy noted the care with which the reporter phrased the details. If you didn't know better, you might suppose Philip Anthony had miscalculated a sharp turn and met his untimely end, pure mishap. And why did Birdy think she knew better, she asked herself. What evidence, besides her own desire for drama and prurience, besides Mrs. Anthony's paranoid victim's slant, turned the story into anything more than these articles indicated? He'd been studying the site of his daughter's death. He'd forgotten to watch the road.

Birdy handed the loop of microfiche back to the woman without having returned it to its box; she wanted to see the woman's displeasure with her. Sure enough, she hissed in alarm, quickly taking the film out of Birdy's careless grasp. From the *Journal* office, Birdy drove down Main Street, passing Jerry's restaurant, the languishing Dora's, the hardware store, the liquor store, Food Land, the Elks Club antler lightbulbs, the Wires Plus van with glowering Ronny behind the wheel, the bars and Bookmobile, eventually attracted without real reason—maybe simply by the fact that there was an empty parking spot, that the building would be air-conditioned—to the Pinetop Historical Museum, which was located in a quonset hut beside the police station. Jesús had told her that in his youth, the structure had been a rec hall, its rounded metal hulk painted to resemble a giant Coors label. From above, it would look as if a can of beer lay tipped on its side, patrons emerging from its doors like foaming brew. Birdy hadn't set foot inside the quonset hut since her first week in town, two years ago.

After dropping her mandatory donation of one dollar in the Lucite box by the door, Birdy found herself alone in the room. From the dimly lighted far end of the hut—curving overhead like an airplane hangar, like a big can—she could hear echoing human activity, someone shifting objects on surfaces, clattering as if cooking.

"Hello?" she called. Tiny round windows occurred every few feet like pricked holes, allowing dusty pipettes of sunlight. Otherwise, the place was lit with fluorescence, tubes suspended from the ceiling on wires, illumination for the local artifacts. There were some mining remains—narrow gauge train track bolts, huge quartz crystals, a rusty little ore wagon—and furnishings from various businesses who'd probably donated them just to clear space for new models— roulette wheel, dentist chair, school desks—and a bunch of dull farm implements, laudatory memorials to the equine, bovine, and porcine inhabitants of the region, and, finally, a whole installation dedicated to detailing different types of barbed wire. This was inconceivably comprehensive, dozens of subtly varying sharpnesses and thicknesses, stars and hooks, mounted painstakingly on wooden boards, labeled taxonomically. Birdy had sent postcards of this exhibit to her friends who collected such kitsch.

Mostly the museum housed crumbling books of photographs. They smelled like authentic history, dirt and mold, leather bindings gone sandy with age. The books were all labeled *These photographs generously donated by Mrs. Homer (Edith) Pack.* Birdy could easily imagine Edith typing each label herself, licking the back with her parsimonious tongue, pressing it on the book, moving to the next one. Her husband Homer Pack was dead, but he had been a photographer, and he'd captured everything he could during his own lifetime, as well as restoring older pictures, sometimes tinting them with hopeful pastel colors, clouds floating by like pink carnations, the snow a jonquil yellow, water flowing Caribbean blue. A hundred years ago, Pinetop had looked like all the other mountain mining towns in the West, muddy main street lined with rickety frame bars and wooden sidewalks, everything flimsy as a movie set. Men and horses faced the camera, surly and stiff, as if the photographer wielded some newfangled weapon he were about to deploy in their direction. Birdy found her own street. Where her trailer now sat had once stood a blacksmith's shed, beside it a stable, and after that the prostitutes' lodgings, their row of little cribs, fussy and fanciful as dollhouses, as if what went on inside them weren't crude one-sided pleasures, distorted business transactions. The women stood with their arms entwined, plump and somber, propping each other up.

In the old photos, Pinetop did not quite seem quaint, not like a movie western, its sound track the jingly noise of a player piano, the laughter of revelers. Instead, it looked like an unhappy place, where life was hard, where people were worn down by living it. The men all sported beards, the children did not smile: it was as if they did not own mirrors. Time had erased them, hadn't it? And swiftly, too. Only Mt. Ajax and Mt. Ballard had not changed in appearance, facing each other over their end of the little town, invincible shouldered giants, smug and pitiless in their constancy while everything below them frolicked and perished, over and over, fruitless pursuit.

Birdy thumped shut the musty book.

Near the rear of the quonset hut lay several sarcophagus-like cases, the huge exhibit of the Basket Maker Anasazi who had once resided just outside town in the cliffs. This display was relatively new, funded by a grant from UNM, down in Albuquerque, and constructed by people who knew what they were doing, and who probably had been appalled by the other rickrack that passed as treasure in the rest of the building. They'd even gone so far as erecting another ceiling over the display, no doubt leery about the soundness of the curved corrugated tin-can roof that protected the remainder. It was not hard for Birdy to imagine the scorn of outsiders, of grad students setting up camp here in the hinterlands of ridiculous Pinetop, where the natives could not appreciate the wonder of their own backyard.

Now that Birdy had recent history to apply to the Anasazi site, she paid closer attention to its more distant past. The tribe had apparently been an offshoot of the Chaco Anasazi, a small band out on their own in the rugged southeastern mountains. By a few hundred years they predated both the Bandelier tribe, up north, and the thirteenth-century fleeing of the rest of the Anasazis. As a group, they were unusually small. "Outcasts," Birdy muttered aloud. "Weirdos. Banished to the boonies like lepers." Sometimes that was Birdy's version of her own life story: doing penance in the fringes, cast out to find her way, to return prodigal or not at all.

It seemed to be the fate of Pinetop to always look puny in comparison to its neighboring communities. That seemed true of the cliff dwellers, as well; Birdy studied the impressive photos of Mesa Verde, its Cliff Palace, and compared them to the local ruins. The Pinetop Anasazis didn't even have a kiva, let alone watchtowers or two-story structures or T-shaped doorways. They used a crude building method, the fundamental principle of which seemed not unlike that behind the common mud pie, something called wattle-and-daub, but which Birdy's father might have named slapdash. The most interesting aspect of the university's unearthing was the grave of a thirty-five-year-old mummified woman enshrined in a little cave off the main rock dwelling, a tomb dug into the cliffs, her body surrounded by a cache of loot. Beads, semiprecious stones, pots, blankets, baskets, a spear called an atlatl. The bones of a pet dog. An unused pair of yucca sandals, waiting alongside her for journeys in the next world. No one knew why she'd been honored by the tribe; perhaps she was considered a seer, a witch, or perhaps merely revered as an elder. Simple survival rated praise. Why not? Birdy thought. At thirty-five years of age, the placard read, she was an elder, her head, for mysterious reasons, flattened in back. Anasazi was the name the Navajo had given the dwellers; who knew what the people had called themselves? Anasazi simply meant "ancient ones" in Navajo. Birdy wondered what tone the word connoted, reverence or ridicule, ancient sages or ancient coots? This woman was an elder of the ancient ones, mature twice over, like algebra. As usual, Birdy was reminded of how grown up grown-ups of the past seemed. Her own parents, for example, bravely breeding children and blithely buying homes, at ages under her own. Here she was almost thirty herself—where were her badges of maturity, her honorable sureness, her integrity-laden adulthood? Many of the world's greats had crashed and burned by her age, leaving their worthy legacies, not to mention their comely corpses. Christ had died at thirty-three; in America, people of thirty could begin plotting their impending campaigns for presidency; in this renegade Anasazi crew, a thirty-five-year-old ruled.

From the back of the museum, a metal pan clanged onto the floor, startling Birdy. "Shoot howdy!" shouted someone. Mr. John now emerged through a door, apologizing as he came. He cleaned many of the town's public structures, possessing the keys to them; private structures were not, by and large, locked, although Birdy certainly locked hers. Mr. John wore his coveralls, an outfit that suited him better than his dress clothes. It would be handy, Birdy thought, not to have to make decisions every morning about what to wear. When he saw who it was, Mr. John said, "What do you want?"

"I don't know," Birdy answered, which was the truth. His approach to Birdy had always seemed confused to her. Like now, not saying her name in recognition, salutation, as if he didn't see her every day during the school year, as if he didn't wash her handwriting from her blackboard, as if he hadn't, just a couple of weeks ago, helped her trap a mouse in her classroom, their two heads bent low together before the suspected hole in the baseboard. His approach, in fact, made it seem as if he did not like her. This had never occurred to Birdy before, and it hurt her feelings that the retarded janitor, mascot of sorts, everybody's idiot buddy, would not like her. What could be wrong with her, to merit his disapproval?

She would have to consult with Jesús, let him convince her the janitor did not hate her, turn it into a joke.

"You don't smoke, do you?" he said, walking slowly toward where she stood, hands on his hips. He had a too-loud voice. There were other ways he revealed his retardedness, by standing too close to people, by his baffled loose lips, his clouded tawny eyes, his no-fashion buzzy haircut, his sudden and unpredictable laugh, the way he concentrated concretely on his tasks rather than performing them while thinking of other things. He was always dedicated to what he was doing, his sole distraction a nicotine habit somebody had unkindly introduced him to years ago, by the look of his fingers and teeth. "I know you don't smoke," he said belligerently. Most of his remarks were prefaced by *I know* or *I want*, as if naming the extent of his knowledge or needs would pin the world down every day, squirming under his thick thumb.

"Nope, I don't," Birdy said, grateful not to have to share anything with him, although Jesús had threatened to invite

Mr. John to join him and Birdy some lunchtime to smoke a joint.

"I knew that," Mr. John said.

"You knew that," she agreed.

"I did." He insisted on having the last word, always. Jesús liked to torment him by making endless exchanges, waiting for Mr. John to give up. But he never gave up. On and on they would go, one inanity after another. Now Mr. John sighed. He was prohibited from smoking without company, and Birdy, having discovered he didn't like her, wasn't in the mood to accommodate. No one else seemed to find Mr. John menacing, but she was never completely comfortable around him. She knew he had topped out at the age of twelve, but she didn't trust twelve-year-old boys, either; she hardly trusted boys at all, even the seventeen-year-old to whom she'd handed over her wobbly affection. Alone in the quonset hut, she kept her attention split between the black and white potsherds beneath the glass before her, and Mr. John, who'd stomped off to sweep. She could hear his broom swishing forlornly behind the postcard rack, his noisy sighs of dejection that she was meant to inquire into.

The retarded were reputed to have depths, so Birdy wasn't surprised when, after he'd finished sweeping, Mr. John began trailing her around, revealing that he knew more than the average bear about the ruin. It was named Velázquez, he said—not quite to Birdy, but sort of in her direction—after the Spanish priest who uncovered the first remnant of stuff in 1692, poking his walking staff into the shallow dirt. The little Pinetop museum held everything that had been discovered; from what had been found in petrified fecal matter, the UNM archaeologists deduced that the small tribe ate squash and corn, nuts and berries, and for water relied on the flow of the Suena Creek, which was now nonexistent, thanks to a dam upstream.

"There's a creek behind my house," Birdy said.

"That's a diversion of the Animas, circa 1880, made by Anglo farmers," Mr. John retorted, quoting a placard. "It wasn't here in the year 700."

"Oh," Birdy said sheepishly, just like one of her students.

There was only the single skull, of the thirty-five-year-old witch woman, the Old Flat-headed One. Using it as a model, someone with a lot of imagination had created a hologram in a lighted box; seen one way, there was the familiar bone arrangement, ape or human skull. Seen another way, the woman appeared, her skin green and incandescent, her chin and forehead only vaguely Homo sapiens. Birdy pivoted her own head back and forth, making the image transpose quickly from skull to face, skull to face. You almost expected the head to talk, so eerie was the motion. Another exhibit featured a diorama, less realistically rendered. Little hominid figures collected around a fire, the ruin site scooped around them like a cupped palm. A figure—presumably the elder—sat in the center of the dwelling, a fire pit made of pebbles beside her, a series of tiny pots and blanket and various crude stone tools near her. Animal pelts, meant to replicate much larger beasts, hung on the walls (cut from a moldy rabbit hide, Birdy thought). Maybe she lived here alone, she and her extended family. Maybe they hadn't been ostracized but had decided to flee a more primitive lot. Then this group would have been at a loss when she died, so they entombed her like a saint and moved on. The Pinetop group of Anasazi had not stuck around to evolve, the way they had at Chaco canyon, two hundred miles northwest of here; they hadn't progressed to building free-standing mud homes, they didn't incorporate the complicated clay firing designs and colors that came later. Some mysterious tragedy had sent them packing, Birdy thought, something their superstitious natures couldn't successfully wrestle with and defeat, couldn't disregard, couldn't sacrifice away. The wind, maybe.

"Mr. John," she said suddenly to her hovering companion, thinking of a more recent mysterious tragedy; the sandals had reminded her that Teresa was found barefoot, her shoes never recovered, evidence her mother believed meant conspiracy. "Do you remember Teresa Anthony? Did you know her?"

"She's dead," he replied promptly, as if the question were predicated on a naive assumption of Birdy's.

"She's dead," Birdy agreed. "Before she died, did you know her?"

"Yes, I knew her. It was bad, when she fell off that high cliff."

"Why was it bad?"

"Because she's dead." He shook his head impatiently; how dumb was she, anyway?

"That is sad, isn't it? Do you know anything about that accident? Do you remember it?"

"She's dead," he repeated.

"Was Teresa a nice girl, to you?" Birdy was thinking of his attention to pretty Luziana; maybe he'd always worshipped the beauties.

"I knew her mother," he went on, nudging Birdy to her part of the exchange.

Birdy sighed. "You don't know her now?"

"Not anymore."

"You don't see her around town?"

"Of course not."

"Uh huh."

"I don't."

Birdy held her tongue. You couldn't expect Boo Radley every time you came upon someone like Mr. John.

Soon he was waiting for her to finish so he could leave; the museum didn't seem to attract many patrons—everyone in town had probably been here at least once, and, unlike other businesses, once was probably enough. As a result, it didn't require much upkeep. He stood at the door fingering his cigarette package, which was zipped into a handy chest pocket. His fingernails, Birdy noticed, were bitten as well as yellow. She bit hers, too. See, she thought, she could find some way to connect with him. He needn't seem so strange; he was just a nervous man-child, chewing his nails.

"You have a car lighter," he reminded Birdy. "In your car."

"The perfect place for it."

"You have a car lighter."

His hair was the thick bristly type that reminded Birdy of toilet bowl brushes. He rubbed it now, itching for a cigarette. "Okay," she sighed. "I'll go with you to smoke." She kept her own pack in the glove box, in the event that she might some day need to cover the odor of pot.

It wasn't until they were seated in Birdy's bucket seats—both doors wide open, just in case Mr. John had visions of ravishment on his feeble mind—that Birdy recalled the last time she'd used the lighter, torching the end of a joint, nearly igniting her own nose.

"Careful," she told Mr. John as he aimed the glowing unit toward his face.

"Care full," he agreed, looking at the hot piece cross-eyed. It was Birdy's sudden mean desire to see him burn himself—she would decide not to like him, either, so there—that made her think of something else. It would make a peculiar burn, a car lighter, on the skin, it would make a tiny bull's-eye target, wouldn't it, pressed against the flesh, just exactly what had been on Teresa Anthony's back. Instantly Birdy conjured up the crime scene, the father prodding the barefoot girl to cliff's edge using his car lighter.

"Makes me dizzy," Mr. John giggled, smiling sloppily at Birdy, sighing luxuriantly. How he loved to breathe smoke.

"Nicotine is a dizzy fellow," she agreed absently, then said, more to herself than to him, "He burned her."

Mr. John's smile faded and his face became uneasy. "I didn't," he said, panicked. "Only the attic burned, not any human beans. The attic, then the other roofs, and some insulation." His ash he painstakingly flicked away from the flammable clothing and car upholstery, out the door in the dirt, as if to spotlight his earnest attention to safety.

"Not you. Teresa Anthony's father." Birdy spoke it in order to solidify the flitting certainty that whizzed through her. "Mr. Anthony. What roofs?" she added.

"Pekkarine's Dry Goods, Gemstone Liquors, The Moon Gypsy Bar, and Buffalo Breath Antiques." This litany he spoke without hesitation.

"You burned all those?"

"Their *roofs*. And one wall of the Whitefront. You can still see the smoke by the fire escape. If you look."

"Huh. You caused a big fire, didn't you?" She pictured the flat roofs downtown ablaze like a big birthday cake.

He rustled himself out of her car, and stood beside the open door, leaning down and in to finish the cigarette in her presence; he was very literal minded about rules. A breeze blew his strange body odor into Birdy's Saab. "It would have been just fine except for the wind. I hate the wind."

Here was another thing to have in common with Mr. John, hating the wind, but Birdy was thinking of her discovery. "Mr. Anthony burned Teresa. With one of these." She held out the now-dead lighter and studied its dull gray surface. Mr. John pulled his face away as if she'd threatened him and slammed Birdy's car door so hard the window rattled.

"You don't know them," he said accusatively, his words

muffled by the door. Funny, no one else had so baldly complained of this inadequacy. He made sure to illustrate dramatically his squashing of his cigarette butt before stomping back into the quonset hut.

No, SHE DIDN'T know them. But she felt as if she were getting to know them. Not so much as a result of reading Mrs. Anthony's book, but as a result of doubting that same book. She read everything in it, then constructed something else, using what was missing between Mrs. Anthony's lines as the incomplete skeleton for her own story about Teresa and her father.

Somebody's Girl, Mrs. Anthony had tentatively titled her manuscript. She was still in search of a sentence to accompany it, right after the colon she planned to insert. *Somebody's Girl: A Survivor's Story of Family Fatality.*

That evening, Birdy took her new clue and hypothesis to Jesús. Using her car lighter, they burned a bull's-eye in a pot holder in his mother's driveway; the paper they'd tried had smoldered into a simple hole.

"Do we have anything that will react like human flesh to this experiment?" Birdy asked.

"Human flesh," Jesús said, holding out his palm.

"Besides human flesh. Something soft, yet durable."

"Silly Putty? A cantaloupe?" Jesús poked the lighter in again, then pressed it once more on the pot holder, making a second eye to match the first. "Symmetry," he explained. Tía Blanca's face looked down disapprovingly on them from the kitchen window. What were they up to, now? She wagged her finger at them: naughty children.

"Do you think this is what was on Teresa's back?" Birdy asked of the lighter.

"Could be," he said, shrugging.

"I hate all the fucked-up fathers," Birdy said. "Don't you? Goddamn lechers. Assholes. Perverts."

"Go, baby, go."

"Pricks," Birdy finished. She looked toward the kitchen window but Tía Blanca had disappeared. "What should I do with this info?" she demanded of her friend.

Jesús waved Tía Blanca's charred pot holder. "It's not really info, is it? It's just a speculation. A smart speculation," he added, when Birdy glared at him, "but what good would it really do, to expose it now?"

"I don't know."

"Mrs. Anthony won't believe it."

"No." Birdy could not imagine how she would broach the subject of the cigarette lighter, the odd mark on the girl's back. She could envision Mrs. Anthony's injured expression, her comprehension of Birdy's ugly curiosity about the events.

"And nobody else is interested in those accidents," Jesús went on, turning to go inside. He seemed to be saying he was tired of Birdy's pet project, that her paranoia no longer amused him as it had used to. When he'd first met her, he told her all he required of a friend was entertainment, someone to make him laugh. She guessed she'd not been holding up her end of the deal lately. School was out and summer doldrums threatened. Now more than ever they needed diversion. No longer were their preposterous colleagues around for sporting purposes. No longer did their students provide fodder. The evening turned a pretty purple in the west, trees spiking into it. In the right light, and ignoring a certain Pinetop inclination toward tire mounds and garish television antennas, the place could seem scenic. Like now. The air contained enough chill to make you glad of the indoors awaiting you.

Jesús said, now gently, "They were a long time ago. History, bub."

"They weren't accidents," Birdy insisted. "They were intentionals." The melancholy sky made truth seem necessary.

"Okay. But so what? What's it got to do with you?"

"Nothing. It's just interesting. If it had been me, I would want somebody to come dig up the truth. That's not so weird, wanting to tell the truth. Is it? Shouldn't somebody be interested?"

"Just for truth's sake?"

"Sure."

He pretended to think it over. "Truth for truth's sake, truth for truth's sake." He snapped his fingers. "I know— your boyfriend. Who else?"

Who else, indeed? Besides nosy Mary Jo Callahan, the last person Birdy wanted to confide in. And why hadn't she thought of Mark, her beau, the only other potential legitimately interested party? Because he hadn't been paying attention to the rest of it. Hadn't read his mother's story, although he seemed to support her writing it. Hadn't been able to contribute much, except that he loved his sister; they got along. She sneaked him out of the house sometimes to accompany her to high school parties. She liked folk music; she knew hundreds of songs, and she liked to drive him around while she sang them. Disbelieving their father's claim of allergies, they'd harbored a stray kitten in Teresa's closet for a few weeks once. When she was sad, she baked cookies or listened to tapes, studying the lyric sheets, rewinding and replaying phrase by phrase until she knew every word.

"Yeah, Mark," Birdy said faintly.

"Go burn his pot holders," Jesús suggested at the door.

BUT WHEN she met up with Mark that night they drank beer and played Scrabble. He had never heard of it before and kept playing illegal words like BOSTON and ETC. He thought phonetic equivalents ought to count.

"What did you all *do* at your house at night?" Birdy asked, remembering her own childhood of family games.

"Why does X get so many points and K hardly any?" he asked.

Birdy didn't have the energy to explain the mathematical occurrence of letters and usage. She liked his flip-flops on his tanned toes, his happy grin when he made ZOO. She didn't have the heart to point out he could have played OOZE and tripled his score.

❧ 7

The next morning Birdy went to the marshal's department where the cherry-topped cars sat all day, and got directed to the sheriff's office, right back by the quonset hut museum; Mr. John glowered at her from the parking lot, where he whirled dirt around with his leaf blower. At the sheriff's office, Birdy was told to sit and wait by a plump woman in an olive-drab police uniform. Her uniform was skintight, buckled and buttoned and tucked and shipshape. Over her dark gleaming hair she had pulled tight a hairnet, as if afraid stray hair strands would dispel the image of efficiency. The effect of such an altogether capable demeanor was to make Birdy feel slovenly and tired. The woman smiled brightly as she slit mail with a long knife and greeted officers as they wandered in, sleepy, bedraggled. The officers looked Birdy over distractedly, perhaps wondering if she were a prostitute or child molester, busted. She covered her knees with her skirt.

The uniformed woman also handled the telephone, which sounded frequently, a tootling noise like a video game. This must be what was known as dispatch. She seemed to Birdy the embodiment of dispatch.

She'd written down Teresa and Philip Anthony's names without comment or expression. This made Birdy wonder if she'd known one or both of them, if she had her own opinions concerning the cases or Birdy's interest in them. She was just too studiously indifferent.

Although the office appeared busy, the sheriff, when he emerged from his interior room rubbing his head, took Birdy in for a long conversation. The cubicle he led her to had no windows, simply a little table and two chairs. From the newly painted white walls dangled a few unconnected and dicey-looking electric cords.

"Don Potter-Otto," he said, wiping his hand on his thigh before giving it to Birdy. It, and its owner, were slightly puffy, as if his skin sheath had been overinflated.

"Birdy Stone," she replied, wondering how his surname was spelled. Like the woman, he seemed confined by his starched olive-drab uniform, he and his dispatcher complementary counterparts, his hair blond where hers had been dark, his skin red in contrast to her brown, the two of them like salt and pepper shakers of law enforcement; they probably had a torrid sexual relationship brewing. He was in his early forties, Birdy guessed, and he liked to stare with his blue eyes deep into the eyes of the people he talked to.

"Lolo says you have interest in a couple accidents," he said, interlacing his swollen fingers on the small tabletop. He wore a wedding ring, one deeply embedded in his porky ring finger.

She explained her role in the editing of Mrs. Anthony's

book, making sure to seek eye contact every now and then, although she didn't really want to. She found it difficult to think when she was looking into someone's eyes. Besides, policemen, contrary to what she'd been promised as a child, had never seemed to her to be her friends. They seemed unwavering and hard, single-minded, humorless—human guns. In dealing with them, Birdy had always worried about being found guilty of something.

"This book," she said now, glancing around at the wires protruding from the walls, "depends on some details of the accidents that are not entirely clear to me." Don Potter-Otto's expression was skeptical, one eyebrow up, as if he'd heard of this lame-brained plan of the woman's before, her damnable book. Birdy had no doubt that Mrs. Anthony would have been a difficult survivor, melodramatic, fragile yet angry, quick to blame anybody but her family, quick to cave in, grief-stricken, when questions became specific, probing, anything less than polite.

Sheriff Potter-Otto said, "You probably don't want my opinion—" Birdy made a quick head movement to indicate she would be absolutely fascinated and nothing but grateful for his opinion "—but I think she ought to get on with her life. None of this hashing up the past is gonna bring those folks back, okay?"

"I think she sees it as a kind of therapy," Birdy said tentatively.

"How long ago was it?" he said. "Seven, eight years?"

"Ten," Birdy said. "1984." 1984. Birdy had been an undergraduate then, in her junior year of college in Champaign-Urbana, sleeping with her creative writing professor, the same one who despaired of ever teaching his students anything. The second class she took with him had been Introduction to Poetry, her thinking being that although she'd had no stories to tell, perhaps she had some insightful lyric moments lurking within her. Alas, not so. In her Post-Apocalyptic Literature class, that same semester, they'd read Orwell's *1984*. She remembered its being a frighteningly inaccurate forecast of the times. She would have to ask Jesús if Pinetop's senior class had been made to read it then, too. If she were still teaching in the year 2001, she supposed she'd make her juniors watch that old chestnut on video, put in their two cents.

She prodded, "You were sheriff then?"

"No, I was the undersheriff then. I got sent to all three accident sites, boom, boom, boom."

"All three?" Birdy repeated, her attention suddenly fixed like an animal in the woods, hearing a snapping limb. She would be ready to react to anything. Three?

"How'd you know about Larry's suicide?" he said, leaning in, "Mrs. Anthony tell you?"

Birdy nodded, an automatic lie. Mr. Anthony's first name was Philip. Who was Larry?

"That was number one, real ugly scene, up at his truck. The thing about Larry is, it is a flat-out miracle he was the only one who died. He was a bad seed, from way back. I used to catch him torching little critters when he was a kid, causing no end of trouble, driving around drunk or doped up all the time." He nodded sagely at Birdy. She shook her head; dang those stewed potheads, those menaces to society. More than once she and Jesús had played out the scene of their entrapment, the breathalizer test, the phone calls, the headline in the *Pinetop Journal, High School Teachers High As Kites; Birdy Stoned.*

"Larry came from an old mining family," the sheriff continued, "you've probably seen his dad driving around in that baby blue pickup of his."

"The old guy with the cowboy hat? And the beard? Always going like four miles an hour?" The man drove Birdy mad, inching along in his monstrous vehicle, facial hair like

ZZ Top, staring stonyfaced at you in his rearview mirror while you honked. She'd assumed he was part of some religious sect that prohibited shaving and accelerating. Stuck behind him, she'd managed to lob a few invectives in his direction, and now felt sort of sorry about it.

"That's him, old Odie Ranta. Their family's been here since the late 1880s, before this was even a state, back when it was a territory. Very old claimstakers, also very tight-lipped. Got incredibly insistent about getting the firearm returned to them. I never understood that, wanting the gun. That was what they kept harassing us about, that firearm. 'When can we have the gun? Where's our gun?' Weapon was a mess. Eventually, we were forced to turn the case over to Luna County. I had to physically remove people from the site."

"Where was that?" Birdy asked, then added, "exactly," as if she knew the general vicinity. As if she knew anything about anything he'd just told her.

"Larry parked by the ruins, in the north turnoff to the lot, kind of isolated. I was the first one there, after the call." He made a grim expression, shuddering like pudding. "You can't believe the blood, head wound in a confined space."

Birdy let this new image assert itself. She wondered how Sheriff Potter-Otto could stand seeing dead bodies on a regular basis, what steps he must have taken to manage it. What he told his wife and kids when he came home at night—or maybe that's what he and Lolo shared, carnage and mishap. "Nothing," he'd say to his wife. "Same old, same old." Birdy was on the verge of probing, her attention wandering from the project at hand to the more sensational one of his job, when he went on.

"We didn't bother with an autopsy, naturally," he said.

"Are there usually autopsies?"

"Now, there are. We send everything—that is, every body—down to Santa Fe."

"Even if the family doesn't want an autopsy?"

He gave her a knowing ironic look meant to communicate how well family could be counted upon to know best. That was *his* job, knowing best. Many factors contributed to the decision, he told her, many, the age and relative health of the victim, how certain the police were about what happened, and circumstantial evidence. "Gotta play it by ear, figure out if what we have on our plate is a crime or not. You'd be surprised, the majority of my job is gut reaction, flat-out human instinct." He sat back, proud of his instincts. Maybe he had one about Birdy.

"But you didn't do autopsies on the Anthonys," Birdy said, to fill the silence.

"We did."

"She doesn't know there were autopsies, Mrs. Anthony doesn't."

He paused, blazing his eyes at Birdy. "She does," he said definitively. "Most families don't want them done, but then later, our experience has shown, it can be helpful. If there's something they forget and bring up later, or they just change their mind, down the road, when clearer heads prevail, and they decide. Now, what was that blood-alcohol level? Or if somebody had a congenital heart condition, or whatever. She knows full well there were autopsies done on her daughter and her husband. Doesn't mean she read the reports. I'm not saying she had to study them. We would have offered her the results, first thing, but that doesn't mean she took them. Doesn't mean she read 'em. We didn't do one on Larry Ranta, like I said. No need to even bag his hands. Cut-and-dried suicide." He paused. "Pardon that rhyme there."

"But the Anthonys weren't cut-and-dried suicides?"

"We saw cause for autopsies, yes."

"Can I see the reports?"

He surveyed Birdy critically, just the way she feared cops would do, as if he could see straight through to her felonious soul. "If she gives permission. I'd have to notify the family and get prior okay. Those aren't open records."

"What if her son gives permission, instead? He's almost eighteen," she added when he didn't immediately respond.

"Is he? Geez, time flies. I don't know." He breathed heavily, catching on—but to what?

"I don't want to make her feel bad," Birdy said quickly. "I don't want her reminded unnecessarily of those times. I'm just interested in what the autopsies reveal."

"Accidents," he said promptly.

"Suicides?"

"I can't really get into that, Ms. Stone, but let me say this: they died of what we call rapid deacceleration, both cases. You fall off a cliff, you die of gravity, basically. No indication of foul play."

Foul play, the same words the newspaper was quick to deny. *Signs of struggle* crossed out in the sheriff's report. Birdy wanted to decry; the whole thing stank of foul play. Well, *stank* was probably an exaggeration. But surely the sheriff understood the paradox he'd proposed: not suicides, not murders, no cause, no effect. Just accidents, two people in the wrong place at the wrong times, rapidly deaccelerating off that irksome cliff. "What about the mark on Teresa's back?" she asked.

He cocked his head, as if he'd heard distant music, as if the wires waving from the walls had transmitted something relevant. "Oh, yeah. I remember that." He squeezed an OK sign with his thumb and forefinger. "Like a test pattern, little teeny thing. Right here." He reached his tightly uniformed arm around his shoulder—Birdy feared a bursting seam—and tapped below the left wing to illustrate.

"Like from a car cigarette lighter?" she asked innocently.

He scrutinized her with a frown. "That's right. That's what the M.E. sent back, car lighter."

"That didn't suggest foul play?"

He rolled his eyes. "Kids," he said, pooh-poohingly. "Always putting their brands on themselves, on each other. You've seen that, up at the high school, haven't you? Cutters? Nickers?"

Birdy had to agree; they did seem to like to rend their own skin. "I thought it was strange that the newspaper didn't really discuss that. I read the articles. They didn't have any scoop at all."

"Different time, different sheriff. Pinetop's a small town, Ms. Stone, and some 'scoop' people just don't want to hear. The sheriff ten years ago was Manny McDonald, and he kept everything tight as the FBI here at the office. No one talked to the press but him. No one was allowed to discuss cases, nothing. You were probably wondering why you couldn't find anything about Larry Ranta in the papers, weren't you? Mac knew his folks wouldn't want it, couldn't bear it. Old-fashioned. He ran the office like a family, he was the commander in chief, sheriff dad, made all the decisions and they were all executive, paid all the bills, took all the shit, pardon my French. I do things different, of course. I have a stack of case reports out there, open to the press. It's pretty unusual for me to yank one, only if it was real sensitive. The press and I understand each other, we have some mutual respect. Manny McDonald never trusted the press to be polite about what they wrote. They did not have mutual respect, no sir. So he looked at everything before it got printed, gave it his personal John Hancock."

"The articles about the Anthonys don't mention anything mysterious."

"Well, they only seem mysterious 'cause they all happened so close together, at virtually the same location. That's something that makes a place nervous, superstitious, or just plain suspicious. But we never found anything particular to say it was anything but a bunch of terrible luck and coincidence. Just one bad piece of road."

"What if Larry and Teresa were a couple?"

"Were they?" he asked. "That what Mrs. A. says in her memmer-wars?"

"No. She doesn't mention Larry at all."

He narrowed his eyes, as if realizing he'd mistakenly given her grist with Larry's suicide. Birdy didn't think she'd make a very good private eye, too clumsy in her interrogation, a blunderer with the witnesses.

Quickly she said, "So you think two suicides and a car crash?"

"No, I do not. I think Larry Ranta shot himself, and Philip Anthony lost control of his car, and Teresa fell. One suicide, two accidents. That's how we left the investigation."

"Teresa just fell?"

"Teresa just fell."

Teresa, Birdy felt certain, had not just fallen. She had been pushed, or she had jumped, and *then* she'd fallen. Right before the force of gravity had taken over, there'd been some other force. It was that moment that Birdy wished to isolate, the critical juncture. She wanted to know the position of the footprints in the dirt, those particular dance steps that were either solo or tango—a father's anger, or a girl's despair, or some lethal combination, a matter of spontaneous combustion.

Maybe it was the result of having spent an hour talking to a police officer in a small room lighted by a naked two hundred-watt bulb hanging from the ceiling, but Birdy anticipated being followed or shot at after her meeting with the sheriff. She thanked him profusely—as if to buy off her unnamed guilt—and left the building with her head lowered, walking quickly in the afternoon sun. She felt as if she were in the middle of a suspense novel or thriller film, sticking her nose where it didn't belong, turning up long-buried ground, doing things the members of the audience knew were foolish. For a few days, she sensed the audience's presence, a stalking wisdom trailing her about, people who knew better than she the trouble she was unwittingly stirring up. Somewhere out there, her readers, her viewers, were slapping their foreheads, shaking their heads, frustrated at her bungled attempts to fashion a story out of this questionable business.

"You aren't making enough money on this to care about it the way you do," Jesús had said to her.

"My mother just needs a friend," Mark had pointed out in a rare moment of insight.

But the story interested Birdy beyond the income, beyond sympathetic allegiance to a writer. She wanted to know what had happened to Teresa Anthony, and why. It annoyed her that everyone seemed so complacent about the past, so uninterested in setting the record straight, so slipshod over the deceased girl. She acknowledged her selfishness: what if it were her body, there at the bottom of a ravine? Would she want the people who'd known her to be satisfied with some flimsy story of falling?

Despite what she'd discovered, Birdy wasn't ready to give up her theory of Mr. Anthony's responsibility for his daughter's death. She had a grudge against a dead man—a stranger, no less—a vendetta with a corpse. But if this new character, this wrinkle in the form of Larry Ranta, had killed himself over Teresa, and if Teresa had been murdered by her father just after Larry's death, then everyone would assume her suicide was in response to Larry's, leaving the father unsuspected and blameless in her slaying. Unable to bear his own Miltonic hell, however, he had killed himself a few days after. Was Larry the older boy Teresa had been seeing? The one Mary Jo had told her about seeing at the Alpine Inn? Was the father jealous of the boyfriend, or merely protecting his young daughter from a mature and dangerous man?

Maybe Larry's suicide had nothing to do with Teresa. Certainly Mrs. Anthony had never mentioned him. The only person who'd seen any reason to breathe the names in the same sentence had been the sheriff, who'd gone to the same scene three separate times in one week; no wonder he linked them.

Birdy wanted to read the autopsy reports, yet did not have the courage to broach the subject. She could ask to see them, and Mrs. Anthony could deny their existence.

Or she could tell Birdy it was none of her business and throw her out of the house.

Or she could dissolve in a weepy heap, the pretense that those reports did not exist the sole explanation for her survival up to now.

The reports could reveal any number of things—violation, volition, virginity—but what Birdy invented as their substance was probably more interesting, more true, than the facts. Furthermore, the key players were all gone. If Teresa had killed herself, hadn't she targeted her quarry, her mourning parents, so sorry they'd done her wrong? And if Mr. Anthony had killed his daughter, well, he'd paid his dues. What further justice did Birdy think she could exact?

Don Potter-Otto had said Larry was a druggie, so Birdy went to Jesús.

"Larry Ranta," he said instantly. "Ooh my God, Larry Ranta. You sure can pick 'em, Bird. Larry was just the kind of dipshit cornpone small towns are supposed to breed. Inbreed, I should say. They put him away in the pen, down at La Tuna, sayonara shithead, but of course he came back, like a big putrid nightmare. Very mean guy, and very dumb, too, but still earned a lot of respect. He was violent, that's what I could never handle. I mean, he'd get wasted with us, and he had some good dope, and he liked to share it, but he had a totally redneck way of being fucked up. We'd all be watching TV, putting on music, making jokes, you know, *Star Trek* with a Blondie sound track, passive entertainment, lazy little stoned pigs. Larry seemed to have a totally different neuro-chemistry, you know? He wanted to go bust things up, do damage, punch people, drive fast. All that nonsense. Very retro kind of 1950s bullshit. When we were kids, I was terri-fied of him. He was always beating us up. Fortunately, I weighed more than he did, by the time we were in junior high. Coulda sat on him, *splut*. What do you want to know about Larry Ranta for, Bird girl?"

"He might have been Teresa Anthony's boyfriend."

Jesús looked disappointed. He was now thoroughly bored by Birdy's fascination with Teresa Anthony; it was all just so much dead history. "Huh," he finally said, shrugging. "I guess he might of. I get the feeling he was a tiny bit hard up, after the pen. Like maybe a high school girl would have been perfect." He hesitated, as if aware that he'd trodden on Birdy's own hard-up-ness, her high school boyfriend. Jesús went on, "He was a few years older than me, maybe even five. He got held back all the time, so I had him in some bonehead English class once. Mary Jo Callahan," he said, smiling. "He used to pop her bra strap." He made pincers and pulled at the air before them. "Larry Ranta, blast from the past. Yeah, I can see him going for a high school girl, after prison."

They were lying on Jesús's mother's front yard, lollygag-ging out there with her terra-cotta, guano-slicked Saint Fran-cis and a bunch of white ceramic ducks. Jesús was supposed to be weeding, but he'd grown weary of weeds. Birdy liked the fact that Jesús's pastimes were sedentary, like hers. In the summer, this came to matter. Mark might spend the day shooting baskets at the school yard, playing softball in the sun, swimming in the river, but Birdy preferred reposing before her swamp cooler, reading books, and Jesús sat in front of his listening to music and smoking pot. In the evenings, he and Birdy used to watch videos; now Birdy spent the evenings with Mark. He came to her trailer after his mother went to bed, either then or on the nights when he claimed to be umpiring or Rollerblading. Their meetings were secret, so it felt good to lounge with a grown-up, now, in full view of the rest of the town. Her illicit affair had the result of leaving her sometimes publicly lonely.

"Know what I heard?" Jesús asked her.

"What?"

"Mary Jo's got a gentleman caller."

"Get out of here." Birdy lifted her head like a lizard. "Who?"

He shrugged. "Someone from out of town, I guess, an import."

"That is nothing short of amazing," Birdy said. "Simply amazing." The news bothered her. Presumably, Mary Jo Callahan's beau would be an adult, of age to go to bars, master of his own fortune. Something occurred to her. "Does he speak English?"

"Haven't met him."

"It's a green card thing," she guessed. "He's fleeing some former Soviet satellite. His aesthetic sense has yet to kick in."

"Try again," Jesús said. "Dream on, girlfriend."

His mother and Tía Blanca then came trundling from the front door of the Fort Avenue fort, across the porch, down the steps, and through the dandelioned grass to where Jesús and Birdy lay. Birdy watched them progress from a sideways position, concentrating on the women's support socks that bit into the veined flesh under their knees. It was like watching trussed hams ambulate toward her. Mrs. Morales and Tía

Blanca both rolled on the sides of their feet, bowlegged, bunioned, old, fat. Each carried a tall colored glass; Birdy thought they were bringing them drinks.

"Novena candles," Mrs. Morales breathed as she reached her son and Birdy. "Saint Jude and Saint Dymphna."

Jesús laughed. "Patron saints of hopeless causes and nervous disorders. They're worried for you, Bird."

The women stood over them frowning. "You laugh ahead, Mr. Knows It All," said his mother. "How many times you see people thanking Saint Jude, in the newspaper, huh? All the time, that's how many." The shadow they cast over Birdy blocked the sun, the light radiating around their heads like halos, as if they were themselves twin saints, Saint Juanita Morales and Saint Tía Blanca, patronesses of inexorable bodily collapse. Their legs seemed to be filling with the full volume of their flesh as it sank, leaving their shoulders bony. "I use to be a Coke bottle," Mrs. Morales was known to say of her shape, "and now I'm a *calabaza.*"

"Gourd," Jesús had translated for Birdy, drawing the wide-bottomed profile with his hands. "*Gorda* gourd," he'd said playfully to his mother.

"Which cause is my hopeless one?" Birdy now asked the women.

"You need to get married, of course," Tía Blanca answered, she who rarely spoke a word, communicating by nodding affirmation to what her friend spoke.

Mrs. Morales said, "There's a novena on each of these. You light the candle, say your novena, everything'll work out. You," she tapped her son in the ribs with her tiny foot. "You get these dandies out of my flowers. And clean up Saint Francis, the bird poop on him, *Dios mío.*" Off she trundled to the house once more, her identical shadow in her wake, the screen banging behind them. Birdy's candles smelled of fruit and spices. Neither she nor Jesús rose from the ground. Lying in cool grass on a hot day reminded Birdy of childhood, of staring into the big blue sky that everyone, all over the world stared into. Birdy had taken comfort in the sperm-shaped floaters that swam before her own eyes, the invisible blots that made her view both imperfect and unlike anyone else's, that went along with her through the years and slid familiarly from one side of the picture to the other, over and over like material dragged by a wiper, pursued by her focus, scooting elusively away then back, and before her now as she looked up at the heavens from New Mexico.

"Why do they want me to get married?" she asked lazily. She liked having Mrs. Morales and Tía Blanca fretting over her life; it gave her permission to reject advice, it gave her a solid stance to rebel against, like an adolescent.

"They want everyone to get married," Jesús said. "Get married, have babies, be happy." He laughed his usual laugh, effervescent as foam from his throat, but for a second, it sounded newly menacing to Birdy, a noxious burbling, a wet jeer, as if he thought his mother's and Tía Blanca's simple pre-scription for Birdy's well-being ludicrous. Perhaps it was ludi-crous, but Birdy wished to diagnose and then disparage it herself. And maybe it was time to get married. Her mother had always claimed that marriage saved her, and Birdy couldn't dis-pute the evidence. Up until her death, her mother's marriage had seemed good, two close friends who still cared what the other thought, who slept in the same bed, who made each other laugh. Birdy had been given the opportunity to marry twice before. The abortion had effectively killed her romance with the poet; and Reg, who'd found her moving in a kind of trance after her break with the professor, had rescued her, someone about to walk into traffic or a river. Reg came along like a crutch, like a host for her then-parasitic neediness. She attached herself thankfully to his affection and began to grow healthy. It seemed ungrateful not to then agree to marry him, when he asked. After all, he didn't ask for much, and he'd been such a kind host, showing her 'round the continent for the last few years, introducing her to his friends and family, involving her in his own parasitic habits, his appendage, his piggy-backed load. Birdy supposed her own return to sense had to do with recognizing Reg's weaknesses, with testing his widths and depths and finding him a pond, not a lake, certainly not an ocean. It was as if she'd wakened from sedation, finally comprehended her own limbs once more as vehicles of their own, willful, healthy. She'd untangled herself abruptly, perhaps too abruptly, leaving Reg a simple note, blaming herself, but how brilliantly free and light she felt, once she realized she needn't marry him, needn't stay with him. She felt as if she'd drifted into a less substantial atmosphere, arrived there only by divine good luck.

"Why?" he'd said, simple and heartbreaking, turning on her his sad eyes.

But maybe the atmosphere was now thinning. A person might slip too far away, untied, unfettered.

"Get married," Jesús repeated in a whining refrain. "Start popping out those babies."

"Fall in love," Birdy added. "There's nothing wrong with that, falling in love."

"Who says there's nothing wrong with it?"

"And what does she want you to do?" she asked unkindly, without thinking.

Jesús filled his cheeks with air, then leaked a squeaky flute through his lips. "My job is to stay right here," he said. "Happy Jesús, mama's fat boy. Hear, see, speak no evil." He moved his fingers from ears to eyes to mouth, kissed them and fluttered them in Birdy's face.

"I wish I could live with *my* mother," Birdy said to him, testily. His sudden and abashed response—he dissolved in hangdog agreement—made her rethink her words. Her intent had been sarcastic—suddenly Jesús seemed like a big twenty-seven-year-old baby—but she discovered she actually did wish she could live with her mother again. What was wrong with living with someone who liked you? Who found you fascinating when the rest of the planet could not have cared less? Her mother had been good company, besides, quiet, humorous, self-sufficient. She needed a few of her vices around—coffee, cigarettes, playing cards, bitter chocolate, gin, mystery novels, arranged in no particular order, augmented by impromptu additions—and she could be perfectly happy for days on end, in any setting. Her amusements went on, with or without company. Asked, she would recount the plot of her book, or teach you how to play variations of rummy, share her chocolate, fix you a drink. An ideal companion would be familiar with the conventions of bridge and the complete works of P. G. Wodehouse. If you insisted, she might join you for a television show, although she found those programs, in general, unexceptional. She could rub your back for a good long time without getting bored.

"You okay?" Jesús asked, sitting up, snapping his fingers in her face. "Woo hoo. Hell-oh?"

"You're lucky," she said.

"Excuse me?"

"You're lucky your mom's alive." Birdy closed her eyes, concentrated on the mashed grass beneath her head, the sensation of some living thing—plant or insect—tickling at her neck.

"Sometimes I wish she weren't," Jesús said, then gave himself two slaps for bad conduct. "Erase, erase. Quick, Bird, change the subject."

"To . . ."

"I know, I know. Wanna be in my Fourth of July float?"

"In the slug bug?"

He stretched, fists way high, and flopped down, pounding

his heels on the ground as if he'd been dropped from a tree onto his back. "I'm thinking love bug."

"Do I have to do anything?"

"Throw candy at children."

"Can I throw it hard?"

"You're cold, girl."

Birdy rolled over and buried her face in the cool grass. "I am not," she muttered to the ground. "I am not."

❧ 8

Luziana Rillos lived only a few blocks from Birdy's house, on the same shady side of town. There was a beautifully arranged vegetable garden on one half of the Rillos front yard, marked punctually by seed-packet signs; on the other half were parked two immaculate, identical, flesh-toned Cadillacs, each showcased on its own turquoise area rug like a frog on a lily pad. Her father and brothers managed to keep the yard and cars (and beyond all odds, the two rugs) in good condition, but appeared to be at a loss at housekeeping. Inside, the place smelled of bug spray, a burning sting in the nostrils. Dishes teetered in the sink and, on the dining room table, an ominous car engine dripped oil into a baking sheet like a basted feast offering. The ironing board supported a heap of wrinkled clothing.

Luziana stood amid the clutter starching one of her flimsy

smocks, wearing a thick-strapped bra and a pregnancy girdle, recommended by the Lamaze instructor to prevent stretch marks and back pain. The scene reminded Birdy of photographs from Third World countries and from the poverty-stricken places more locally located, the jarring juxtaposition of mechanical hardware and clean white cotton, of motor oil and human flesh. These were the places of sickening accident, the ferment created by blending or misusing elements: children drinking drain cleaner instead of milk, playing with switchblades and loaded guns instead of harmless plastic toys. Young females with their distended bellies who didn't connect sexual sport to this dreadful swelling.

Birdy had come to take Luziana to her final Lamaze class, a celebratory Saturday brunch under the elk heads to which former Lamaze graduates were also invited, bearing their offspring and their war stories.

"Hey Miz Stone," Luziana called, hefting the iron in welcome. "You know I flunked World Leaders? Gotta do summer school. Old Whack-off." The students' favorite target, Mr. Whacker was six years overdue for retirement. He once told Birdy that he still slept outdoors all summer, listening to the wildlife. Without warning, he'd thrust his pointed nose at her and squawked, imitating some creature. Birdy had jumped back, startled. Afterward, she always pictured him like a corpulent corpse in his backyard, staring up at the stars with a savage grin on his face, arms crossed over his chest, communing with nature.

"Where are your brothers?" Birdy asked, wondering if Luziana paraded around in her underwear in front of her male family, curious again about the identity of the baby's father, feeling queasy at the notion that this house, too, held some incestuous intrigue. Luziana planned to use her secret like an ace, withheld until most valuable.

Birdy looked in vain for a place to sit.

"The boys are at soapbox racing," Luziana said. "Down in Alamagordo. But you know Miz Stone, I've been getting these pains in my tee-tee, and all tight everywhere. Maybe I'm having contractions?"

Birdy's heart fluttered, but Luziana simply ironed, blandly. Her due date was still three weeks away, and she seemed to believe the baby already had a definite birthday. ("A Cancer," she had told Birdy despondently last week. "I don't even get along with Cancers. My mom was one.") Plus, Birdy and Luziana were scheduled to visit the Albuquerque maternity ward day after tomorrow, a day trip down the mountain, one Jesús planned to act as chauffeur on, since he knew his way around town. The ob/gyn who came to the Pinetop clinic had been sick last week, so Luziana hadn't had her weekly exam. Maybe she was in early labor. Maybe it was going to be up to Birdy to diagnose it.

"You know what?" Luziana said. "I finally got a crib, go check out my bedroom." She tossed her head toward the small hallway. Birdy stepped carefully past the bathroom and a dark bedroom before coming to Luziana's. She recognized the white and gold furniture from her own girlhood; its appeal must have been especially hormonal. The crib, also white, was nearly as large as Luziana's canopy bed. It was festooned with blankets and pillows and stuffed animals. The two beds sat beside each other, the other furniture crowded against the walls, a narrow path burrowed out between. Luziana's baby would probably like all the garishly colored posters hanging on the walls, never mind that they were of half-naked rock singers whose faces were contorted with the effort of their art.

"That's nice," Birdy told her as she returned to the dining room.

"Mr. John bought it for me," Luziana said. "Isn't that sweet?"

"Well. Hmm. I don't know about accepting gifts from Mr. John . . ." Birdy trailed off. What did she know, anyway?

"Why?"

"What if he starts thinking he's entitled to . . ."

"To what?"

"I don't know. To being your baby's father. Or something."

"I don't have time to look a gift horse in the mouth," Luziana said, snapping her blouse before her and eyeing it critically. "Shit," she said, leaning suddenly on the board, the iron plopping down on its hot face. "Look at that," she said, pointing to the floor. She stood in a puddle. "My water broke all over my bike shorts."

Four and a half hours later, Birdy could hear her from the little delivery waiting room at Albuquerque's Memorial General; Birdy had been sent out when Luziana required restraints and an epidural. One look at the anesthesiologist's needle made Birdy weak in the knees. Nothing was like Lamaze. No opportunity for deep cleansing breaths or calm focal points. If she'd offered Luziana a lollipop or neck massage, she felt certain the girl would have sunk her teeth in her arm. Luziana had been screaming like someone was killing her for at least an hour. Jesús, who'd been, mercifully, unbusy and willing to drive them down, now laid his hands over his ears, hear-no-evil style. If she was useless, Jesús was even more so. "We got to get stoned," he kept telling Birdy. "I can't take this. You want some Valium?" He produced a palmful of yellow pills, Vs etched out like valentines in their middles. "They aren't much, little five miggers, but they're something."

Birdy wondered how Mark Anthony would have behaved, had he been here in their place. He was the appropriate age to become a father to a teenage girl's baby. He would be the attentive other, present at her side, sturdy where Luziana was insane, young along with her in his complementary way. Suddenly Birdy wished she could put the two of them together like Ken and Barbie—or Skipper, she supposed, Skipper and the appropriate-size boy doll, whose name no doubt would be Sparky—the correct ages and genders, the he and the she, the parents and the infant. She herself would gratefully defer to them both, squeeze out of the trio like a sly matchmaker, erase her own stopgap role in each life.

Wasn't she just getting in the way of the normal pattern of things, an interruption in the weave?

Then she imagined Mr. John, sitting here in her place, itching for a push broom to take care of the littered floor. He was the father, she believed. Luziana was the kind of girl who might have felt sorry for his virginity, offered herself as a kind of charity, made a gesture modeled off the lessons learned in public schools: mainstreaming the handicapped. Nothing made more sense.

"Do you inherit mental retardation?" she asked Jesús.

"Did I?"

"Does one?"

He shrugged. "Why? You think I'm fucking with my chromosomes? I'm no sperm donor."

"I was thinking Mr. John might be the father."

Jesús shook his head dispiritedly. "Doubtful. Let me get your opinion, Bird. Who's the genius who named hospitals 'Memorial'? And bus stations and airports 'Terminal'? Who's in charge of this shit, anyway?"

"I thought you took a Valium."

"Four. They haven't kicked in yet."

Poor Luziana screamed and screamed beyond the swinging aluminum doors, her voice eventually, finally, falling into a wrenching guttural helplessness, *unh, unh, unh,* the sound of a dying animal, subsumed by the noise of professionals around her, encouraging her, reprimanding her, ebbing and flowing, ordering her to push, then ordering her to wait, to breathe, to hang on, repeating her name as if to keep her from giving up in the rugged surf. And then, at last, there was the riveting shriek of a baby, *waaaa*, a noise that sounded as if it had been long bottled, dying to make itself heard. Like Luziana's jumbled house, this sound, too, rang discordant, misplaced in the clinical atmosphere.

Birdy and Jesús looked at each other, eyes wide. Birdy felt certain Luziana must have died, since her voice had so abruptly disappeared. "Luziana," Birdy said, breaking into a panicked sweat, feeling wholly responsible for her student's death; it was just like a Victorian novel, moral retribution, God would punish her for having such a skeptical appreciation of His ways. She promised herself she would no longer sleep with Mark Anthony, she would call UNM and admit her tampering with his file, she would phone his mother . . .

And then there was Luziana's regular childish nonplussed voice, saying, "Oh my God, she's so big, holy shit, somebody look at her thumbs, these dwarf thumbs run in my family, oh my God . . ."

Jesús began clutching Birdy's wrists, tears in his eyes. "She's fine," he was saying. "You can stop, everything's cool, you can stop. Crying. Birdy." Birdy had to put her hands to her face to understand that she was, indeed, crying, sobbing, in fact, her heart overloaded with some dubious emotion.

THE BIRTH announcement in the *Pinetop Journal* claimed that mother and baby were both healthy, although the child had yet to be named.

"Not Mongolian," Jesús assured Birdy.

The newspaper not only didn't mention the lack of a father, it failed to note Birdy's heroic attendance. Hadn't it been Birdy, sitting in the backseat of Jesús's cramped slug bug while Luziana convulsed on the passenger seat, who'd kept the girl from leaping from the vehicle? "Do you realize this baby has to come out my *vagina?*" Luziana had screamed more than once as they sped down the road. "Out that tiny hole? It's like shitting a basketball, fuck, fuck, fuck!" She'd torn Jesús's mother's rosary off the rearview mirror, scattering beads on the floorboard. Through all of this, Birdy had implored calmness, her voice measured, not unlike the sexy spiritual guide who'd led Mrs. Anthony on her daily audiotape journeys. Fiercely, Jesús piloted the bug and valiantly, Birdy coached.

At one point, she'd said, "Do you want me to contact the father now?"

"Shut up, Miz Stone!" her student had responded.

Now the newspaper ignored their invaluable assistance. Birdy felt overlooked, minimalized, shorted. Even in this podunk hellhole, her name would never appear in the newspaper, her presence would not be noted or appreciated, nor would she be missed if she took it into her head to skedaddle. Mark would come sniffing around her trailer in the evening like a mutt hungry for the bitch in heat, and she'd be gone. Who would miss her?

As if to augment Birdy's sense of smallness, her sister phoned to say she was pregnant again. Birdy, fresh from the experience with Luziana, groaned.

"Aren't you going to congratulate me?" Becca demanded. "Ever since Mom died, no one uses their manners anymore."

"Congratulations," Birdy said, wondering what other instances of absent manners Becca alluded to.

"This time it will be a girl," her sister reported, as if she'd mail-ordered, checked off the female box. "Due Christmas day." Just like a UPS package.

"Congratulations," Birdy repeated. Then, in the expensive sizzling silence of the long-distance phone line, she asked after their father. He was fine, Becca said, going on to detail his fervent attentions to his new children, his two little identical sons. His new wife was Colombian, beautiful and demure, with a charming accent that made everything she said harmlessly cute. Birdy had appreciated this about her while still believing her father should have honored his first wife's memory by waiting longer to spring to connubial action. Plus, the new wife was precisely opposite from Birdy's mother, who'd been stern and wry, tall and domineering, a tough flat-chested woman with a raucous cigarette laugh. Choosing someone so different from her—plump and innocent, friendly and guileless— seemed an insult.

But many of her father's actions seemed like insults to Birdy. Just before she graduated from college with her BA in English literature, she'd realized there wasn't much she could do with such a degree, hardly more than what she'd done after her last graduation, from high school. When she presented this problem to her father, he'd recommended she become a paralegal. He'd read somewhere that English majors made fine paralegals. It wasn't until Birdy was in her last semester of her education certification that she realized the affront his advice had been. She'd rankled in retrospect. Why hadn't he suggested she go to law school and become a full-fledged lawyer? Why did he assume she would never be good enough for that, only for the underling position, the paralegal?

When she presented this evidence of her father's lack of confidence to her sister, Becca shrugged. She'd married a lawyer; she probably didn't think Birdy had what it took, either. Their father hadn't expected much from either one of his daughters, Birdy decided, except respectability. His overriding fears during their high school years had seemed to be promiscuity and drug use. As long as they brought home decent grades and didn't get pregnant, he seemed to believe they were fine. Birdy assumed he would have other expectations of his new sons.

"Consuelo has given me a bunch of nice baby stuff," Becca was saying over the phone line.

Who was Consuelo? Then Birdy remembered: her stepmother. She had a stepmother, like an abandoned princess. In the beginning, back when she and Becca were allies, they'd referred to her as Consuelo the Concubine. Birdy couldn't imagine bringing up that name now with Becca. All of her relations were becoming mere acquaintances, their shared jokes dated and obscure. When Becca finally asked her, obligatorily, what was new, Birdy didn't know where to begin, so she didn't. "Nothing," she said. "Just nothing." In their earlier incarnation as siblings, Becca had played the voice of reason, flatly frank when Birdy seemed about to plunge headlong into something reckless. Birdy used to knock upon Becca's door, sit on her canopy bed, have her notions dispelled or ratified. Becca, she'd always believed, *knew*. Becca was on the right course, and Birdy's job was to keep her in sight, use Becca's accomplishments as markers for her own. Later, there'd been visits to Becca's sorority house, then phone calls to her suburban home with her husband, the noise of dishwasher or television in the background. It had been Becca who'd sneered, long distance, at Birdy's plan to go live in a castle in Italy with her poet professor. Birdy had canceled her reservation, based on Becca's complete confidence in the sheer ridiculousness of the idea. A castle, for godssake, what would she think of next? It must have been clear, by then, that Birdy was no longer on the same track as Becca.

What, for example, would her sister have made of the current state of Birdy's affairs? Living in a dumpy trailer on the shady side of town, smoking pot with her best friend the homosexual, dating a seventeen-year-old ninny, investigating a melodramatic teenage suicide?

"When are you coming home?" her sister asked.

"I don't know."

"This summer?"

"Maybe."

Birdy couldn't see herself in Chicago; it was as if the place had become a movie on a screen, on Mrs. Morales's screen, a bunch of meaningless silver dots far away from her, a thing you could entertain as an idea but not as a real destination. She had to confess that she felt uncomfortable thinking of it as home. The house she'd grown up in had been sold; her father's new residence was in Evanston; Becca lived in Skokie. Home had been dispersed along with her mother's ashes.

"The kids are getting big," her sister threatened. "If you don't see them soon, you won't recognize them. They won't recognize you."

"That might be okay; then you can introduce me as someone else. They didn't like the old me much, anyway," Birdy said. Small children like her nephews intimidated Birdy; they had no scruples about saying just exactly what they thought, pointing at a person and laughing uncontrollably.

"Oh, come on." Becca was exasperated. She'd never tolerated self-pity well. She didn't have time for it. Self-deprecating remarks were wasted on her, as she would be more likely to agree than not. "Reg called here, one day," she said before hanging up. "He was at the airport, just flying through, called to say hi."

"Hmm," Birdy said. She could imagine him smoking at O'Hare, muffling his breathy exhalations while talking with her sister. He liked to keep in touch with people, even after there was no real reason to do so, as if he had a lot of friends. He liked to phone a local, wherever he was, and say hi, ask after the children. She supposed it was endearing—Becca certainly sounded endeared to him—but Birdy considered it mildly pathetic. Her heart did a shame-and-pity wince in memory of her own unkindness to Reg.

"He's getting married," Becca said triumphantly.

"What?"

"Yeah. Some girl he met in New York." Becca was being too casual, suggesting that she'd known all along Reg would get snapped up by some lucky girl, and wasn't Birdy sorry now?

"Bully for him," she said sourly. Her annoyance was with her sister, not Reg.

Toward Reg she felt only relief: now she was not responsible for his unhappiness. "Maybe I'll mail him a fondue pot."

Her sister said, "Well, I guess that's everything," as if they spoke often, as if this were a weekly bulletin from the heartland, as if they'd heard each other's voices often in the last fifteen months.

"Take care of your baby," Birdy made herself say cheerfully. "Jerk," she said, after they hung up. How her mother would have grieved, to see the two of them like this. Sometimes her mother seemed to Birdy like her conscience, and she didn't enjoy it, since it had no realistic boundaries. This haunting was as excruciatingly exacting as the haunting of a god, a saint, a whole castigating religious faith, as if her mother held the key to her moral fortune, knew her through and through, saw into her shallow petty heart—saw into it, and decided it was not beyond repair. Birdy couldn't tune her out, couldn't hide from her scrutiny, couldn't combat a sense of needing refurbishment. The dead had that advantage.

On an impulse, Birdy phoned the Anthony house. If Mrs. A. answered, she'd hang up, like a prankster, like a girl with a shy crush. But it was Mark who picked up the phone.

"It's me," Birdy said, realizing it was the first time she'd spoken to him over the telephone. Her ridiculous life, she and her boyfriend unable to phone each other freely.

"Oh." Did he recognize her voice? Or maybe he wasn't sure how to address her, accustomed, as he had been, to calling her Ms. Stone. Mostly he was too busy *un*dressing her to bother *ad*dressing her.

"Can you talk?" she heard herself say.

"Okay."

"Your mom's there?"

"Sure."

"You want to come over?"

He paused. "I can't, Rus."

"Rus? Who the hell is Rus? What about later?"

Another pause. "I have to go on a date tonight."

"A date?"

"My mom is making me." There was noise on his end, his mother voicing some objection to his phrasing, his laughter. "Really," he said to Birdy. "She thinks I'm getting introverted."

"She thinks you're turning queer." It seemed that all her men were spurning Birdy. Maybe Mark, like Becca, expected her to dredge up jealousy. Not likely. "Who with?"

"Elizabeth Eversman," he answered, speaking her name as if she had that old-fashioned affliction, cooties; Mrs. A. could be heard registering another complaint. "*Ow,*" he said, in response to what must have been a swat.

"Have fun," said Birdy flatly.

"She's really dull. Yes she is, Mom, she is." Commotion ensued, a muffled exchange. Elizabeth, who'd graduated a year ago, had been in one of Birdy's lit classes. Mark was right; pretty enough, Elizabeth was extremely pallid and had almost no effect. In her essays, she'd always pursued a family values angle, promoting her own clan's Mormonism in the strenuously polite way that was their method. After graduat-

ing, she'd stayed at home with her parents and sisters, working at their family video store that refused to stock R-rated
movies, wearing her name tag.

She was never Beth or Liz or Betty or Libby; always Elizabeth, all four syllables, like the queen of England.

"You have a thing for older women," Birdy teased. Mark
laughed then, tentatively relieved, his exhalation over the line
making the hairs on Birdy's neck rise. She wanted him to
materialize before her; she wanted him to put his mouth
there where she'd felt his breath.

"I'll probably be home by ten," he said.

"You gonna kiss Elizabeth good night?"

"Should I?"

"Use your judgment, big boy."

"Don't you fall in love," she whispered, after he'd said
"Good-bye, Rus," and hung up. It was only then, her silent
trailer surrounding her, that Birdy recalled Elizabeth's
Reader's Journal, the notebook Birdy had required that particular class to keep, her own promise to check their entries
without actually reading them. In these entries, they were
supposed to reveal their personal responses to the stories and
poems they read, the things they might not feel comfortable
divulging in class before their pitiless, scornful peers. Birdy
had been amused by Elizabeth's properness, her confessions
of either not understanding or being offended by hedonistic,
heathen themes and their attendant crude language. Then
one day Elizabeth had turned in her notebook with her own
story in it; *Please Read This!*, she'd underlined and highlighted
with thick overlays of ink. Birdy read (she'd been reading
many of the students' entries anyway). The story concerned
a girl who fell in love with a boy, the boy who seemed to reci-
procate her love, the girl's ensuing sacrifice of her virginity,
and then the boy's instantaneous discarding of the girl.
While Birdy was happy that "Jessica" had been deflowered,

she regretted "Brent's" unkindness; it would only confirm what poor Elizabeth had been told, that nice girls did not mistake sex for love, did not expect respect after making themselves vulnerable. What caught Birdy's eye, what she remembered most distinctly, was the story's unconvincing conclusion: "And Jessica did not care if Brent ignored her, she simply did not care. Their love was not intended to be and Jessica knew she would soon fall in love with her intended he would realize how special she was and love her right. She did not care about Brent she was carefree and she laughed aloud as she saw him walk away alone across the empty football field."

Birdy's comment, in the ubiquitous red ink of her trade, read: "This is a touching story, Elizabeth. You have a flair for clear sentences. It would be okay, you know, if Jessica were hurt, in the end, by being betrayed. Her pain is what would reveal the emotional center of the piece." She didn't go so far as to say that the pain was what had driven Elizabeth/Jessica to write the story in the first place, that the "laughed aloud" part had practically broken her reader's heart. "Come see me, if you want to talk," she concluded her red comment. Elizabeth made no further mention of her creative entry— and no other ones like it—and though Birdy waited for the girl to arrive weeping at her desk some afternoon after class—thankful for understanding, for permission to grieve— that never happened, either.

In fact, Elizabeth seemed to have grown even more distant in her relations with both Ms. Stone and literature, as if both had offended her.

Now Mark was going on a date with her. It was not difficult to picture his hands roaming Elizabeth's body; like clay figures, Birdy saw them together, their soft brightly colored parts meshing and mushing. It was as if this date with Elizabeth were already a part of Mark's romantic history, some experience toward which Birdy could decide to feel a minor indebtedness.

She stared at the telephone, as if it was responsible for her terrible mood. She would give it one more chance to exonerate itself. Jesús answered on the first ring, as if waiting for her call. When she told him all her news, he suggested psychedelic mushrooms.

"You need modification, Ms. Bird."

"Let's go to the ruins," she suggested.

"Party on," Jesús said.

They ate the mushrooms on a cheese pizza, washed down with Gatorade to quell both dehydration and nausea. Jesús had been doing drugs for so long he had strategies for nearly every side effect; he would be an exemplary spirit guide, Birdy thought. She would hand herself over like an eight-year-old on an airplane, flying alone, waiting for assistance gate to gate, solicitation and caretaking. They drove his slug bug out of town, hurrying so that the mushrooms wouldn't take hold until they were safely at the ruins, installed in the hollow space, snug. Birdy pointed out her favorite road sign, the orange one showing a piece of the cliff breaking off, a rock suspended midair. Given its location, she couldn't help imagining arms and legs and head on the little chipped icon: BEWARE FALLING BODIES.

They stumbled to the dwelling, Jesús in the lead, holding her hand, the sun starting its setting furor behind them. Their view was of the pink sandstone facades of the facing mountains, Pinetop an H & O scale cluster of toys in the distance, the blinding sunlight reflecting as if from mirrors from a few aluminum roofs. Piñon trees dotted the landscape like scrappy train set shrubbery. The cliff house held them like a lap.

"Once I got stoned once and spent the whole night staring at the stereo," Jesús said. "I thought I was on an airplane, looking down at a city."

"Once once, staring stereo," Birdy said. "You could write songs."

Birdy had done mushrooms before. Then, she'd been very happy for about three hours, crawling around the empty apartment of a high school boyfriend's father, who'd just moved his furniture out, laughing so much her face ached the whole next day. She and the boyfriend spent the high chasing his nervous cat, making love on the floor while laughing convulsively, mesmerized by the miracle of padded carpeting, riveted by the view of Lake Michigan, lights from Navy Pier appearing like stars, forming new constellations along the pattern of modern piers and roadways, as if Birdy and her boyfriend were floating without sense of up or down, defying gravity.

Gravity made Birdy think about falling, rocks and bodies. Her mood plunged, as if she'd forgotten something crucial, like breathing. "Don't let me fall," she cautioned Jesús.

"Relax, Bird girl. Give in." He spread his arms as if to embrace the cosmos, as if to welcome crucifixion. He thumped his chest, then wheezed, kneeling to find a piece of charred wood. With it, hunched over like a primate, he headed for an empty space on the rock wall.

"But if you look out at that town and think it's just a stereo, then anything could happen. You could twist a dial and end up down in the bottom."

"This canyon is filled with broken glass," Jesús said. "Decades of beer bottles. An anthropologist could write a dissertation on the strata."

"Did you bring a flashlight?" she asked.

"Nope."

"Matches?"

"Nope."

"Breath Saver?"

"Nope, nope. No emergency provisions whatsoever. No flare, no snakebite kit, no water. And nowhere to go for a while. So relax," he repeated, distractedly. And Birdy made herself surrender to the ecstasy. He seemed like a big woolly bear to her, friendly and protective, a savior like his namesake—only less dour about the enterprise. Nothing could happen to a girl in his care; he had no sexual appetite or angry vengeance to get in the way with girls. Even now, he was probably writing rules on the walls. No hurting the girls, she imagined he wrote. Take good care of the girls. Soon Birdy dug up her own piece of charcoal and joined him. Although Jesús had a knack for pictures—he'd made three cartoon panels, a bunch of ravens and mice—Birdy never felt artistic inclination when armed with a marking implement. What came to her were words, always words, commentary and criticism and correction and simple vocabulary curios; she scratched a few of them on the smooth red wall. *Splat, Kilroy, avuncular, impertinent.* Along with words, she loved her handwriting; it was elegant, recognizably Palmeresque, even in black soot. And she loved Jesús's comic strip, his beleaguered rodents, his fascist predators. She turned to see him smiling widely at her.

"Va-va-voom," he said. "Hello musha-room."

They laughed although nothing was funny. Sometimes laughter seemed to Birdy better than anything, better than sex or food or foot massage. Also more intimate. Laughing hard with Jesús felt almost like a betrayal of Mark Anthony, who never made Birdy howl with hilarity. Beware, the seductive power of a sense of humor.

"Being really funny is like a secret weapon," she told Jesús.

"So's body odor," he replied. "Flatulence, bad taste in clothes, a wet handshake—there are a thousand ways to keep people away from you. Are those ants or raisins?"

Birdy picked one up, turned it in her hand, her mind turning its identity simultaneously. She knew yet could not name this pebble. "I know it more profoundly than words," she thought she told Jesús.

"Mouth it," he said. What could he mean? Like "wing it," as in behaving without plan? Or perhaps she was meant to kiss the little stone. To eat the morsel. "Mouse shit," he repeated, when she looked vacantly at him.

Then she was laughing again, and so was he.

"I might have peed my pants," she said. "Don't make me laugh anymore, please."

The wind swept through the gorge then as if to sober her up, in its wake a tumbling of dust and paper and grit, the consequence of frivolity. Something yellow across the canyon caught Birdy's eye, a shirt, she thought—no, a dress, a girl, Teresa! Birdy watched the garment calmly, veteran of stoned delusions, interested in why she had instantly seen a *dress* rather than the item's true identity. She associated the cliff dwelling with Teresa Anthony, so her brain made a puppy chow sack into a girl's dress. Getting high, like most things, was becoming more and more about her own mind than the curious world. The sack settled among the broken glass, looking even more convincingly human. There Teresa had landed, too, in the sparkling litter.

"What's that look like to you?" she asked Jesús.

"The gossamer thread uniting us to the cosmos," he replied. "Attached at our navels. Why?"

"Just wondering."

"You happy?" he asked later.

"Yes. I think mushies make me mushy." More than anything, she wished it were possible to be in love with Jesús, that she could begin a conventional life right here and now, do something that in years to come would represent the beginning, her own commencement, of happiness. She began to leak tears: for one kind of happiness, which was his company, and for one kind of loneliness, which was also his company.

FOUR HOURS later, their high was subsiding. Stomach-pain messengers were finally able to clear the logjam of their nerves to arrive at the translating stations in their brains. Birdy thought of Mrs. A.'s theory about train cars wiping out in the body; she felt unquestionably derailed. She and Jesús irritably cruised Main looking for something bland and filling.

"Pudding," Birdy begged. "7Up and saltine crackers."

"Beware the curse of the sphincter," Jesús had warned.

"Meaning?"

"Diarrhea."

"Oh yeah, diarrhea." Ever since they'd started coming down from this trip, she'd been remembering why, last time, she'd sworn not to do mushrooms again.

They both saw the lighted sign of Jerry's at the same moment: a peaceful oval, revolving slowly in the night sky like a beacon of salvation, lighthouse in the turbulent, hungry sea, advertising SHAKES, STEAKS, PANCAKES as it patiently spun.

"Perfect," Birdy sighed, already savoring the creamy comfort of mashed potatoes.

They hadn't been seated two minutes before Mark and his date appeared. Birdy blinked, unconcerned, certain that he was a manifestation of her high, a residual hallucination wandering through. Hadn't she just seen a whole array of things that weren't, probably, really there? Or only half there, the other half supplied by her revved-up, polluted, turbo-loaded imagination? Semaphoring vultures and animated rocks and a bloody sunset burbling like a lava lamp?

"Bird," Jesús hissed, leaning conspiratorially over the flecked Formica table.

"Don't look now, but your love bundle is here."

"He's a figment of our imagination," Birdy said. "He's a special effect."

"Nuh-uh." Jesús staunchly shook his head.

Now she frowned. "Do I have black all over my face, like you?" she asked him.

"I have black all over my face?" He snatched up his stainless steel knife and held it before him, inspecting his reflection. "Shit. We should have done a presentability check in the parking lot. No wonder people are staring at us."

"People are staring?" Birdy gazed around. In a fog until this very moment, she hadn't registered others in the dining room, hadn't heard the upbeat muzak, couldn't recall which of the many uniformed women strutting around like hens bearing coffeepots was their waitress. And what were they doing at this table, situated like a floor show in the exact center of the room instead of huddling in some discreet corner booth? It was exactly like being wakened from a dream. Except that she wakened to a kind of nauseating nightmare, her face and clothes filthy, her hair full of grass, her bowels more than irritated. Before she could flee to the women's room, Jesús had leapt up to dash to the men's.

"You ready to order?" a waitress asked. Her tan uniform scared Birdy, as if the woman might be authorized to make arrests.

"Mashed potatoes," Birdy said. The names of other foods would not come to her; what did one eat? "Uh, green beans. Bread, please, that big Texas toast thing. And some pie, banana creme, and crackers, and scrambled eggs. And tortillas."

The waitress said, "Like, à la carte?"

"Yes, exactly like à la carte. Two of everything, one for me and one for my friend." She and the waitress looked thoughtfully at Jesús's empty seat. "And 7Up," Birdy added. "Three of those."

"Coffee?" She held the pot before Birdy's face like a witch and swirled its evil contents.

"Oh my God, no. 7Up, 7Up." Birdy imagined her stomach to look just like the coffee, a viscous whirling gritty brown mess. A familiar refrain began to circle in her brain: if only I survive this ordeal, I promise never to get high again. Birdy couldn't count the number of times she'd sung this tune. Why were all her resolutions so weak?

She sneaked a look at Mark's table. He smiled at Elizabeth Eversman, nodding his head eagerly, in a way he never did with Birdy. He said he'd go home by ten, and it must be later than ten. Wasn't it? Where was Birdy's watch? On her wrist she found only the pale band of sunless flesh. Elizabeth's hands, under the table she shared with Mark, shredded a napkin. Birdy couldn't bear to witness it. What if Elizabeth were in love with Mark? Who was Birdy to deny "Jessica" a better match than that asshole "Brent"? And what if Mark were in love with Elizabeth? What if his sheepish behavior over the phone earlier were merely a ploy, meant to remove suspicion? What if he were tired of Birdy, and wanted to find someone young, someone he could borrow the car for, drive to a dark lookout and maul like a normal teenager? Elizabeth probably had a domineering dad for Mark to dread meeting, a curfew, a brassiere with tricky clasps. What if he wanted Birdy for one thing only, and a girl his own age for all the rest? For the first time, Birdy understood that he, too, would have cause to question their affair, would have reason to be embarrassed or reluctant. She was just like a whore, waiting in her trailer for her one john to come pecking at her door. Just like a whore, except making no profit. A pro bono prostitute.

When she focused again, there sat Jesús, beaming at her from across the table, his face clean, his hair slicked back, his buttons all buttoned. "I have been born again," he declared, hand raised in a papal gesture. "Go freshen up, Bird, it'll do you a world of good. I feel like a new man, like I urinated away my high. A flush."

"Urinated," Birdy pondered.

"It's a funny word," Jesús agreed.

"Too many syllables, but I can't think about it now. Have they spotted me?" she asked.

"What did you order? I'm starving." He turned his coffee cup right-side-up with a clang. "And I need some java, pronto."

At this, Birdy stood, lunging from the table toward the safe haven of the bathroom. Midway sat Mark and Elizabeth in a window booth, neither looking toward her. Their willful refusal to see her made Birdy begin to cry. In the bathroom, she locked the door and sobbed, inhabiting the yawning blackness of her own head for a few minutes. Even there, distractions entered. Across her eyelids flew a couple of leftover purple squiggles, some red crosses and yellow arrows she watched even as she wailed. Slowly she finished, concentrating on Lamaze breathing techniques she'd picked up with Luziana, pant blow, pant blow. She sat for a long while on the toilet, respirating, picking sand burrs from her socks, letting the weepy red heat drain from her cheeks. Then she braved the mirror.

Things were not as wretched as they could have been; her face, except for a Lent-like smear above her eyebrows, seemed fine. The hair could be explained by a convertible ride; her bloodshot eyes, the little pinpricks that were her irises, nobody looking at her casually would make out. By the time she flushed, slapped her dusty jeans, washed her hands, and blew her nose, she felt rejuvenated for the passage back to her table; just as Jesús had touted, she felt she'd left a lot of her high behind her in the bathroom.

Now that she'd ascertained her own appearance, she took stock of Mark's. He had dressed up for his date, pale blue oxford shirt still pressed from its rectangular plastic wrap, chinos, loafers with old Abe Lincoln in the slots. Elizabeth wore a flowered dress. They looked across the table at each other with their young clear eyes, Elizabeth facing Birdy, her features, if lackluster, also composed, sober. Immediately Birdy felt bedraggled again, adrift out here between islands of aid.

"Miz Stone," Elizabeth said as if naming a museum piece. Mark's shoulders flinched, which calmed Birdy. She could confront him, find out right now if he still loved her.

"Hi Elizabeth, how's tricks? Mark." She stopped at their table so they could both look her up and down. She was prepared to award them to each other, already forecasting her future, the return to quiet evenings with her books. Maybe she'd finally give old Anthony Trollope a roll, he was good for a year or more. . . .

"What's the matter with you?" asked Elizabeth.

"Asthma," Birdy said, wiping her nose. "How are you?"

Mark's glance rescued Birdy—his wet brown eyes, lashes long, flicking nervously down, then up—rescued her from jealousy, from foolish thoughts of giving him up selflessly to Elizabeth. She perceived his ardor for her plainly. He loved her. His pleasure at her arrival, despite the circumstances, was pure and left her breathless. His eyes went from their polite interest in Elizabeth to a smoldering and complex atavistic sort of swoon over Birdy. A pink splotch bloomed on his cheek; she trusted that he felt a similar bloom in his chinos, a certain thickening. His desire registered like heat in her sternum. When she touched his shoulder, she could feel his urge to cover her hand with his, felt the muscle shimmer, the reflex checked. Maybe this was better, this forbidden love. Maybe openness would ruin everything.

"Have fun, guys," she said, moving away, giving Mark's shoulder a final stroke, teacher to graduate.

"Everybody happy?" Jesús asked. Many individual plates sat on their table, big white faces, each with a single expression on its nose: discrete food items, one per plate.

"What is this?" she asked, attracted to the assembly of china, to the virginal presentation.

He shrugged. "*No se.* You ordered. How's your boy?"

She sat and spread her napkin in her lap, hoping she would remember all the other conventions of being a normal diner at a restaurant. "He's my boy," she said.

"Of course he is. Who wouldn't be? If I were straight, I'd be your boy, too."

"Really?" Birdy was touched; a tear, left over from her emotional mushroom glut, squeezed heavily out, like mercury. She was also famished. There were so many plates teetering before them, they couldn't help busting a couple. They broke beautifully, solidly in half like two phases of the moon. The tip on the table—as well as the debris—was extravagant.

"Do you know what I actually considered doing if Mark didn't want me anymore?"

"What?" Jesús asked. They were buffooning their way through the two sets of glass double doors to the parking lot, pushing, pulling, jockeying around the glass, trying not to trip or leave smudges.

"Reading Trollope."

"Good God, doggy. Narrow escape."

"I'll say."

𝒜 9

Birdy was laundering her lingerie in the kitchen sink when Mr. John came to call. He pounded with unnecessary force upon her trailer door, and Birdy's heart quavered guiltily as she envisioned Sheriff Potter-Otto standing there, an unhappy expression on his face. Instead, there stood Mr. John with the unhappy expression.

"Tell her to let me see the baby," he said bluntly.

Birdy played dumb. "Who?"

"Luziana. Luziana," he repeated, a sob, the sound of her name tacitly sad. Stella. Lolita. Desdemona. The name of every lamented, lost girl there'd ever been.

"I can't make anybody do anything."

Only the aluminum screen separated them. Mr. John stood on the other side, his chest rising and falling. She glanced quickly at the door's little laughable lock, having no intention of letting him into the trailer, although she couldn't have stopped him if that's what he wanted. It was bright outside, and he grimaced disagreeably against the glare. "Tell her to let me see the baby," he said again.

"Luziana is very overwhelmed with her baby," Birdy said, aware as she spoke that she had no idea how Luziana was; perhaps the girl was underwhelmed. Perhaps the baby looked cute now instead of ratty and constricted. Fatuously, Birdy went on, "It's hard to be a new mom."

"I want to help. Tell her to let—"

"You must respect Luziana's wishes."

He reached for his chest pocket, his cigarette pack, like a talisman, just to touch its trusty bulk near his heart. "I want you to tell her to let me see the baby. She won't come out of her house. I want to see the baby." He did not inflect, his voice registered no valleys and peaks, as if he were barking, an animal yapping in distress.

"Mr. John, you have to let Luziana alone. Her brothers might hurt you. She could call the police. She wouldn't do that," she added swiftly, when he flinched. "But you shouldn't make things hard for her. Going to her house is inappropriate."

"I want to see the baby. I like babies. I like her."

"She likes you, too. But your relationship with her was a school relationship. It can't happen at her house. A school relationship stays at school. You see?"

Behind her, Birdy heard her backdoor open and then close, felt a brief cross breeze on her bare legs, heard a basketball hit the floor and roll. Whoops. Mark had come over, on his way home from the high school court, carrying groceries for his mother. He set the bag on the table, put something in the refrigerator, knocked the ball out of his way. On the stoop, Mr. John shaded his eyes with both hands, leaned forward and pressed his large-pored nose to Birdy's screen, looking for what had made the sound.

"Birdy?" Mark said.

"That's Mark Anthony," Mr. John told her. He met her eyes through the netting. "Hello, Mark Anthony," he called out, still looking at Birdy, as if he were greeting her.

"Hey, Mr. John. How's it hanging?"

"It's hanging fine, Mark, thank you, how is it hanging with you?"

"Oh," Mark said, trying to sound nonchalant. He held one of Birdy's damp stockings in his fingers. "This was on the floor," he explained.

"On the floor," said Mr. John, chiming in with the last word, as usual. Birdy's face burned but she stared right back into his tawny eyes, daring him to compare her affection for a student with his.

"He'll tell," she bemoaned, later, on Mark's chest.

"I don't think he will. I think he keeps secrets pretty well."

"I hate to think the secrets he keeps. But even if he doesn't tell, he'll know. That's almost as bad."

While his mother's ice milk melted on the kitchen table, Mark kissed Birdy's forehead. "Just a secret between us, you and me and Mr. John."

"Among us," Birdy said. "Among, not between."

MOST OF Pinetop participated in the Fourth of July parade. There was hardly anyone left to be the audience, just old people and diapered children, a few serious, flat-faced Apaches from Ridgepole who'd come over for the day, a handful of ill-advised tourists getting out of Albuquerque's heat. A man on a bicycle who'd been loitering around town since school let out. Birdy put on a 1970s costume—orange platforms, black fishnets, white lipstick, metal cake-cutter dug into her stiff teased hair—and pelted the crowd with Fireballs. Ahead of Jesús's love bug warbled the Whistlers, a strange display the volunteer fire department had dreamed up years ago. Birdy had never seen anything remotely like it. Ten men and a few boys had painted their bare chests and bellies to look like faces—nipples for eyes, navels for mouths—while their real faces were covered by giant papier-mâché hats they held up with their hidden arms. Suit jackets were fastened below their waists, arms dangling, no pants to speak of, and their booted feet stuck out stumpily below. Their belly buttons were painted lewdly open, lipsticked holes, and a tape recording accompanied them, whistling an eerie melody from the sound system of an ancient fire truck.

"Yuck," Birdy said. "That gives me the creeps."

"Spooky," Jesús agreed, "but what can you do? It's tradition."

"Thank God you're here to tell me what to expect."

Jesús pointed over his windshield. "The flubber blub is Manny McDonald."

"The ex-sheriff?"

"Don't you love the way he shakes?"

"I think it's obscene." Like most obscene sights, Birdy couldn't take her eyes off it. Grown men wavering down the street, undulating their pale flabby flesh, immodest in their relative anonymity, bright summer sun beating on them remorselessly. She felt sorry for the marching band in their hot woolen regalia, uniforms old and ill-fitting, hats like torpedoes upended on their heads. Their necks wobbled under the burden. The fire chief felt inspired to blast his air horn now and then just to keep the procession lively, chortling in the driver's seat.

"The fire ladders are made of wood," Birdy commented to Jesús, raising her voice over the combined noise of the Whistlers and Jesús's *Saturday Night Fever* sound track.

"Now you know why the place burned down twice."

The float following Jesús's car was all about chain saws. CORDLESS BUT NOT GUTLESS, its banner read.

"Stayin' alive, stayin' alive," sang the tape while Birdy hurled fistfuls of candy at the spectators. Among them she located Mary Jo Callahan hiding in a doorway, scowling as she shielded her features from the sun, her hand, sure enough, secured to the hand of a man. Jesús swerved the bug toward the two of them, and Birdy tossed some candy. Mary Jo waved wildly with her free fingers. Her man was a small one, but otherwise ordinary looking, most likely a legal resident of the United States. Neither old nor infirm, not unkind or stupid. Birdy tried to talk herself out of her cynicism; mightn't a man enjoy Mary Jo's company, see beyond her unattractive yet superficial features? For a second, Birdy thought of her own boyfriend and of the response her holding hands with him on Main Street would elicit. She found herself in the unusual circumstance of envying Mary Jo, of wanting a smidgeon of what she seemed to have. Birdy might have once believed that being involved with a younger man like Mark would make her young herself, make her feel closer to him, to teenagers in general, to the jolly bon vivant of youth. That had seemed to be the case with her poet, who had brandished her before him like a shield or prize, as if her youth proved his own, crumpled the thirty years between them, his virility verified. And it seemed to be the case with her father, whose young wife and new babies had provided his new lease on life. But Birdy had discovered that being with Mark served usually to point up the ways in which she'd changed in the twelve years that separated her from him. As a result, dating him made her feel old, older than she was. Downright ancient, she thought.

She cringed as she noticed all the video cameras. Here was her Pinetop posterity—and she'd come dressed like a clown.

The procession ended at Jerry's parking lot, the front end of the line collecting in a clotted crowd as they waited for the final floats and tottering bands. Water bottles and sunscreen circulated. The Whistlers swept off their giant hats, dripping sweat, smearing their painted tummies and downing beers. Cheerleaders and pom-pom girls brought up the rear, while Sheriff Potter-Otto trailed them in his cruiser, light revolving woozily. Coincidence or maneuver, the man stationing himself behind the behinds of twenty scantily clad teenage girls?

Following the parade, the volunteer firemen formed two lines, one on either side of Main, and shot one another with fire hoses, the force knocking them off their feet, into storefronts, spray falling over the crowd in a welcome mist. Birdy picked out firemen she knew: Ronny, her bad date from last year, as well as the butcher, the basketball coach, Deryl Whacker, Hal Halfon, and Mark's friend Mike, who was already eighteen. If she remained in Pinetop, soon she'd know other of the volunteers. She might donate money to their fund, buy her own American flag and attach it to her trailer. She'd appear in more and more of the town's videos, that familiar-looking woman with the yellow hair, hanging out with Jesús Morales, what in the hell was her name? What had she been doing there, anyway? What ever had become of her?

When the hosing was done, everybody proceeded to the town park to eat barbecued beef and drink beer. "And after that," Jesús told Birdy, holding out his fingers to number the steps, "everybody goes home and sleeps in a bloated drunken stupor until it's time for fireworks." Birdy had been awakened that morning by dynamite, two big booms that shook her trailer and made her think of apocalypse and that Lolo the dispatcher swore were nothing to worry about.

"Why dynamite at daybreak?" she'd asked.

"Tradition," Lolo had said. "Always done it, always will. Every year, somebody calls to report the Second Coming."

"That would be me?"

"Yessir. You're our alarmist, this year."

The firemen set off the dynamite, Jesús told her later, and they put on the fireworks. That way, if there was an accident, they'd be there, prepared. "Although usually they're pretty drunk by the time it gets dark," he conceded.

Mark's sister had died on the Fourth of July; the Anthonys did not attend the parade or barbecue, Mark had explained, although they did bring chairs outside at dusk and watch the display explode over the little town. The celebration must seem cruel to Mrs. Anthony, unintentionally rude, a communal faux pas. In the afternoon, while everyone else guzzled beer and then slept it off, she and Mark would take flowers to the graveyard.

Birdy thought one or the other of them would invite her to come along, and felt excluded when neither did. Jesús offered to squire Birdy about the picnic with his mother and Tía Blanca, but Birdy didn't really want to make small talk with other teachers in the glaring sun over a soggy plate of baked beans and side of beef. Summer was for rejuvenating one's tolerance for one's fellow instructors. So she went home. Now that the sun shone on her bread box house all day long, she wished it would go away. In the kitchen she kicked off her platform heels and shed her fishnets, stuffing both in the garbage. After lying down for a few minutes, like a pie in an oven, she decided to take a drive.

But there was nowhere to go in Pinetop. Smoke rose from the barbecue pit, carrying the smells of charred skin, beef, and chiles; trucks were parked along the road, float leftovers caught up in the wind and in the tree branches. Time hung depressingly over Main Street and the closed businesses, passed slowly as Birdy navigated the empty streets in sluggish second gear. Everybody had somebody, today, except her. They all knew what to do, where to go, how to have fun there. From the middle of a weedy vacant block, three boys ran in front of her car as if they'd been waiting for someone to come kill them. She honked, furious, but they only waved, the way everyone in Pinetop did, as if hailing neighbors were what the automobile horn had been designed for.

Birdy headed out of town as if she weren't coming back, fast, aimed downwind from Pinetop in her aerodynamic old Saab.

The day was brilliant, the highway glistening with mirages, like a long greased slide, and soon Birdy realized where she was going, where the chute led, where her appetite propelled her. The little stone ruins stood out in high relief, flesh-colored against the deep blue sky. The blankness here did not depress her; the absence of humanity did not remind her of her loneliness so much as make her relish her solitude. Perhaps the Anasazi had migrated north in the summer, fleeing the heat. Perhaps one fall they had simply not made it back, greener pastures, something like that. Maybe they just got tired of climbing up those damn rocks every day, leaky clay pots of water straining at their necks. She parked where Larry Ranta had killed himself, pulled her emergency brake, and opened her door.

The wind in the trees sounded like a running stream, a welcome illusion. Along the trail to the cliff house lay clues— a beer can, a bicycle chained to a spruce, a child's grubby blue mitten, an empty film canister, another beer can, the ubiquitous ribbon of audiocassette tape fluttering in the scrub, one more beer can—clues, but to what?

Inside the dwelling, the air was cooler but not fresh, as if emanating from a source metallic and deeply cold. The hieroglyphs Birdy and Jesús had added in their mushroom bender were streaked, the words illegible but still recognizably words, symbols of some embarrassing bygone emotion. Birdy sat on a ledge and surveyed the site with a domestic eye. She recalled the diorama from the quonset hut museum. The undying fire would have been there, in the center, the bowls and baskets nearby, blankets and pelts on the walls, stone tools. Living was simple, really, reduced to the essentials of sustenance and warmth, the orange embers glowing faithfully. You'd reach the end of the day content just to have survived it, no room left over for boredom or angst. Birdy thought she should do more of that herself, be contented with her tiny trailer, her paltry job that paid the rent and put some form of food on the table. As for finding a mate and propagating the species, well, maybe that would come later. They farmed, the Anasazi, so they'd had to store their grain and they'd had to mash it and prepare it. At the museum, crunching corn had looked highly labor-intensive, a daylong project, two rocks with the blue kernels ground between into a heartrendingly meager powder. When they weren't preparing food, they'd practiced their potmaking, sculpting and slapping and smoothing—often just to watch the thing split in two like a gourd. They'd kept a few animals, turkeys and dogs, and probably had to dream up something to feed them, too. They'd had no leisure time to contemplate their relative unhappiness. What was unhappiness, to the Anasazi? What would they make of that sixties vexation, the vapors? When their leader, the thirty-five-year-old woman, had died, their days here were over.

What if they were all women? Birdy wondered. What if that were the reason they'd ceased to exist? A clan of women in the caves, either by choice or not. It would explain their quiet, unambitious existence; without men, there wouldn't be the impulse to storm other camps, make war on either man or beast: no Homeric rage to spur them, none of that. Basket-weaving females, vegetarian females, nurturing their pets. No tension, no competition, no aggravation.

Dull life, she granted, living without men; she couldn't

imagine it. And not being able to imagine such a lucid, sensible state of existence depressed her even further. Shouldn't a sane person desire peaceful enlightenment? Nunnish and pure? She looked down toward her town, Whoville, where the natives were getting plastered before setting off explosives.

She felt wise, up here. It was curious that Mrs. Anthony had not capitalized on the site, which seemed a perfect mystical resource for her story. This maybe should have been the woman's first instinct, to see some connection between the people who'd once lived and died there, and her own family. Why hadn't she probed the metaphysical import of their position? Couldn't the Ancient Ones have carried off Teresa and Philip, sacraments of some sort? What, given Isadora Anthony's temperament, made more sense? Why be satisfied with an illegitimate Egyptian pharaoh infant when the Anasazi were so conveniently situated right around the corner?

In a past life, my tiny daughter was left crying in a cornfield when sacred eagles came and pecked out her eyes. Blind, she tottered to the edge of a cliff, calling her mother's name, Mama, Mama, and then stepped off like a bird whose wings were not ready to yet fly . . .

Mrs. Anthony's prose style: she was practically channeling it.

Outside the dwelling the sun shone severely. Down in the ravine lay the puppy chow sack, faded now, looking nothing like a girl's body. Some grasshopperlike insects made a searing sound like a metal saw in the dry air, vaulting by and landing in the sand, pausing and then hurling themselves up again stickily as if they might intend to adhere to Birdy. Aside from them, she heard nothing except the infrequent car from the highway. The contrast between blue sky and pink rock caused a fierce vibrant tension in Birdy's gaze, one she could barely stand to witness. She found a large rock she could lie down on and lay back, closing her eyes, grateful for the inces-

sant breeze, feeling it blow across her face and steal the moisture from her lips.

She was wakened by a voice. The light had changed, as if
many hours had passed, and her dreams had been so alien—
in time and place and character—that it took Birdy a
moment to gather the elements of herself into a current
coherence. Someone far away, around the other side of the
cliffs, was yelling into the chasm. "Hey," the voice said, and
then the faint echo answer came, which must have been what
prompted the calling. "HEY." Pause. "Hey." Pause. "HEY."
Pause. "Hey." The presence of another person, along with
her vulnerable sleeping, made Birdy nervous; wasn't this the
way the world's Ted Bundys worked, waiting for nubile
young women to show up alone out where no one could hear
their cries for help?

Nubile.

Maybe that's what had happened to Teresa; she'd been
lured to this site and raped, forced over the edge when the
man was done. Maybe her promiscuous reputation had pre-
ceded her, tempted some neighboring degenerate to come
gunning for her, or some heavily tattooed friend of Larry
Ranta's, hellbent on avenging his friend's wretched suicide,
his cellmate from La Tuna who thought Teresa thought she
was hot shit, too good for his bud. Birdy picked her way
down the cliff, over the sandy path past the beer cans and the
bicycle, toward her car, hustling away from the range of the
voice. "HEY," it continued behind her, fading, its echo nearly
imperceptible.

But your average avaricious rapist didn't trouble himself
to travel to obscure natural landmarks and wait for victims to
show. Your standard assailant went for the fertile feeding
grounds, college campuses and jogging paths in city parks,
heedless women hanging around like fish in a barrel.

Whenever she was actually at the ruins, it was difficult for Birdy to believe that Teresa had been murdered. Probably she had planned her death, the drama, the seclusion, she and Larry both, good kids gone bad, misunderstood, unappreciated, neglected, forsaken. The place seemed like a fine one to select as your last place, the gesture satisfyingly grand, here in the presence of the Ancient Ones, this view a magnificent ultimate one, the drop before Birdy's feet intoxicating. It was far easier than anyone would acknowledge to end your life. Also far more alluring than it should have been; Birdy could feel the tug—gravity, Sheriff Potter-Otto had named it, fundamental stuff—even as she feared it. Maybe you wouldn't fear it if you didn't so keenly perceive temptation.

But whenever she thought about Teresa at her trailer, Birdy believed the girl had been murdered, hunted ruthlessly to the end of the earth, left with no choice but to fall off.

Only after she'd reached her trusty Saab and started safely for home—locking her doors, speeding away—did Birdy realize that the voice she'd heard could have been yelling "Help" instead of "Hey." She accelerated at the idea, trying the two different words out aloud, "Hey. Help. Hey, help." What could she have done, anyway? she asked herself. Couldn't a cry for help be merely another ploy on the part of a crafty rapist, enticing a woman close only to hurt her?

Was this the mark of paranoia or merely good sense? When every human gesture had to be weighed? Or was this simply akin to her shifting conviction about Teresa's death, one sure story when she stood at the ruins, another when she was at a distance?

Back in town, the only other person on the streets was the cyclist, wearing his cyclist clothing. He lifted his gloved hand to her as she drove by, and she honked, like a native. At the sheriff's office, she slowed and studied the blank windows, debating her duty to tell Lolo what she'd heard at the rocks. In the end, she just went home.

THAT NIGHT, after the fireworks, Mark came to Birdy's trailer bearing flowers, a bouquet of wilted faces, their stems leaving a bitter dust on her palms. "They grow around Teresa's grave," he explained. Birdy imagined the headstone among the bright colors, the solid rock of death anchored in the frivolous flowers.

"What's it say on her tombstone?"

"*Our Girl* and her name and dates."

Birdy felt a need to cling to him, long and hard. His clean clothing and puzzled embrace bespoke a purity she wanted to absorb, make her own. He stroked her hair like someone stroking a horse mane. For once, this did not bother her. He shifted his weight when she poured her own against him. This was another lesson of manhood he would need, sea legs for the rocky tipping of life's boat. It seemed to Birdy she'd been neglected physically, although he'd held her only the night before.

"How'd you like the fireworks?" he asked, just to make conversation as she butted against his breastbone.

"Oh fine," she said. "Dandy." The display originated practically in Birdy's backyard, just across the stream on a little lump of city ground. Even now, the firemen's flashlights sent fractured beams here and there, their trucks and hoses still running, their voices drifting in through Birdy's open windows along with the mustardy exhaust of sulfur. She didn't bother to mention that she and Jesús had smoked marijuana and lain on her trailer roof, heads on the tires—Jesús speculated that the tires' function was to keep the lid on Birdy's house—the prospect of a burning spark descending on their bodies thrilling them. She'd been so happy to see Jesús, when he showed up at her door with a joint, she'd kissed his nose.

"How's your mom?" she asked Mark, leading him by his hand to the bedroom.

"Bummed, just like every Fourth. It's like having a birthday on Christmas—everybody celebrating makes you feel bad."

"Is her birthday Christmas? I have a niece due on Christmas."

"No," he said, looking confused. "February tenth. Or maybe twelfth. I just mean that remembering a death on the Fourth—"

"Oh," Birdy interrupted. It was either his logic that was fuzzy, or her brain. She pulled off her shorts and T-shirt, which seemed suddenly heavy, saturated with smoke. She wanted to slap all their parts right smack together, skin to skin. She needed to be truly held. "Was your father a volunteer fireman?" she asked, stretching on the bedspread, beckoning.

"Yes."

"Did he ever paint his stomach and walk half-naked down Main Street?"

"No, you have to be an Elk *and* a fireman to do that."

"I see. Why wasn't he an Elk?"

"Maybe he didn't want to have to be a Whistler on the Fourth of July. I wouldn't want to, either," he assured Birdy, beginning to remove his shirt.

"What a relief! Although you'd be the best-looking Whistler out there. Not that that would be such a distinction. Were you ever in the parade?"

"No, only Teresa. She was a flag girl."

"Really? Think of that—a flag girl. What's a flag girl?"

"Like cheerleaders, only with flags. They waved to some Michael Jackson song that last year, the one about so-and-so is not *duh duh.*" He hummed thoughtfully, slipping off his watch. It had a tendency to beep, generally right in Birdy's ear, and she'd banished it to the hallway.

Birdy pictured Sheriff Potter-Otto trailing the flag girls, watching the place where their little skirt hems and ubiquitous long hair met. It occurred to her that there might have existed, somewhere, a video recording of Teresa Anthony's last Fourth of July parade, waving her flag. Birdy cheered, sort of, at the notion. It would be novel to see the dead girl in motion, living her tarty teenage life, slashing the air with two flags . . .

" 'Billie Jean,' " Mark said at last, pleased with his memory. "That song."

"Hurry with the clothes," she complained. "It's too hot for clothes. Did your dad help with the fireworks, on the Fourth?"

"Sure. He had to get the barbecue pit going, too. Some years he set off the dynamite." Mark's disrobing always amused Birdy, the way he looked down, chin to chest, as he unzipped his pants, one palm against his sucked-in abdomen so that he wouldn't snag his short hairs. "Can't be too careful," he said.

"So your dad was out lighting fireworks the night she died?"

"Probably. I'm pretty sure he would have been." He hopped onto the bed with Birdy, which made the trailer rock, and scooted up beside her. "Here," she said, directing his fingers to her bra cup.

"Why did your mother say she had to wake him?"

"I don't know. Did she say that? Maybe it was late. They didn't wake me. Didn't tell me until the next morning. I knew just by looking at my father's face that Teresa was dead." For a moment he stared through Birdy into memory, then came back, smiling. "My dad was wearing his fireman boots, black ones. He had forgotten to strap them up. You know the kind I mean? They're like kids' snowboots, with the buckles and all. Him in his rubber boots, standing in the kitchen crying. Unbuckled."

Birdy's image of the suspected murderer changed as Mark remembered him. She'd seen the father's slick face atop his suit jacket and necktie in the family photo and she'd grown to dislike him by virtue of the crime she believed he'd committed. But now he stood undone in the gloomy Anthony kitchen, wearing open-mouthed black galoshes, grief-stricken and speechless.

"If it was late," Birdy said, shaking her head to disrupt the image, her own excursion to the cliff dwelling that afternoon fresh in her memory, "how would they know where to find her? I mean, if she was missing, and everybody was watching the fireworks, how would they know to look at the ruins? At the bottom of the ruins?"

"I wouldn't know," Mark said—in the way Bartleby must have intoned that he would prefer not. Mark's voice seemed older to Birdy as he neatly cut off this discussion, and she liked that about it. Resignation was a grown-up trait, she thought. Or maybe massaging her bra had simply distracted him from thoughts of history.

"Because of Larry," Birdy answered her own question. "Because that's where Larry had gone, just a few days earlier."

"Larry who?" Mark asked, nuzzling her neck.

"Larry Ranta. He died a few days earlier, at the ruins. You knew that."

"No, I didn't."

He'd been seven years old; his sister's taboo love life with an ex-con did not involve him. He would have been fast asleep as the parents discussed it, the first in a series of crises, the crises specific to raising a girl. Birdy suddenly recalled waking one morning as a teenager with her panty hose sawed off at the knees, no memory of having cut them. It had been hilarious to her, but, of course, it wouldn't have been hilarious to a parent. She said to Mark, "Maybe you should ask your mom about him. No, on second thought, don't do that. I'll tell you." And so she told him about the older boy's suicide, careful to keep her theories on his father's guilt out of the story.

"What's that got to do with my sister?" he asked after a moment.

"Maybe nothing."

" 'Maybe'?"

She sighed. Their hands still wanted each other and circled willingly, but their bodies had staked slightly distant claims on the bed. Outside, a cat began a plaintive, sickening wailing. This had been happening more and more often, some black skinny thing abandoned in the neighborhood, howling until someone took pity. Birdy swore it wouldn't be her. The animal's noise made her ache, plucked at a little-used nerve in her inner ear, behind her eyes. It seemed to her that more and more creatures were discovering where she lived, coming around uninvited, like Mr. John. Finally, Mark's fingers worked their way to unfastening her bra and then landing on her skin, pressing gently, as if in search of lumps, then being joined by the fingers of the other hand on her other breast. He watched his own roaming palms as if watching the hands of a stranger crawl over her body, and Birdy watched his eyes, which crossed as his hands intersected in her lap. She tried to feel disdain for his excited ineptness, but instead she got carried away, as usual, by what his touch inspired. Good-bye, brain, she thought as she switched off the lamp, hello lust, you hussy. Those panty hose from long ago were gnawed off by just such an impulse. In her brain, Michael Jackson's breathy falsetto sang "Billie Jean"; outside, the cat stayed a good long while, crying right under the bedroom window, as if it knew precisely where the people were, and what they were doing.

❧ 10

Not long after, the monsoon season insinuated itself upon Pinetop. All day the sky pressed down on the town, oppressive and sultry as a steam bath, muggy, unbreathably hot, the muttering clouds in the distance finally bursting into rain in the late afternoon, torrents flinging themselves like ocean waves upon the storefronts and fields and hot parking lot pavement, take that, take that. Birdy's trailer developed leaks and she set coffee cans around the floor, invariably knocking them over when she rose in the night. Poor night, after days such as these, arrived a listless, pale thing, stars hardly visible under the weak cloud cover, the heat only barely subsiding.

She promised herself she would end her affair, would exhaust this bad habit as she had exhausted others—she'd quit smoking, hadn't she? Broken herself of gnashing her teeth, never failed to fasten her seat belt. It hadn't particularly reminded her of her relationship with the poet professor, but now it was starting to. Maybe it was the existence of their respective mothers, Mark's and her own dead one. She'd had to keep her affair with the poet secret from her mother, too. And she certainly wouldn't have discussed her current romance with her mother, if she were alive.

What was it about mothers that made you have to hide your sexual self? Or was it just because Mark was still, technically, a child? A grown-up's ward, innocent, unfinished, immature.

But hadn't all of Birdy's other boyfriends been immature? Reg with his scamming cheapness, his daily forages for drugs and food and rock and roll? The professor with his relentless, self-conscious policing of every simple conversation, his readiness to find infraction, stale or insincere usage, that, and his hypochondriacal schedules and rules, no food after six P.M., no conversation before Tai Chi? If Mark Anthony was immature it was only in comparison to men older than himself, Birdy rationalized. For his age, she considered, he seemed right on track. Sophomoric, yes—but he was a sophomore, more or less.

Besides, youth wasn't simply a matter of beauty or potential hope. You might wish a boy had a history, ponderings to talk about. But maybe there was something to be said for a blank slate. Mark hadn't done anything long enough to have it show on his face, and in that dark nasty cavity of the soul where, in others, bad deeds are stored, he harbored very little, possibly the barest whiff of regret, perhaps a tiny nugget of remorse, guilt like a marble rolling harmlessly around. His grave mistakes were all ahead of him. He didn't even have a single filling, not a glint of silver when he opened his mouth, nothing but ivory and saliva. He wasn't young enough nor small enough to be treated like a child—nor was he fragile with age. He was instead sturdy with fullness, robust, bones calcified, testosterone boisterous, every tributary clear and thriving, from the heartiest thickly pulsing jugular to the tiniest peppy penile capillary.

Maybe his fitness explained why Birdy sometimes had the urge to hurt him. Youth lacked humility. She wanted to see something besides easy joy on his face. She wanted something besides flawlessness to show on his skin. So on his shoulder she might leave the imprint of her teeth, a perforated ring enclosing a bruised plum of flesh. She might bend that hard penis into a right angle. She was breaking him in, her very own picaresque hero whose adventures would serve to mellow and season him. Her professor, she recalled, had used to stop in the middle of sex to take Birdy's long hair and wrap it in a single skein around his fist, pull it taut behind her as if to test the tensile relationship between it and its follicles, as if to tie Birdy to the headboard. Pain, she thought now, he'd wanted to see her suffer, although not too much, not for too long.

"Ow!" her loved one would cry. And then she would apologize, insincerely.

She and Mark continued to land in bed together, her sheets wrinkled and soft from so much sweaty use, the bedroom the center of her little home. On the trailer roof, the swamp cooler shuddered and chugged, sending a thin rusty drizzle down the metal exterior wall and across one of Birdy's windows, following the path of an old stain she'd always noticed but never understood the source of. Her body liked his body, there could be no denying it. He hadn't much to say, but ultimately that did not matter. The innocent confidence of his urges, the earnest pleasure of his release—these served to convince Birdy that all could not be wrong in the world if their bodies could find joy so simply.

In between episodes of lovemaking, she and Mark watched television or ate snacks. Alone, Birdy would have read books, but that was a solitary pursuit, and one she'd more or less forgotten, her library books overdue, her fat classics waiting on their shelves like history: they'd be there when she came crawling back. Together she and Mark tried to find TV satisfying, passing over the dull domestic shows (cooking, repairing old houses, caring for babies), disliking each other's taste in sitcoms, disagreeing about movies (he wanted action, she satire), and holding their breath in the face of talk show candor (women who loved men who wanted to be women, people who had sex over their computers, first cousins and siblings who married each other)—afraid to find their own May-December vignette under scrutiny, Birdy supposed, its outraged antagonists, its lewd proponents.

Occasionally she landed on WGN, her hometown cable network, and surveyed the city's data: weather, sports, celebrities, politics, the familiar skyline, as seen from somewhere in the middle of Lake Michigan, on the news trailer. She made sure to point out the landmarks to her boyfriend, civic pride ignited by his awe. World's tallest building, city of big shoulders, home of Michael Jordan, Oprah Winfrey, old Saul Bellow, and America's worst public schools. She still remembered the job fair she'd attended downtown, the legions of unvisited inner-city booths, their attendants snapping gum, and the long lines for the plum suburban interviews, Naperville, Winnetka. She recalled her own directionless ambling, ending at the far end of the Marriott ballroom in the Western States section, finally before the Pinetop sign, hand-lettered, the size of a postcard.

Nobody lined up to talk with that recruiter, either; the pay was unbelievably low, approximately half what Birdy had been told by her professors was the national average. The interviewer looked as morose as Birdy felt. Ultimately, this was the only job Birdy was offered. Two days after she accepted, her mother was diagnosed with cancer. Fate—what a piece of work.

After WGN, Birdy chose stand-up comedians. Make me laugh, she dared them. Mark's television preferences reflected a predictable demographic: he liked music videos, their bathroom humor, the raw erotic posturing that displayed a self-absorption and absence of irony Birdy found spooky. He had his very own facial expression to wear when listening to music, eyes sullen, lips like a shelf, jaw jumping with the drumbeat. It seemed to kindle something savage in him, something hard and wild.

In both cases—comedians and videos—Birdy felt antsy, as if some integral part of the dynamic were missing. She paced around a lot, rearranging knickknacks. Perhaps this reminded her of her relationship, which also seemed curiously incomplete. Over time, the emptiness would fill, she guessed. He would grow up; they would begin conversations with "Remember that time . . ."; they might someday joke about the cradle-robbing origins of their affair. Mark would look back fondly on his impetuous youth. "You chased me shamelessly," Birdy would declare.

They ate microwave potpies, sweating through the miserable heart of the hot summer. Birdy was often tempted to let Mark know she'd stayed in town on his account, that he was responsible for her heat rash and water retention and glistening face. But he seemed to understand his role of champion: since Birdy never tired of hearing how much the students liked her, Mark resorted to compliments when conversation flagged. And it was Birdy who counseled Mark on his first semester's college courses, providing him with some pleasure (A History of Jazz) as well as rigor (Intro Trigonometry). Because Mark had no particular past of his own, and no way of knowing how to either elicit or respond to Birdy's past, they were truly intimate in little more than sexual ways, and all of their dates took place on the surface of Birdy's spongy rental bed. Some people got to know each other at work, Birdy reasoned. She and Mark had a slightly alternative common ground.

He had not been an exemplary student—far from it, average, and below, in all respects except lasso turning. But while he might be a dim bulb in the classroom, in bed he shone. Unlike his mother, he wanted to do precisely what Birdy advised. He was a quick study, learning immediately where to touch her and how, mastering the art of foreplay, practicing diligently on caressing without seeming to be in a hurry, excelling in gentleness, and passing with flying colors body rhythm, heart articulation, the surging urge of his own pure passionate expansiveness. Virginal, he'd been an open book, on which Birdy had engraved her own desires, inscribed the private methods. She was his tutor, he her prize pupil.

She asked herself what made her so hungry for this? And when would her craving sate itself, wear out, move on to devour its next victim?

MEANWHILE, a stranger had ridden into town, that stranger on a bicycle. He'd circled dimly at first, peripheral and impending as the monsoon fronts, and Birdy had seen him only half-consciously as he toured Pinetop wearing his cyclist's regalia, gleaming black tights, vivid Lycra jersey, bulbous plastic headgear from which sprouted a tiny mirror like something from the dentist's office, like a single antennae. She waved, he waved. She waved, he waved.

But it was as if he circled on an ever-tightening spiral, zeroing in on his quarry.

He camped at the ball park. He showered at the laundromat. He ate bananas outside the QuikMart. He smiled at everyone as he sailed by on his bike. Rumor had it he would build a treehouse, that he also owned a unicycle, that he was a crazy disinherited Du Pont. Wherever you went, there he was, cruising pointlessly around.

"He's beautiful," Jesús had said, and though it was not unlike Jesús to point out the beautiful, it *was* unlike him to pursue it, at least in Birdy's limited experience with her friend. But something like sonar had made the cyclist and Jesús locate each other. Evidently, they'd met in some other level of living, their mutual subsets overlapping, a zone Birdy could have predicted would not include her, push coming to shove. Now, in the rainy season, on the rare occasions when she saw her friend, he had part of his attention newly tuned, and to another frequency.

This made Birdy angry although she knew it was unjustified. Just a few months earlier hadn't she deserted Jesús, with the same lame hormone-induced excuse? Hadn't erotic adventure always taken precedence, always, always, always, a code girls pledged allegiance to in high school and never forsook?

When she finally met the cyclist, in Jesús's mother's living room, she noted that his legs were as smooth and hairless as her own. In fact, he seemed better at defoliating himself than Birdy ever had been. She usually got hung up around her ankles.

"I am Jesús's friend," he said, extending both of his hands like a Venus fly trap to snare hers. If he was Jesús's friend, Birdy wondered what she ought to call herself. Jesús was no help, planted in his BarcaLounger, totally tongue-tied, infatuated. He scratched the Naugahyde with his fingernails, unconscious, a rasp under the rumble of the swamp cooler.

Tía Blanca glowered as she brought out beverages from the kitchen, Cuba libres all around except for the cyclist, who, naturally, requested bottled water. Birdy decided she would loathe him not because he was handsome, not because he seemed smug about his power over Jesús, and not even because she envied his calf muscle definition. No, she would loathe him because he wouldn't drink a Cuba libre, the prig.

"Jamie," Jesús uttered, when a name was required.

"*Jaime,*" the cyclist corrected, overpronouncing the Spanish, Hi May. He was white as the driven snow; Birdy rolled her eyes at his acquired ethnicity. He'd begun his sojourn in March, ridden all the way from Phoenix on the scenic route, through the Gila, touring Indian ruins and hot springs. He settled himself on Tía Blanca's ottoman, straddling it, leaning forward, which made both Birdy and Mrs. Morales pitch back into the sofa. Tía Blanca trudged once more into the kitchen to concoct some bottled water. It was Saturday, time for Mass, time for cinema, yet here was a guest. Because Mark Anthony was busy, a last campout with his high school friends, Birdy and Jesús had planned to watch *Alfie,* a movie she remembered seeing on TV long ago, Michael Caine the inveterate womanizer, bopping chippies all over London while Cher crooned in the background.

The video box sat right over there, waiting enticingly on the giant television. And in Jesús's Altoids tin rested a pair of joints, also waiting.

But here instead was Jaime prattling on about his bike tour over hill and dale, sending long frank looks in Jesús's direction, while Jesús deferentially tucked his head, like a stunned turtle. Jaime's teeth seemed unnaturally large and white, his hair, despite lunky helmet, slicked down like wet tobacco. His cycling shoes pristine, ankle socks like a Catholic girl's. He not only knew all about New Mexico and its Native Americans but also the sum total species of wildlife he'd encountered on his travels, recalling every incident of flora or fauna, then, grinning remorsefully, forgivingly, complained of truckers and other angry drivers who'd made his journey perilous. "Not perilous enough," Birdy muttered.

Mrs. Morales listened to him with a bored scowl on her face, arms crossed over her chest as if questioning his alleged sincerity. Tía Blanca had decided not to return from the kitchen and pantry, and Jesús stared simple-mindedly at the floor, his hands now gripping the recliner as if it might be capable of either bucking him off like a bronc or folding him in like an oyster. Maybe he would have liked that, Birdy thought, a dramatic exit. Jaime held way too much sway, anybody could see it, could feel it in the laden late-afternoon air, and he didn't deserve it, Birdy believed. He was not a good person, no matter what he knew about the natural world, no matter what he abstained from. How did she know this? She didn't know how.

Someone, somewhere, had told him to make eye contact with every member of the audience. When Birdy wouldn't let hers be met, the cyclist made a stab at flattery.

"*Great* earrings," he told her; she was wearing one yellow plastic cocktail monkey hooked by the tail through the hole in her lobe, and one green. They'd come from the Everything For $1 store.

Jesús echoed this compliment. "Great," he said, he who'd been there with her and hooked a monkey in each nostril.

"They're just toys," Birdy said.

"So creative," Jaime insisted.

Mrs. Morales noisily drained her Cuba libre and asked, apropos of absolutely nothing, "How old are you?"

"Twenty-two," he answered promptly, so promptly you could tell he didn't consider the question rude, he was just that young.

"Don't you have a car? Why do you ride your bike to these places? Why don't you take your car?"

He laughed, as if she were joking.

"The journey's the thing," Jesús said, his first particular utterance this afternoon. It was the sort of comment their

Pal, Hal, might have made, opening the school year, something that might appear on a hopeless poster in a Pinetop High hallway, but not something Jesús would say. He'd been overtaken, Birdy thought, body snatched by a pod person.

"*Pues,*" said his mother, rising from the flowered sofa in her flowered dress. She nodded to Tía Blanca, in the shadows wearing a similar dress, two bouquets. "You want to join us for Mass?" she asked Jaime, daring him to waste any more of her time. Was it the shaved legs that irritated Mrs. Morales? The suspiciously avid nature-boyness? Or simply the concrete evidence of what had been her son's abstract predilection? *Puercas afuera,* Birdy thought: pigs outside.

Or maybe Birdy projected all the hostility. Maybe Mrs. Morales liked Hi May just fine.

Jaime stood, flytrapped Mrs. Morales's hand, and said, "Thank you for the invitation, but I think Jesús and I need some time alone."

"*Hmph,*" said the mother, claiming her hand, leaving, taking her old housekeeper with her.

Jesús shot a pleading look in Birdy's direction: *Don't go,* it said. Or possibly, *Please go.*

"I love your mother!" Jaime said, falling back onto the ottoman, this time with his gorgeous legs splayed, his eyes suddenly hungry instead of innocent. He stretched his limbs so as to showcase their stringy muscles, like a vain dancer. He was bad news, Birdy thought, bad, bad, bad. "And your aunt, they are so authentic."

Both men turned in Birdy's direction, Dr. Jekyl and Mr. Hyde. Authentic what? she wondered. Jesús seemed helpless, hostage to his own cravings. She had never known him so thoroughly at a loss for words. She felt like coaching him into his lines, reminding him of how he hated phonies and made sport of overt sincerity. *Irony,* she wanted to shout. But he was as opaque as a stranger to her. Did he want her to leave? To stay? To shoot him? "Well," she said, testing the waters. "I guess we could watch *Alfie* some other time."

"I guess," Jesús sighed.

She told Jaime it was nice meeting him, suffering those hands around hers once more, then departed from Mrs. Morales's fort, knocking his bicycle over as she went. It gave her pleasure to see its rear tire spinning uselessly above the cement.

THE NEXT DAY, Wednesday, Birdy arrived early at the Anthony home to find herself alone. She'd not been there alone before. For only a moment she sat in her car contemplating her next action. Like Goldilocks, she trespassed, into kitchen, living room, bedroom, briefly testing the wares of each. The house was prissily clean, as always, and she could hear the clock ticking over the stone mantle. Mark's room she avoided, although she made a short visit to Mrs. A.'s, studying the vast closet of plastic-bagged clothing, mild odor of dry cleaning chemical. The air rustled as she swung the door open, plastic shimmering. Had she all the time in the world, Birdy might have investigated every dresser drawer, but she contented herself with the top one: stockings stuffed in Baggies, arranged in rows by color, light to dark. All this suffocating plastic sheathing: it wasn't exactly unexpected, just scarily confirming.

Like a good snoop, she did not neglect the bathroom medicine cabinet. Everything ordinary, mouthwash, estrogen, jumbo laxative, lavender bath crystals, plus eight bottles of algae. You'd think one would be enough. Capsules full of pale dust, ranging in shade from gold to green to black, another apparent scam Mrs. Anthony had swallowed in her quest for the miraculous. Birdy twisted open a bottle just to get a whiff of the sea. On the back of the toilet sat a crocheted doll, her fat buttercup yellow antebellum skirt hiding a spare roll of toilet paper. "Oy," said Birdy, then made her way to the kitchen.

The room she concentrated on was the one that had been Teresa's, behind a closed door off the kitchen, a room apparently added on to the adobe home, molded against the house where a window used to be. Even Birdy, unversed as she was in carpentry, could see that the room was an afterthought, tacked on late and clumsily, perhaps originally intended only for storage: barrels of dry goods, sides of beef.

According to Mrs. Anthony's book, she had been unable to leave Teresa's things where they'd lain, had packed the contents of her bedroom into boxes, dispersed the furniture and clothing. The personal objects, papers and trinkets, Birdy herself possessed, report cards and wallet. Now the room was for sewing. Still, Birdy had wanted to see it, check out the closet for a message penned on the wall, some sign that there'd been a cry for help.

She stepped down as if into a cellar; the air was cool and stale, the room closer to the earth, clammy with the odor of mushroom and snail and other damp inhabitants. It was kind of a stumbling step downward, off the warm oak floorboards and onto the cool tile, chilly smooth, seeming to lie just above the dirt. Why had they made the girl sleep here, in a second-rate room off the kitchen like a scullery girl, like Cinderella, instead of with the rest of them? Birdy gasped at the sight of the dressmaker's dummy—for a second, it could have been another intruder, waiting there to grab her. It would have served her right, entering if not outright breaking. Headless, limbless, the dummy resembled an exclamation mark, emphatically declaring something from the center of the room. It wore a bright orange blouse without sleeves, pins stabbed everywhere like voodoo. An old sewing machine sat under a window, obscurely menacing, as vintage machinery often seemed to Birdy—as if the Singer at some point in history might have been a device of torture. On the walls, dimly visible, there hung prints of flowers in small ornate frames. Plastic shelving held cloth and pattern packages, spools and magazines and pinking shears and buttons and bobbins and zipper plackets, all itemized as neatly as the objects in Mrs. A.'s bedroom. Birdy could only guess at what might have hung on Teresa's walls before her mother cleaned up, what icons and idols had sat on the shelves, what clutter and funk and stink might have defined the place, the style the girl had seen as her own. Teresa had been only a few years younger than Birdy, and, given the fact that Pinetop was at least a few years behind Chicago, it was possible they'd shared some passions, some smutty books, some disturbing music. In collecting her own box of remnants from her own home, Birdy had been horrified to discover her teenage self, all the cheap jewelry she'd stolen, the inane quotations she'd thought lofty, the tacky preoccupation with pornography, the sheer quantity of *stuff* that had made its way into her young life and then stayed there, subject to anyone's perusal and judgment.

She was glad Teresa's things had been given away. That must have been step one in Mrs. Anthony's attempt to relieve whatever pressure she felt swelling in her heart. Let objects be objects, trash be trash, let it all be gone. A draft seemed to swirl along the floor, catching errant threads; Birdy knelt, hair sweeping the tile, to look under the shelves, saw a brilliant slit of light where the floor and the wall did not quite meet. Daylight leaked in, as in a cave. From that opening she thought she heard a car's motor, approaching. When she crossed to the window and parted the sun-bleached curtains, she discovered bars.

Through the bars, she saw the Anthonys' car turn in from the road.

Out the door Birdy hustled, careful to close it, hurrying

through the kitchen and into the sultry outdoors, around the front, walking like someone with legitimate business, someone who'd been knocking on the backdoor, maybe calling "whoo hoo," vaguely annoyed that her appointment was late. She counted nine windows on the house, and only Teresa's had bars. It was something you might never have noticed. Did someone think a set of bars would keep a girl in? Contain her like a toaster cozy, like a Tupperware seal?

Mark drove slowly up the road, parked beside Birdy's car, and automatically went 'round to open his mother's door for her.

"How're you doing, Mark?" Birdy asked brazenly.

"Fine," he said, eyes skipping over her.

"Fine, thank you," his mother corrected, rising from the vehicle. "Have you been waiting long?"

"I just got here," Birdy said.

Mrs. Anthony plucked a pink thread from Birdy's hair, flicked it to the ground. "Well, let's get to work, shall we?"

This would turn out to be their final official editing session. Mrs. Anthony had been gaining confidence in her work as it neared the finish line, its bulked-up and bullying substance, less intimidated by Birdy's expertise on matters literary. Clichés, she had decided, were fine; they spoke the truth, that's why people had been repeating them for all these years. And she flatly refused to believe in the subjunctive. "If I were a bell, I'd be ringing," Birdy had cited *Guys and Dolls* to strengthen her case. "If I *was* a bell," said Isadora Anthony stubbornly. But if Mrs. A. were a bell, she'd be cracked, like the big one in Philadelphia.

"I'm shooting baskets," Mark told his mother later, disguised as an innocent athlete, saggy shorts, giant shoes, ball casually lodged on hip. "I'll be home around ten." Now he would take the car to the school, walk to Birdy's trailer, wait for her. Birdy's attention now forked, half tracking his progress, while devoting the remainder to reading the last chapter of *Somebody's Girl.*

"That's the way we talked to each other," Mrs. Anthony was insisting.

"No?"

"We did."

Birdy had circled a long exchange of dialogue among the Anthony family, father, mother, son, and daughter, and now tried to cajole Mrs. A. into admitting that her family partook of normal discord at the dinner table. Mrs. Anthony, possessing some occasional savvy about timing, had intuited that the final scene of her book ought to be one wherein both Teresa and Mr. Anthony were still alive, the last ordinary meal the family had shared. Birdy praised this good sense, while offering perfectly modest suggestions about the conversation, which seemed awfully portentous, everyone pledging their undying affection, their wholesome regard for one another.

"A little spat would read more realistically," she claimed.

Mrs. A. shook her head, like a terrible two-year-old. It was the first time Birdy could recall outright refusal.

"He said this? Your husband? That his love was neverending?" Even cornball country western singers had the grace to twang a tad ironically at that.

"He did." She would not relinquish her mushy vows. She did not believe a reader would find the scene anything but tender, heartwarming.

"I see. Well, surely you disagreed about something? It's just not natural to have a family get along this splendidly. In fact, it's totally suspicious. There has to have been some friction somewhere. Let's just say Mark threw his three bean salad at Teresa. Even a little thing would help with the verisimilitude. In my family, for example, I used to lick the silverware when I set the table, spreading my germs around, a bit of what you might call domestic revolution." Mrs. Anthony merely crossed her arms, disgruntled, looking out from under her eyelids as if Birdy had confessed, finally, to being unfit, absolutely unqualified for the position she held. Why was Birdy always inserting her own irrelevant family affairs into Mrs. Anthony's? Birdy stubbornly waited for Mrs. A. to acknowledge the workaday grievances of any group of people living together. "So maybe the kids did things like that, things they shouldn't have. Maybe Teresa was acting all sweet because she was planning to, I don't know, *escape*, run away . . ."

"She wasn't."

". . . or maybe she was trying to seem older than her years, maybe she had a boyfriend who was less than desirable . . ."

"She did not."

"Maybe she was just plain difficult, like teenagers are, like they're supposed—"

"She wasn't. Was not."

"Really?"

"Really." The two women stared at each other as if they were having a fight. Maybe this *was* a fight; certainly they disagreed and felt passionately about it. Despite the muggy heat, Mrs. Anthony was impeccably dressed, as usual, chest puffing beneath her silk blouse and ascot. It all seemed related and reprehensible, the impeccable clothing and the barred window, the fabricated last supper and the hidden dirty autopsy reports. The place was a regular cottage industry of cover-up.

Birdy, feeling there was little left to lose, leaned over the pages and said, "Have you ever wondered if Teresa and your husband—"

"*This* is the way we were," Mrs. A. interrupted, patting her pages, her face flushed a smoldering red as she seemed to understand all that Birdy was hinting at. No one dare imply that Philip Anthony might have been a suspect. "We couldn't," his widow emphasized, "have been," she said, "happier."

They sighed heavily, at an impasse. They gave up on each other at precisely the same moment, the manuscript on the table between them like a disputed contract, a divorce decree, a child each thought she owned and was maybe prepared to have torn in half.

"I think that will be enough tutoring," Mrs. Anthony said at the same time Birdy said, "Maybe somebody else should read this thing." And that was that.

What Birdy could gloat about was the fact that, when she walked out of Isadora Anthony's house with her last twenty-four-dollar check signed by the woman's quaking fingers, she was going directly to Mark, her son. She was going to remove his clothing and put her naked flesh right up against his. If Mrs. Anthony thought she'd won anything, she was sorely mistaken.

Canned, Birdy felt stung and touchy. When, a few evenings later, there was a knock on her front door—a sound that in the past wouldn't have particularly alarmed her—she hid her face. She expected a posse of some sort.

"Who is it?" she whispered to Mark, poking him in the chest as he peered through the curtains on the side. She shoved him over to see for herself. There stood Luziana, toe tapping, hip thrust, head tilted upward in the model's swan-necked pose while she scratched a bite behind her earlobe. She wore her baby haphazardly on her chest in a sack contraption. She rapped again, clearly said "Shit," and turned around, plopping down the steps, stopping at the curb to look once more at Birdy's door, then heading up the street, now absently scratching at the baby's scalp.

"I hope she didn't see your flip-flops," Birdy said, of Mark's muddy shoes between the doors.

Mark still whispered. "She still hasn't given her baby a name. I heard it was because she might put her up for adoption."

"What?" Although Birdy might once have advocated for adoption, she felt somehow as if everyone, herself included, had devoted too much energy to Luziana's baby to let it be snatched by strangers now. A collection for Infant Rillos had been taken up at school; others had donated clothing and a carseat and a wind-up swing that jerked forward and back like a metronome; Mr. John had provided the bed; and Birdy herself had bought Luziana that expensive pack sack. She felt guilty, watching the girl wander down the block. She hadn't been a very loyal friend, visiting Luziana's house only once since the baby's birth, the place as uncomfortably moist and fetid as a terrarium, all those sour infant body fluids in exchange, the Rillos menfolk standing around befuddled and useless, averting their eyes when it was time to nurse. The child was a big chunk of a girl who Luziana claimed was sucking her dry, Luziana unceremoniously hoisting her shirt and plopping her swollen freckled breast in the infant's face. "Baby," she called her, when she needed a signifier.

"Adoption might be good," Mark said, stumping back to bed, his erect penis leading him like a dowsing rod. "My sister was adopted, you know."

"What sister?"

"My only sister." He threw himself onto Birdy's bed as if it were a deep swimming pool and he had a great distance to fall. "Actually, she was a gift."

"What are you saying?" Birdy stood over him with her hands on her hips, convinced he was suddenly revealing a religious fundamentalism, one that indulged in strange metaphorical idioms, not unlike his mother's peculiar vocabulary in her tome: *life footprint,* she recalled.

But Mark proceeded to too-casually explain that the family down the road had given his family Teresa when she was eleven. "When she got her boobs," he said shyly.

"What?"

Birdy hurried to locate the family photo, uncovering it among her unpaid bills and unanswered letters, noting this time that Teresa bore no resemblance to any of the family members, Mister, Missus, or Mark, who, she noted, looked just like his father, as she had presumed. All of the faces meant something different to her than they had used to. Skittery Mrs. A., sweet Mark. Teresa's was finer, darker, cast from another batch. "The neighbors gave her to your parents?"

Mark nodded, patting a place beside him for Birdy to occupy.

"Gave her? Who gave her? There was nothing legal?"

"I don't know, her mother. She wasn't getting along with her mother. Because of her boobs. Her mother had a new husband and she was jealous. Teresa just came to live with us, like a baby-sitter. She baby-sat me."

"She baby-sat you?"

"Yeah."

"Because of her breasts?"

"Yeah."

"The neighbors dropped her off, and she moved in."

"Right. Why are you repeating everything I say?"

"And you don't think that's just the slightest bit *odd?*"

"To baby-sit?"

"No." She swatted him with his own photograph, wondering why his mother hadn't asked for it back when they'd severed relations, it and the articles, and the box of papers, Teresa's orange suede wallet with its ratty little papers. "Odd to take a child from the neighbors and pretend she's your daughter."

"I guess," he said. "I never really thought about it."

He'd never thought about a lot of things, Birdy knew.

"And your mother never mentioned this, not once. She let me believe Teresa was her daughter."

"Teresa *was* her daughter," Mark said, sitting up, suddenly indignant. Because he was young and dense, Birdy could forget to be careful. "She was my sister. The very first thing I remember had Teresa in it, when I was like three." He went on, scratching his sideburn, his erection a crumpled pouch between his legs, "My parents had a baby before me, one that died, a girl. So Teresa sort of became a suffragette."

"A what?"

He turned away angrily when Birdy laughed. "Surrogate," she said, sitting beside him on the bed, then added, "This whole thing is un-fucking-believable. There is not one mention of an adoption in your mother's book, not one single solitary word." She felt a specific raging humiliation, imagining all the people who must know this basic secret about the Anthonys. The town was simply too small and necrophilic not to know that Teresa had been adopted. Everyone must know, mustn't he and she, every man, woman, child, and pet? And didn't that leave Ms. Stone not in the catbird seat but in the dunce's corner, sitting there stupidly under her pointed cap?

Although Mark didn't seem to think less of her for not knowing.

"The neighbors were Italian," he said later, after they'd made love and he was falling asleep on her. "They moved away, to different mountains." *Segregate,* Birdy thought dreamily, *surfeit,* trying to think of other words he might have misused in attempting to find the right one. She envisioned herself seeking out Teresa's original family, pressing buttons on the telephone, talking to operators and Department of Motor Vehicle personnel in all the mountainous states, the whole wide West. Doing something, maybe, that no one else had done. Now the girl's long name made sense. Signaigo, not Anthony. Now Birdy understood why Mr. John, concrete thinker, insisted he didn't see Teresa's mother anymore. Perhaps Birdy would be the one to inform the Signaigos that Teresa had died ten years ago, perhaps they'd not heard that news. Was there anyone who knew less than Birdy about the whole ghastly thing? Of course, to Teresa's original family, the girl had died before then, when they'd given her away. Hadn't she? Wouldn't that be the only way you could leave a child behind?

"Mark," she whispered. He slept deeply; that adult trait of fearing the worst, of being able to rouse himself in an instant to face his most dread nightmare, had not visited itself upon him yet. She shook him, his smooth shoulder in its smooth socket under her palm like an elegant gear shift. "Mark, you have to go home." In her bathrobe at the door, she asked him what his first memory had been, the one featuring his adopted sister.

"Just swinging," he said groggily, stepping into his crusty flip-flops. "On a tire swing in our yard. Later there were wasps in the tire and we couldn't swing, but before that I can remember looking up through the leaves, you know how the sun shines through tree leaves?" He tousled his plenty-tousled hair.

"Those were the trees you cut down?"

"Yeah, a lot later. I just remember her pushing me in the swing, her face and the leaves. Sometimes the smell of new tires makes me remember it, or just touching a tire."

"That's called something."

"What is?"

"I don't know, remembering with your senses, touching and smelling."

"I gotta go." He kissed her upper lip, taking it gently into his mouth for a moment.

After he left, Birdy sat on her stoop surveying her little town. Next door, a fat woman lived with a fat dog, feeding it tubs of margarine. She suspected the A-frame on the corner to be occupied by an addict of some sort—he kept such strange hours. Down every street a house, inside every house a family, among its members many secrets, and behind every single face a more profound privacy. She'd supposed the Anthony autopsy reports were her answer to the question of Teresa's death; now she saw there was no answer. The story of a life, even a young one like Teresa's, was a thing like a rose, layered, densely tiered, and you could remove all the petals, methodically, logically, with scrupulous candor and care, and still reach something at the center just as complicated and entirely hermetic and puzzling, petaled in a way that defied peeling.

She looked into her darkening town as if it were the sky overhead, just that vast and inscrutable.

AFTER THIS revelation, Birdy's curiosity in Mrs. Anthony's project shifted to a more sublime regret, sadness of a higher, more diffuse magnitude. There were new characters to contemplate, whose motives seemed gothic or surreal. You might as well entertain the notion of an asteroid striking your planet: the finer details faded to folderol. Like Mrs. Anthony, she no longer could see the possibility of a coherent shape. The story was too hopelessly snarled, and although Mrs. Anthony didn't even *want* to untangle it, Birdy didn't think it was feasible, anyway, even with the desire. No doubt Philip Anthony had found himself attracted to the girl who'd been given to them, and then insanely, homicidally jealous of her boyfriend. Yardbird Larry Ranta would have been a boyfriend simple to despise. And no doubt Mrs. Anthony did not want to acknowledge her own failure, did not want to admit that she, too, would be driven to give away the girl with breasts, pass her around like a hot potato, like a loaded gun, no one willing or able to hold her long. Teresa's real family, apparently, had departed soon after bestowing Teresa on the Anthonys. They never looked back, it seemed, never wondered what became of their girl, good riddance, bad rubbish.

If everyone wanted her gone, who could be called guilty when it actually came to pass?

Oh ho. Birdy considered this in light of her own estrangement; she hadn't spoken to her father for over a year. Was this lapse her responsibility or his? Who had abandoned whom? Like a child, she had been testing him, waiting to see when he would remember who and where she was. But unlike the parent of a child, he had not played along. Her mother would have. Her mother wouldn't have been able not to.

Perhaps her father thought of it as desertion; in his version of Birdy's life, maybe she was always giving somebody the slip. She tried this on to see if it fit. Her mother had died, true, leaving Birdy without tether, but Birdy had flown the coop before it happened. She'd fled her mother's sickbed, ditched Reg at the altar, left her spurned poet back in Urbana. Even her baby, that scant shrimpy mishap lodged deep and insensible inside her, too tiny to know better or be abject, she'd forsaken. A body abandons another body, no longer holds its hand or whispers affectionately at its ear.

So who was Birdy to cast stones in Mrs. Anthony's direction? Wasn't this house of hers—gleaming, fragile, refracting—also made of glass?

"I'M BLOWING this clambake," Jesús said, the next time Birdy saw him. It was Mass night once more after a long absence, the two of them had a movie date. Mark was weatherproofing his mother's home, sealing the place in more plastic, preparing her for the winter ahead, the one she would have to survive without him, and Birdy had been glad for the excuse to spend a night with Jesús.

Only half attending, she said, "What do you mean, you're blowing this clambake?"

"I mean when you've gotta go, you've gotta go. And I've got to go."

Onscreen, Grace Kelly and Bing Crosby constituted a peculiar couple, Grace a dowdy wife and Bing her morose drunken husband. William Holden was playing an asshole stage director banking on Bing's comeback, and there was a dead child in the scenario, a four-year-old son Bing had somehow lost sight of while ogling his own celebrity. "Go where? In what way, 'go'?" Birdy asked, distracted. She liked the Princess of Monaco's looking less than lovely, and Mrs. Morales had two swamp coolers flooding her living room air, so the temperature was tolerable. Still, the night was too muggy to flick a lighter, to ignite marijuana, too hot for anything but beer, in tall bottles from Tía Blanca's freezer. Birdy and Jesús had experimented until they knew to leave the bottles for exactly seventy minutes, so that, instead of solid ice, what emerged was a slushy substance of tiny gold crystals that slid tingling down the throat. A half-dozen empties stood on the coffee table beside the hammer and nails. Another six waited in the deep freeze. Jesús, who was generally shy about exposing his belly, had removed his shirt in deference to the heat, and thrown it onto the neglected ski machine in the corner. Birdy could not help staring at him, his smooth brown flesh over a generous paunch, dark hairs rising over him like a bowed arrow pointing to his groin. Since she'd met Jaime the cyclist, Birdy had seen Jesús in a different, less benign, light. His sexuality was no longer hypothetical and hip, but tangible, to be reckoned with.

He said, "I mean 'go' as in, past tense, gone, history, adieu, bone swar, I'm bailing." One palm slid against the other, his hand aimed toward the window. "Outta here, see ya, sucker."

"Who will be my friend, if you go?"

Jesús had spent the past week away, driving the cyclist back to Phoenix with his bike strapped to the slug bug bumper. Birdy hadn't thought much about it, Jesús's fling, devoting most of her time to Mark, whose belly, she decided, was simply unforgivably firm. She would work on softening him up. Since the school year was impending, they spent even more time at her trailer, letting the light blur into dusk, the daylight heat into dark heat, the visible into the invisible. Sloppy, slippery, nearly unconscious. Summer had come to seem like one extended monsoon, the muggy swelling of anticipation, and the sultry burst and flood. Her body had never felt so synchronized to the elements. So her attention had been with Mark, not Jesús; if she'd ever taken a minute to actually figure, she would have convinced herself she had the whole school year to attend to Jesús, catch up, restore order, talk, talk, talk. Everything she'd not told Mark would have been saved for Jesús, jokes, insights, confidences, the complaints of age, Birdy filled like a reservoir with chatter. Now, he said, "I've got a job lead, Bird. The Jesuits in Phoenix want to make sure their little whitebread guys get that hot habañera bilingual thing."

"Jesuits?" Birdy said scornfully. She felt stupefied by the beer, by his news, giving herself permission to respond more adroitly tomorrow. It seemed to her that somebody was pulling a fast one on her, snapping open a trapdoor beneath her feet.

"Yeah, Jesuits. I'd hafta quit drinking, too, no drinking, no pot smoking, no, no, no. They do random testing."

"Oh my God."

"Not to mention that it's not that good for you."

Birdy thought of the cyclist, sipping sanctimoniously at his bottled water, stretching those shimmering muscled legs.

"My salary would practically double," Jesús said hopefully. "And maybe it's time to grow up, hop on out of the nest. A boy can't live with his mother his whole life, can he? And I could lose fifteen pounds in a week if I stopped sucking down this stuff." He slapped his bare paunch, then lifted the clear Corona bottle and finished his slush. "Just get a load of Bing, there. And remember *Lost Weekend*, Ray Milland dragging his ass all over town on Sunday morning, hocking his girlfriend's leopard coat for booze? No thank you, none for me." He burped behind his fist.

"Oh, you're not like him."

"Name one significant way in which I am not like Ray Milland."

"Well, for starters, you're not under the delusion that you have a book to write."

"How do you know?"

"Anyway, he wasn't hocking the coat for booze, he was trading it for his gun." Birdy particularly remembered this part because that's where she'd attached herself to the movie, the temptation to make stirring suicidal gestures.

"*The Bottle*," Jesús quoted, pointing at his forehead fanatically. " 'I've got it all up here!' " He laughed, open throated, then said flatly, "This town's small, Bird. Way small. You know it is. I've been here, done that. Now it's time to move on. If it were you, with a new job, I'd be giving you hugs."

Birdy pulled herself out of the soft sofa and made her way to his chair, where she fell onto his lap like a hound dog. "Good luck," she said soggily into his damp chest hairs.

"Don't go. Don't leave me with those fools in the lounge." The Ideal World swelled ahead of her like an airborn toxic event.

"Not everything is about you, Bird." He put his sweaty arms around her but, even sloshed, Birdy worried that his embrace was insincere, perfunctory, someone coddling a drunk. He smelled powerfully of his wonderful cologne, but in some important way, he'd already gone, put himself in his slug bug and left Pinetop like a bad dream. She was already nostalgic for this scent. Or maybe his embrace was lackluster because he worried that she was trying to seduce him, that his naked chest—or maybe just his naked affinity for the cyclist—had pushed her over the edge of yearning. And what did he mean, not everything was about her?

"What's this Jesuit school like?" she asked, settling herself in as unsexual a manner as possible on his knees, unsticking her forearm from his belly, pledging to get interested in his future.

"Small, private, K through twelve. Outside the city in an old dude ranch. They renovated the horse stalls for faculty housing. You want to know the truth, I thought I noticed a beasty odor in there, kind of piss-on-hay, but maybe not. It's near Jaime's apartment. If I get the job, I'll get to teach art as well as Spanish," he added. "That's what we call a perk in this biz."

"Near Jaime," Birdy said skeptically. In her mind, she put the two of them together, roving around with their droopy genitalia, but homosexual sex continued to tax her imagination. "Are you sure you wanna quit everything, leave everybody and move there, for *him?* Are you sure he wants you to?"

"Your point being. . . ?"

"I mean, he seemed maybe fickle."

"Fickle?"

"You know, like a tease. Like maybe he was leading you

on, like playing you for a fool. He's so young. And that job is not for sure, is it? You'd be going there for hardly any reason. You don't even know him, he just came here out of nowhere and made you drive him home, you hardly spent any time with him. I mean, did he buy gas?"

Jesús abruptly stood, scooting Birdy from his lap into the warm seat he'd left.

"I just don't want you to get hurt."

"Bullshit. You just don't want to take me seriously."

"I do," Birdy said, wondering if she did.

"I can't finish this movie, Bird, it's depressing the hell out of me, Grace wearing off-the-rack and old Bing in the bottle." He snapped the remote like a switchblade, clicking off the screen without waiting for her to agree.

"I was kind of hoping William Holden would seduce Grace. I'm sorry, Jesús, really. I *do* take you seriously, I'm sure he's a nice guy, I'm sure he likes you." She was bad at bluffing; no wonder she'd not been able to stick around comforting her dying mother. What could you say to a person who was dying? What could you do besides cry? Now all she could picture was Jesús's humiliation, when he discovered what a sucker love had made of him. She had no faith in happy endings, none whatsoever.

He was rewinding the tape, clinking empty bottles, gathering up the packing materials to send the video back to the club. He yanked the ceiling fan chain with enough force to rock the massive hardware. Dispatch. Dazed, Birdy watched from the chair, feeling sick, wondering if he wished the fan blades would land on her, sever her like a rat in a blender. "You don't go gaga after undeserving hunks, only I do that," she said, sacrificing poor Mark in a last-ditch effort to win back her friend, trying for lightness, doing, she supposed, exactly what Jesús had just accused her of doing, steering the conversation toward herself. "I'm the only one that stupid."

"That's right, Miz Stone," he said singsongingly without turning from his chore.

Foul! she wanted to cry, *you told me to!* she wanted to remind him. But had he? Had he done anything but be her booster, encourage what her heart—dragging her body, ball and chain, along behind—had already decided to stake and claim?

"I'm going to bed, bub," he said tiredly, meaning that Birdy was not invited to wait until Mrs. Morales and Tía Blanca returned from church. Meaning, Birdy wouldn't get a plate of enchiladas and rolled tacos and hot refried beans, wouldn't get a second feature, wouldn't get even a tiny dose of the women's reflexive mothering. She looked at the cluttered walls as if to imprint upon her retinas the arrangement of their contents, as if she might never be welcome inside to view them again. All the smiling siblings and grandchildren, so unsurprised to see her banished.

"I'll call you," she promised at the door as he was closing it between her and all of them. *Puercas afuera,* indeed.

A FEW DAYS later Mrs. Anthony accompanied Mark to Albuquerque; classes started the following morning, both at Pinetop and at UNM. Their sedan was stuffed full of Mark's clothes and books and size-twelve double-E shoes, a small microwave oven to prepare his urgent adolescent meals, weight-lifting equipment to tone his hard adolescent body, and an elaborate stereo system to sate his tedious adolescent appetite for gruesome music. The car sagged under the weight of its load. Birdy hoped that somewhere in there rode the talking picture frame safeguarding her photograph and distorted voice. He navigated the big burden by her house, as she'd requested, and she stood on her porch in the same shorts and T-shirt he'd peeled off of her the night before, waving good-bye to him with one hand, holding a half-peeled orange in the other. Mrs. Anthony simply looked out the passenger window, her fair face troubled, her fine hair blazing in the sun, some dawning recognition seemed to light her piercing eyes.

"Attractive nuisance," Birdy whispered, of herself, hoping that's what she was. But she'd lost her appetite for the orange, and threw it in the street. Her neighbors surely wouldn't notice or care.

In Birdy's bed the previous evening, Mark had wept, a boy who maybe had not wept since the deaths of his sister and father. When his eyes were wet they appeared more than ever like daisies, like stars, profuse lashes stuck together, offsetting their fathomless black nuclei. "I love you so much," he sobbed to Birdy.

"You love sex," she told him, panicked nonetheless; what could this display foretell? His feelings, never mind that they were inchoate and clunky and spawned from who knew what, touched her. That he felt them, that was enough. He proclaimed his willingness to give up college, disappoint his mother, ruin Birdy's career—all of it, just so they could fall into bed together.

Young love: able to leap tall buildings, mightier than the sword, abiding none but its own dumb laws.

"We'll write letters to each other," she placated him, handing him a paper towel with which to blow his nose. "We'll talk on the phone," she promised. Both of these pursuits seemed so flimsy, so unlikely. What would they have between them, once they couldn't grope each other? Mark's education under Birdy's tutelage had been of the physical variety; where in the wide wide world did they think mere words were going to get them? Where had words ever gotten them?

Dear Sweatheart, he would write.

He hadn't wanted to leave her trailer; he moped on the bed, he cried at the door, eyes as sad and beseeching as Birdy had ever beheld. On an impulse, he grabbed up her hand and kissed the knuckles, like a knight. When she thought of him later, she would run her fingers over the ridges, his lips recalled there, brushing across in an ardent chapped whisper.

She loved his love, she thought, if not him himself.

Their slow-moving car, like a parade float, disappeared down the street, which seemed suddenly hushed, the neighborhood gone still as a sucking vortex with absence.

SHE DIDN'T think to organize a going-away party for Jesús, so Mary Jo Callahan did, instead. Penitent, Birdy arrived first and was shown around the little bungalow as if she ought to aspire to such a dwelling in her future, as if Mary Jo's situation ought to offer her hope.

"You can get a mortgage loan easily if you have any savings to invest in a down payment." The vocabulary alone terrified Birdy: savings, investment, mortgage. She had noticed in people a tendency to indoctrinate others when they'd made commitments—married people wanted you to get married, new parents wanted you to have babies, home owners wanted you to buy a house. Alcoholics wanted you to drink. People didn't want to float alone in their boats, in their kettle of fish. Perhaps the dead had that same urge for fellowship. Perhaps that explained the insistent call of her mother and Teresa Anthony, the lure of their voices, their desire for her company.

Her desire for their desire.

"And you can buy points," Mary Jo added slyly.

"Ah," Birdy said. Points: now you could buy them as well as make and score them.

Mary Jo's house smelled of potpourri, as if a funeral had

just been held there. The decor was of a different sort than Birdy's, despite the fact that they shared a love of books.

Mary Jo's were collected in the room she called the library, up to the ceiling on expensive wood shelves, a ladder on wheels at the ready. The books were alphabetized, their flyleafs (fly*leaves,* Birdy wondered?) no doubt bearing Mary Jo's name. At Birdy's trailer, books lay waterlogged and neglected, holding up lopsided furniture, their spines cracked and their pages bent, abused, often unfinished, resting against one another indiscriminately, Elmore Leonard atop Marcel Proust, *Jane Eyre* wedged between *Valley of the Dolls* and *Sybil.*

"How's Isadora Anthony's book coming along?" Mary Jo asked.

"I don't know," Birdy said. "I was dismissed."

"Oh . . ." Mary Jo touched Birdy's arm.

" 'Oh' what?"

"Nothing."

"What?"

"I bet I know why she let you go." Mary Jo positively glowed, simpering, preparing for Birdy to bite.

She sighed, waiting to hear that Mary Jo had known all along about Birdy's illicit love affair with Mrs. Anthony's son. "Why?"

"Because you told her you thought Mr. Anthony might have pushed Teresa over the cliff." Her eyes were bright, maniacal, and she was standing far too close for comfort.

Birdy didn't respond, which seemed to be a response.

"See, that's what *I* did," Mary Jo said proudly. "That's why she fired me, last year. I used to be her tutor."

Of course, Birdy thought. Of course Miss Callahan had been the first choice. Of course she'd tracked Birdy's progress over the same ground with such crazed concentration. Of course, no wonder, no wonder, of course: her brain was making all the noises of discovering the right-in-front-of-your-face truth. *Duh,* her students would have intoned.

Mary Jo went on with a great deal of satisfaction; she'd been waiting so long to mention this to Birdy. "And when I saw the autopsy reports, well, that was the straw that broke the camel's back. She couldn't deny what they said. So she let me go." Mary Jo pursed her lips and jiggled her head like one of those loose-necked toy animals in the rear windows of cars. Birdy was dazed, mortified, furious, but she refused to let any of it show. She would ask no questions. She was renouncing nosiness, to hell with curiosity, although it occurred to her that this was a convenient excuse just to be plain rude. She could not bear the idea that she had followed the footsteps of Mary Jo Callahan, planting her soles right where her colleague's had tread before her. Thankfully, the doorbell rang, and Mary Jo skittered off to answer.

"Dolt," Birdy said, of herself. Moreover, how had Mary Jo actually gotten access to the autopsies? There was a connection somewhere, to the dispatcher or sheriff or some deputy, an inside advantage, a tricky network at the local level that Birdy could never have infiltrated. She felt somehow manipulated by Isadora Anthony, but to what real end? Enabler to the liar, she supposed.

Mary Jo had invited strictly school people to this party, all the dullards Birdy had complained about from the teachers' lounge. They started arriving in pairs, Edith Pack with Felicia Oppenheimer, Hal Halfon with his wife, Mr. Schweinbraten with Mrs. Schweinbraten, the football coach with the basketball coach, Hugh Gross with Derek Whacker, Jesús's mother with Tía Blanca, and Jesús with Mr. John, as if having found a substitute for Birdy's companionship. Mr. John carried a jar of stuffed olives.

"Hello, Mr. John," Birdy said as sweetly as she could muster.

"How is it hanging?" he said mechanically, if not provocatively.

All year she would have to worry about his barking out what he knew about her. He would be the loose cannon of her life, rolling about the halls of Pinetop High. Maybe she would take up cigarette smoking again, just to buy his loyalty.

She began drinking too much of the pink champagne punch; her evening's activities were, alternately, the filling of her glass and the emptying of her bladder, from the punch bowl to the bathroom she moved in a slow relay. People's voices were acquiring a strange muzziness, as if she were wearing earplugs or listening to them from inside a fishbowl, and when she set her glass on the table, it hopped to the floor, popping like a lightbulb.

"I'll get it," Mary Jo said instantly, the mess cleaned and a new glass in Birdy's hand in no time. Mary Jo was that kind of hostess.

Birdy hadn't been stumble-down drunk in ages; she'd crossed a line without realizing it. Alcohol was a thick inebriate. It made her slow and gluey, a body made of molasses. She embraced poor Jesús a hundred times, she couldn't help herself, oozing, apologizing again and again, extolling the virtues of Jaime the cyclist. "You're forgiven," he said, the first time laughing, blessing her like the pope. "Go, my child."

Now that he drank nothing but sparkling water, he seemed to think she'd blown her cool, and foisted her off on his mother, who, having dragged a dozen children into this world and through the Pinetop public schools, did not lack for opinions to offer the other guests, teachers. Becoming drunk alone made Birdy melancholy; she missed her boy. She realized that the next time she saw him, she would be thirty years old. He had never asked when her birthday was—age lay so heavily between them, they never brought it up, permitting it instead to fester underneath like cancer, unmentioned. Besides, while he looked toward the future, Birdy had entered an age where she might wish for her own past. "Thirty's not so old," she said defensively to Hugh Gross, who happened to be within earshot.

"I wouldn't go back to my twenties for anything," he agreed. He wore a sweet expression tonight, his wide brown necktie with its smiling paisleys hanging around his throat. Why hadn't she fallen for Hugh? He would have a wonderful stereo system, she wagered, and know a lot about music. Even the kind she didn't particularly appreciate might be redeemable, if she met with the proper enthusiast. Maybe she could get used to his schizophrenic face, next to hers on a pillow.

Birdy said, "Aren't these lights awfully bright? It's like she's expecting shoplifters," but Hugh had disappeared and only Mary Jo heard her, her ugly features briefly afflicted by Birdy's criticism. To make up for this rudeness, Birdy began eating the goodies Mary Jo had prepared, small rich things, gummy in the mouth, difficult to swallow, lousy with those candied fruits she hated so. "Delicious," she murmured, longing for a simple potato chip, a familiar starchy product to start soaking up all this champagne she seemed to have guzzled. Why didn't urinating help? Jesús passed by and Birdy clutched at him again.

"Bird, you're smashed," he noted. "Get a grip, girlfriend."

"Don't be mad at me," she begged in his ear.

"I'm not mad," he said. But he was cool, unintoxicated, unintimate, and that seemed to Birdy worse than mad. He wasn't coming along for the ride.

Hal Halfon was talking about the Anasazi. Someone from a museum in Santa Fe was threatening to seize a blanket from the Pinetop Historical Society. Those big-city know-it-alls didn't think Pinetop could properly care for their treasure. "The weave is anomalous for the time and area," said Principal Hal. "They're saying they need to store it in a climate-controlled case, out of the light. Otherwise, it will disintegrate."

Birdy frowned, casting herself back in the beer-can-shaped museum, trying to locate the rug under discussion. It was, apparently, hanging unprotected on a wall, gravity unraveling its ancient fibers, sunlight burning away its vegetable dyes. The other teachers stood unanimous in their disapproval of the plan, despising snooty Santa Fe for trying to rob them of their heritage. "It's a slap in the face," declared Edith Pack. Mr. Whacker was reminded of the British Museum's making off with all the loveliest and most valuable parts of the ancient world. Mary Jo suggested that the historical society could hide the blanket somewhere and hang a counterfeit to deceive them. Mrs. Morales, queen of exhibition, did not see why a blanket should not be on display rather than hidden in a drawer.

"It should be properly stored," Birdy heard herself say. Her fellow party animals glanced askance at her; what a turncoat she was. "This place isn't prepared to care for it properly." She noted that she'd successfully navigated *properly* the first time she'd said it, but the second time had seemed botched by too many consonants.

Mr. John seemed personally affronted. "I clean the rug every week," he said to her angrily, "with my Dustbuster."

Birdy winced. Hugh Gross put on an aggrieved face and said, "Perhaps we should raise funds to preserve it."

"Pickle jars!" Birdy said. "More pickle jars with chump change in them."

"Ah," said her Pal Hal, chin lifted, nostrils flared. He smelled conflict; as mediator, he was hot on its trail. "Maybe a revenue bond would be more successful," he pronounced. Birdy, only momentarily of interest to her colleagues, was forgotten. She set herself down in a straight-backed chair, registering its sharp angle at the small of her back, and told herself to stay bent at this identical right angle, not to slump, not to speak too loudly nor smile too broadly nor burst into tears. She would sit erect and watch alertly, wait for others to come to her. No more champagne, no, no, no. From this position, she scanned the room like a motion detector, careful to keep her eyes wide open instead of drowsy slits, avoiding the glare of Mr. John, of Tía Blanca. There was a pile of gifts over there, on the buffet. Had they been there before? Was this someone's birthday? No, Jesús's going-away party. Gifts. They had all brought gifts. How had they known to do that? Had Mary Jo mentioned it, and Birdy, busy kicking herself for not having thought to throw the party, simply not heard? Maybe this was a grand conspiracy of Mary Jo's, designed to dishonor Birdy in Jesús's eyes.

She finished her drink, yet, lo and behold, somehow it was filled again, like a trick cup, like a cunning trap.

The Santa Fe conspiracy died down and Jesús began opening the packages: mouthwash and deodorant, a dribble glass and a backward-running watch, a subscription to the *Pinetop Journal,* postcards and bumper stickers of his hometown—consummate corniness, every one of them, Mr. John's half-empty jar of stuffed olives the finishing touch.

Just what her mother had warned her against: showing up empty-handed. Birdy's mother made a custom of bearing gifts, flowers, toys, bag of pretzels and bowl of mustard, bottle of champagne, held before her like offerings against her own undesirability, as if they would cover the cost of hosting her. Birdy's heart ached to remember it, her mother's fear of social blunder, her wary care of rebuff.

"I don't mind," Jesús said afterward, when Birdy apologized for her lapse. The two of them had stayed to help clean up, Birdy doing hardly anything except keeping herself from stumbling into a spindly antique.

"Okay," she confessed to Mary Jo as she swept beneath the table. "Okay, tell me about the autopsies."

"What would you guess was in them? What have you imagined?" Mary Jo looked craftily at Birdy, leaning on her broom.

Jesús answered for her. "She thinks the dad did it, got jealous and tossed her off."

"I also think she might have killed herself," Birdy said.

"She thinks Teresa was the victim of a plot," Jesús said.

"I think she had tragedy written all over her," Birdy tried to explain. "From the minute her first family gave her away till her second one killed her."

"What'd the reports say?" Jesús demanded of Mary Jo. "Did she have sex the night she died? Whose semen was it? Was she wearing her panties? Who burned that hole in her back? Did the coyotes get to her before the sheriff? Was her neck broken before she fell, or after?" He cleared his throat as if coughing up a lung. "Won't everything be swell when we know *just exactly what happened*?" Both women stared at him. He smiled then, innocently. "Y'all think you're in a murder mystery, but I'm here to tell you this is just plain old life. If you want my opinion, Isadora Anthony has the right idea: just make up shit and believe in it. I'm going to put that on a coffee cup, some day. *Make up shit and believe in it.* I rest my case." He took a paper bag of trash from Mary Jo's floor and disappeared into the kitchen with it.

"Well," Birdy said.

"I'll be right back," Mary Jo claimed, leaving the broom and following Jesús. A moment later, they could be heard laughing at something together. Wasn't that the living end, Jesús laughing with Miss Callahan? Birdy rose regally and strode out the door, stealing one of her hostess's crystal ashtrays just for good measure.

In the driveway stood Mary Jo's boyfriend, a potted plant

in his arms. Could it be that Mary Jo would wind up with two friends in her house while Birdy staggered home alone?

"Where are you from?" she demanded.

"Pardon?"

"From whence do you hail?"

He was quiet, plant on his hip while he aimed his remote control at his car. "Las Vegas," he said as the lock thunked secure. "Why?"

She aimed herself down the hill toward her trailer, saying not one more word to the American boyfriend, ashtray against her ribs. Could she be arrested for drunken walking? Would Sheriff Potter-Otto pull up and insist on a sobriety test, align her clumsy gait, make her find her nose with her fingertips? If she stopped, or passed out, perhaps that could be called loitering or vagrancy. In Chicago, when she was a little girl, she'd misunderstood the signs warning the cabs and cars. " 'No standing'?" she'd cried, indignant, all of seven or eight, interpreting the written world for the first time. "Why can't we stand? What's wrong with standing?" Belligerently she would hold herself motionless under the sign, waiting to be ticketed.

At present, she wasn't sure she *could* stand—not still, anyway. Momentum seemed to be carrying her onward, preventing her sodden body from sagging to the ground, where it seemed more logically to belong, where it seemed to long to be. The ashtray slid from her fingers and smashed into a hundred glittering bits on her sidewalk. She could scarcely believe she made it home—was this her door, this her living room, this her warm kitchen? After a long stop in the bathroom—speaking aloud to herself, guiding herself step by step, from toilet paper to aspirin to light switch—Birdy phoned Mark's dorm. She wanted to talk to him, say good night, hear him flatter her. He seemed like the only person left who loved her, whom she hadn't somehow poisoned by negligence. The phone on the other end ratcheted in her ear as if it shook when it rang. A boy finally answered, then went away for so long a time Birdy nearly fell asleep as she waited, then returned to let her know Mark Anthony was not in his room. "May I take a message?" he asked. Now Mark lived among people who knew the difference between *can* and *may.*

"No," Birdy said. "You may not."

She didn't want to lie down because she knew the room would begin spinning, and she hated that spinning. There was nothing for it but to begin eating, peanut butter and jelly sandwiches, cookies, anything that would sit like a sponge in her stomach. Aloud and alone, she told the item about Jesús that she knew and had never spoken: "He shaves his nose." Still, she felt no better.

From outside came the caterwauling of the stray, *yow, yow, yow.* How could it sound so miserable, and nonetheless live? Finally Birdy had had enough of that cat. She flung open the trailer's backdoor and let the thing in.

"You got your way, idiot, now what?"

The cat stuck to the kitchen's perimeters, slinking along the cabinets, winding behind the trash can. She was a scrawny black thing, a witch's cat, a few white hairs on its head that Birdy had the instantaneous insane desire to pluck. "I'm allergic," she lied to it, slamming the door between the kitchen and hall. "You stay in here." It seemed suspicious of the milk Birdy set down for it, as if accustomed to cream instead of skim, then began lapping quickly, settling on its skinny rear haunches, closing its eyes while white drops collected on its whiskers. Birdy watched attentively, afraid of blinking, afraid of losing focus. She did not want to wake in the morning on her kitchen floor, face in a bowl of sour milk, strange cat on her neck. As soon as the milk was gone, the cat cleaned its cheeks and forepaws, a rattling purr coming from its chest. It coughed a few times, sneezed, wandered around the trash can again, then raised its tail and made diarrhea on Birdy's rag rug before the sink.

"Goddamn," she said, stunned. "Why on the rug, you little asshole? Look at all this ugly linoleum, a hundred square feet, and you shit on the rug." Drunk, she couldn't much care about cleaning it up tonight. Out the back door the rug flew, but the cat refused to be caught. Birdy lunged after it half-heartedly, then left it in the kitchen and went to her spinning bed.

❧ 12

A new hairdresser opened shop across the street from Birdy's trailer. It was called Tencha's Fatal Look, a name that made Birdy optimistic about Pinetop's prospects as a town: edginess, irony, humor. Tencha was a tiny young Hispanic woman with an enormous amount of hair. Her hair looked as if it would soon overtake her, like kudzu. Birdy's thirtieth birthday fell on a Saturday, and, as luck would have it, Tencha was not busy that morning, just sitting on the front stoop of her shop in the sunshine holding a cigarette in her long manicured claws, looking bored under the breadth of her coiffure. Birdy wondered if Tencha's hair was flammable. Finally she summoned her lonely courage and went over to get a cut.

"What is permanent makeup?" she asked, sitting in the chair and reading the prices of treatments listed on a placard before the mirror. She hadn't been to a hairdresser in years. Usually, when she remembered, she trimmed her own split ends with her toenail clippers.

Tencha unfurled a plastic sheet the size of a shower curtain and fixed it around Birdy's neck, saying, "I, for example, have permanent eyeliner." She pointed at the black feathered rings drawn round her eyes. "Never smudges, never washes off, won't streak when you bawl."

Birdy was aghast. "Like tattoos?"

Tencha nodded her heavy mound of hair. "Okay, like tattoos. Your boyfriend, he never has to see you with your naked face. Save you an hour a day or more. You are always ready for the party."

"But you can never change it."

"I've had mine for three years and I never wanted to change it." In the mirror, Tencha gave Birdy a challenging look. She stepped up on a little stool in order to see the top of Birdy's head.

"Do a *lot* of people get permanent makeup?"

"Tons," said Tencha acidly.

"Wow."

Along with makeup, Tencha advertised bleaching, waving, color, pedicures, acrylic nail application, and waxing—facial, body, and bikini line. Birdy was tempted to ask what training credentials and health codes existed for such an establishment, but Tencha already seemed touchy, and, since Birdy wanted a nice haircut, she tried flattery instead. "I love the name of your store."

"Tencha's Total Look? Just saying what it is. The total thing, head to toe, and I mean toe."

"Oh. I thought it was *fatal*. Tencha's Fatal Look."

"That would be a terrible name." Tencha made a pissed-off face in the mirror, pulling at Birdy's stringy yellow hair with her fingernails. They were long nails, made of a petroleum product, so thick they looked deformed, like a set of red-capped pens.

"How old are you?" Birdy asked.

"Twenty-six," Tencha answered suspiciously. Teresa Anthony's age, just as Birdy had guessed. This would have been Teresa, had she survived, a pretty girl with a flair for permanent wave. That was all; destiny probably had less than noble intentions for most, Teresa among them. If Birdy needed to regret Teresa's death, perhaps it would be wise to think of Tencha from now on, living the life Teresa had missed, wandering ahead on the road Teresa hadn't taken, winding up in her own bland hometown with her hands in someone else's sudsy hair.

Wasn't that the saddest thing yet?

"How old are *you*?" Tencha asked.

"Thirty. Today." The women locked eyes in the mirror.

"You a teacher?" Tencha asked pointedly, as if she'd finally put together all the pieces, read all the clues and come up with the verdict. Birdy knew her haircut was doomed now.

"Yeah," she admitted. "English."

"I always hated English," said Tencha, pincing a pair of sharp scissors from her pocket.

THERE WAS one phrase of Mrs. Anthony's that Birdy liked to turn over in her head. Instead of *in and of itself,* she'd written *in enough itself.* This was one malapropism Birdy was willing to find worthy. Too often things were in enough themselves. For example, the one VW bug she'd loved so well, now gone to Phoenix with Jesús inside of it. He had brought by all of his drug paraphernalia to bestow on Birdy, big malodorous bagful, that, and a fussy kiss on the forehead.

"See ya scum," she'd said.

"I'm going to send you anonymous postcards," he told

her. "And they're going to be totally incriminating, bad-ass pictures. People at the post office are going to be checking your skanky self out." He blew his nose after they embraced. "Take good care of the Hoov," he reminded her, meaning his favorite bong. There was a perfectly fine joke to go with the name, but Birdy forgot how to find it funny.

"Sadness," she told herself as he drove away, the puttering bug so nostalgic and snappy, full of beans. "Sadness and woe."

Thus the fall term began and proceeded, dreadful without Jesús.

It also proceeded without Mr. John. Jesús had his new job, his new love, to explain his leaving, but there was no explanation for Mr. John's having done so. Birdy immediately assumed the worst, of course, that Mr. John had attacked a child, sodomized a sheep, along those lines. The other teachers weren't talking, not to Birdy, anyway; they'd closed themselves to her, she thought, reverting to their former attitude, suspecting the outsider again. Hadn't she tried to give away their valuable Anasazi blanket, just ready to fork it over to the first stuck-up egghead from Santa Fe that walked into town demanding it?

Probably Mary Jo Callahan had begun a rumor about Mark Anthony—not an explicit one. Mary Jo was afraid of explicitness and preferred innuendo, instead. Her phrasing would be suggestive, *consorting* came to mind, possibly *fraternizing*. Birdy had been *consorting* with a student. The problem, Birdy saw, was that she hadn't befriended Mary Jo the way everyone would have expected, hadn't looked up to her, hadn't gone to her for advice. Two unmarried English teachers, the soppy lit lovers, quoting pithy poetry at each other, one a kind of mentor, the other a willing apprentice, two single babes going ironically out on the town some Friday night, drinking big colored drinks, collecting the cocktail parasols and swords, giggling at school the following Monday, the rest of the faculty amused, charmed, naming them "The Girls." Birdy had snubbed her, she supposed. Mary Jo's passiveness was aggressive in nature, like most everyone else's.

Fuck it, she had to keep telling herself. That, and that she could always tender her resignation. *I must tender my resignation,* she rehearsed, liking the sound of it, the nineteenth-century delicate swellness of it, as if she'd been diagnosed with something unmentionably terminal and must hasten to the seashore, anon.

One of the new graduates took up Mr. John's job at the school, Buddy Lopez. He was a friend of Mark's, and most days, Birdy believed he was ignorant concerning her affair, believed Mark had not told, bless his earnest heart. Buddy wore blue jeans instead of a khaki jumpsuit, and shot baskets over lunch with the boys. He was a bright spot in Birdy's semester, fresh blood, lively where the rest of the faculty looked tired. He loved making puns, which seemed to be his way of coping with his new job, coining stupid jokes all day long, repeating them to whoever would listen. Birdy appreciated his goal of making people laugh. She much preferred him to Mr. John, toward whom she had no sentimental attachment whatsoever. Good riddance, she thought. Maybe he'd drowned in the stream or burned up in his hovel, taking what he knew about Birdy with him, leaving Luziana alone with her baby.

"I'm going to *pun*-ish you," Buddy would greet her in the morning. And that was fine with her. His physique was not unlike Mark's; they'd both had their dark hair trimmed by the Pinetop barber in the only style he knew. There were times when Birdy caught herself looking twice at Buddy, her carnal side excited to recognize the object of her affection, then quickly realizing its mistake in deflating disappointment. Sigh. At times, on days when she succumbed to paranoia, she was convinced he not only knew about her romance with

Mark, but planned to use his knowledge against her, pull her into his janitor's closet and have his way with her, gasp in her ear, rut in her pants. She was afraid her reputation with the students had come undone, a loose fringe they could pick at with their fingers, denude her, leave her without recourse.

But these moments of hysteria were rare. She supposed she should be comforted to discover that she wasn't going to make a habit of seducing her boy students; that Buddy did not interest her was a good sign, she decided, indication that she had some integrity, some faculty for discrimination left. But all it really made her see was that she must be in love with Mark.

After her drunken attempt to reach him, Birdy determined she would let him call her, the way boys were supposed to. He did so occasionally, from the dorm. He was lonely, he told her, although she could hear the pleasant ring of voices in the background, the camaraderie of early evening meal gathering, life plaiting itself in a healthy textured weave without her. He wanted her to come visit, then he covered the receiver to answer someone, then returned to her and his loneliness. Birdy was skeptical, but in early October she rented a room at the Hilton near campus, where Mark showed up after intramural football practice.

She'd sort of forgotten how much she liked the way his thick eyelashes stuck together.

"You cut your hair," he said. Birdy reached up to feel her bob, surprised, as usual, to find skin where once there'd been hair. Tencha had shorn off more than Birdy had planned. After their early skirmish, the two women had been silent in the shop, Birdy shrinking under the raspy blades, watching as skeins of hair fell to the floor, pondering the many years it had followed her around, growing blamelessly down her back. Tencha had said, "You're lucky you're a blonde cause that means the gray doesn't show so much."

"Lucky me," Birdy had said.

Mark had made a few changes, too. In honor of being a college boy, he'd sprouted a goatee, which made his mouth and chin look dirty. His clothing, previously under the purview of his mother's tidy eye, now hung out where once it would have been tucked in.

"Nice shirt," Birdy said. He looked down, forgetting what he had on. "I love that color, is that chartreuse? That Hi-Liter green?" He shrugged. His grass-stained knees brought a smile to her lips. They embraced in the lobby, the first time ever in public. He smelled of dirt and exertion and cotton and shampoo, was a big warm form welcome in her arms. Instinctively Birdy glanced around, as if for her townspeople or his mother. As if she were notorious. No one in the lobby—not the pudgy desk clerk nor the businessmen nor the maids—seemed to notice. In the face of this collective neglect, Birdy pinched Mark's firm rear end.

"Hey," he said, pulling away to grin at her.

"What happened to your tooth?" she asked. He had a snaggle in one of his top front teeth where he hadn't before. That, combined with his facial hair and mod rumpled clothes, made him look older, as if he'd been on the road a while, seen some things, caused some trouble, maybe learned how to wail on the harmonica.

"Oh, golf," he said nonchalantly. He'd told her his major would be phys ed. What had she expected, she asked herself, brain surgery? Philosophy? Already she could conjure a future involving his return to Pinetop High with his bachelor's degree, where he would be head coach and driver's ed instructor. He would wear those peculiarly hideous coach's shorts, a whistle around his neck; he and Birdy would share bag lunches in the teachers' lounge, hold each other's knees beneath the table while crunching carrot sticks. It wasn't unthinkable, Birdy was thinking.

They rode silently up the elevator. Birdy's room had the pleasing feel of a big-city hotel, the illusory sway of the upper floors of a tall building, and overlooked the intersection of two interstate freeways. Mark stood next to her at the glass door to get his bearings, finally pointing out his dormitory as if it were now magnetic north. After that, neither of them had much to offer by way of conversation. Mark explored the room, noting its improvements over his shared dorm room. Birdy thought it was more appealing than her home, too, cleaner, less flimsy, and without the odor of kitty. They ended up at the foot of the king-size bed, each waiting for the other to make a move.

"Have you heard from your mom?" she asked, sitting down. She could imagine Mrs. A. turning her creative juices toward her son, thick envelopes arriving full of her ongoing correspondence with herself.

He nodded, joining Birdy on the glossy bedspread.

"Did you know that she'd hired Miss Callahan, before me, to help with her book?"

"Sure."

"Miss Callahan came to your house?"

"Mom went to hers."

"Why didn't you tell me that?"

"You didn't ask." He shrugged guilelessly. "I figured you knew."

"I didn't know."

"I worry about my mom sometimes," he confided. "I used to do most of the shopping and stuff."

"It's funny how people get on just fine when you give them independence," Birdy said. She thought Mrs. Anthony needed some cutting off. "Just fine."

"Yeah. I used to tell her about everybody, too, you know, bring home the news for her. She always wanted to know who I'd seen, what they'd said, what was going on. I sort of wonder if she's lonely, there. That house." He swung his head, weary. "I've been thinking she was kind of afraid of going into town, you know, like one of those whatchacallits, angoraphobes."

"Agoraphobe," Birdy corrected. "An angoraphobe would be someone afraid of rabbits. Or maybe sweaters."

He smiled, showing his broken tooth. Perhaps when they kissed she would nick her tongue on it, taste blood.

"Did you ever tell her about me?" Birdy asked.

"About. . . ?"

"No, not about us, just about me, me at school."

"Well, she was more interested in the old-timers, the people who've lived there for so long. I'm sorry," he said.

"You don't have to apologize." She laughed. "I was just curious. Maybe your mom should get a job."

"But she doesn't know how to do anything. Except be a mother."

"Being a mother is hard," Birdy said, thinking of her own mother. "Being a good one," she amended. "Being a bad one doesn't seem very challenging at all."

"Are you saying my mother isn't a good mother?" Mark asked.

"No," she lied.

They were silent for a moment. Finally Mark asked, "How's Mr. Morales?"

She told him about Jesús's new job, about Jesús's new friend. His disappearance reminded her of Mr. John's, so she told Mark that.

"My mother would want to hear about Mr. John," he said. "He's been there forever. I wonder what happened? I hope he's all right."

"Why does everyone love that damn janitor so much?" Birdy asked, suddenly incensed. No one was ever going to love her the way they did Mr. John; was that her problem?

"He did nothing but leer at girls and burn down buildings and come bang on people's doors. And SuperGlue, let's don't forget the SuperGlue. Why does everyone find him so fucking adorable? I do not get it."

"I guess we just knew him for so long . . . I don't know. Because he's retarded. Why do you hate him?"

Birdy considered. "I don't hate him," she lied again.

"What SuperGlue?"

"Never mind." Birdy shrugged to get rid of the subject. She could hear Mark breathing and coordinated her own to match. Outside the semis passed, endlessly unknotting the interchange, on their way to the coasts bearing the products of the country's landlocked states. It would be nice to ride in a truck, look down into the laps of the other drivers, sleep in hotels, eat greasy food. Go somewhere. Birdy pictured the sprawl of the United States, scanning for a place that stood out, called her name, waited for her. But nothing responded. There was no place. She reached across the bed and put her fingers in Mark's hair as if to hitch herself to him; he instantly nudged against her hand like an animal returning the pressure of a caress, asking for more. His head was warm, solid; Birdy had the need to cradle it against her breasts. "I got a kitty cat," she said softly. "To keep me company." Things were fine, now that they'd begun touching. He undid her clothing like gift wrap, like someone who saved the stuff for later use, touchingly careful, as if Birdy were fragile or expensive inside it.

"Sometimes I feel like crying after sex," Birdy said, after sex. She said it so she wouldn't do it.

"Really?" He had grown garrulous, giggly, as they made love—naked, in bed, it seemed the whole procedure came back to him, this thing called their relationship—and lay confidently with his hands crossed beneath his head on the bleached hotel sheets prattling on about his classes as if he hadn't spoken to anyone in days. Clearly he didn't feel like crying. He went on about college life as if he'd discovered it, as if it were a great secret club the likes of which most people could not imagine, much less hope to join. He told her about a Hawaiian party his dorm had recently thrown, one with coconut drinks and grass skirts and the speared heads of pigs. He made Birdy wistful for her own college days, when her future life had used to stretch before her like a smorgasbord, endless and fruitful, all she could eat, when she felt she could hop in her car and drive anywhere, the continent as easy to navigate as a game board.

"So," he said at last, remembering to turn the conversation her way, "how's Sock Probs and Am Vals this fall?"

"I wouldn't know," she said. "That's Mary Jo's problem this year. Buddy Lopez is the janitor," she offered, by way of news.

"Yeah, Buddy. He's a funny guy."

"Mark, where did you get that shirt?" Tennis ball green suddenly did not seem like a color either he or his mother would have been drawn to. Only a girl would have selected that shirt. A sorority girl. An earth-mother girl. A punk rock girl. "Are you dating anyone?" Birdy asked, flopping herself closer alongside him, her breasts near his face, daring him to tell her anything but the truth, the whole and nothing but. She tried to sound as if she asked without hidden motive, as if she were simply an interested former teacher, and she wondered which answer, yes or no, would make her more anxious, or if neither would upset her. As a teacher, wasn't her concern supposed to be in his continued success? His promotion?

He blushed, scratched his new goatee instead of his sideburn, went cross-eyed under her flesh. "Not exactly *dating*," he said, then added, "My dorm's coed, you know." As if his falling in love might be out of his hands, these girls in the halls, girls in the bathrooms, everywhere, girls, girls, girls, looking him over, inviting him to join them, outfitting him in funny-colored shirts.

"That's great."

Later, after they'd swum in the hotel swimming pool, shopped in the hotel shops, dined in the hotel dining room, and returned to Birdy's room to order drinks from the hotel bar, Birdy asked if she was going to meet any of his new friends. She asked not because she felt the need to acquaint herself with more college freshmen, but to measure Mark's reaction to the idea.

"If you want," he said. "We could go sit around the dorm, I guess." He checked his watch as if gauging where everyone would be, then frowned as if trying to fit Birdy there among them. How would he introduce her? she wondered. Would he ask his roommate to please vacate so that he and Birdy could snuggle on the lower bunk? Would she have to run to the floor above or below in order to pee? She felt an old ugly feeling wash over her, one she recognized from her own college days, when she'd loved the poet but still suffered some unbecoming shame at introducing him to her friends. He had this bald spot, some fleshy jowl business, and antiquated opinions . . .

Mark said, with not very much enthusiasm, "There's a kegger at one of the frat houses. My roommate's going."

"What's his name?"

"Byron, but we call each other Roommate, or Matey."

"*When* is it that you'll be twenty-one?" Birdy asked.

"In three years," he said. "September first, 1997."

She sighed, leaving her own recent birthday unmentioned; they were both Virgos, it turned out, so what did she expect? "We can watch nasty TV," she suggested at last. "The triple-X station."

"Cool," said her boyfriend.

SHE LEFT Albuquerque troubled. A part of her past had
come uninvited into her present, like a canker sore, something sleeping quietly for years only to arouse and erupt.
Over spring break their first semester together, Birdy and her
poet had gone together by train from Champaign to St.
Louis for a few days. He had friends there—older than Birdy
by ten years, younger than he by twenty, former students, she
found out. They stayed with a woman who seemed reluctantly to be their host, assigning them a bedroom in her
unfinished attic—folding table and chairs, a trouble light
hanging by an orange cord over a thin foam mattress pad. In
St. Louis, where their relationship did not have to be hidden,
he became uncomfortably demonstrative, touching her face,
holding her shoulder, gripping her hand when they crossed
streets. Once, when they thought their host was safely away
at work, they'd made love in her bedroom, downstairs, where
there was heat, a real bed, a functioning toilet. Of course
she'd come home unexpectedly. Then there was some scrambling and averted eyes, some bedclothes-clutching, tiptoeing
away with sheets where there ought to have been shirts. Bare
feet.

And that wasn't the only humiliation Birdy had had to
suffer in St. Louis that spring break. She could have sung her
very own St. Louis blues. The worse thing, worse even than
being discovered in bed, was their evening at the movies,
when one of the poet's colleagues from his department—500
miles misplaced—had showed up several rows ahead of
them. The poet had been licking Birdy's face, an activity he
liked but that Birdy found bewildering, uncomfortable, odd,
and which left her vaguely sticky. She let him, figuring she
simply didn't know about this courting ritual, she was only
twenty, after all, there at the Crest Theatre, him busy tongu-

ing away at her cheek. She saw the unmistakable form of Professor Schulte enter, the department's regal Romanticist, a divorcee in her early forties, tough in class yet, according to the poet, who seemed to know all the secret foibles of his associates, fragile as a china figurine outside academe. What was she doing in St. Louis? Dr. Schulte took a seat a few rows ahead of them. Birdy hoped that she was the only one of them who'd noticed the others. But then the woman turned unerringly and met Birdy's eyes, gave her what Birdy's father would have named a withering glance. Why had feminists of Professor Schulte's generation bothered to do everything they had done, the woman's look seemed to say, just so the next set of girls to come crawling out of subjugation could wind up the playthings of old men? Or maybe she had designs on the poet herself: she was single, after all, and middle-aged. Perhaps she resented Birdy's having snapped up one of the few unmarried professors on campus. Or maybe Birdy reminded Dr. Schulte of her own daughter, which seemed the most likely explanation, and this look—pity and disappointment and annoyance at once—was the complex one Birdy's mother would have given her, if she'd been there.

Or maybe the public face-licking just disgusted her.

Birdy was glad to return to Pinetop, happy to have seen Mark, happy to have him three hours away. Their relationship was a tug-of-war, her affection one minute zealous, the next slack, the rope she held onto ambiguous.

Mrs. Anthony finished her book in late October. It was only coincidence that Birdy found out, as they ran into each other at the post office, Mrs. Anthony bundling her manuscript in a box. They hadn't seen each other since the day Mrs. A. had driven Mark out of town. Although Mark had asked Birdy to look in on his mother, she'd put it off, pretending to herself that she would do it soon. Mrs. Anthony wasn't, after all, going anywhere.

"How're you doing?" Birdy asked her, bending to retrieve her mail from her compartment. Given an opportunity, Birdy would have been perfectly willing to supply at least part of what Mark did for his mother, pick up some groceries, fill in the details of Pinetop scuttlebutt, such as she possessed.

"Absolutely fine," Mrs. Anthony said. They were studying each other's hair. Mrs. A.'s had been recently dyed, the red vibrant, deep, making her face seem even more faded. She wore a black wool suit with a bright orange blouse. Halloween was coming; this was the shirt Birdy had seen in Teresa's old bedroom, pinned to the dummy.

Birdy resorted to the obvious: "You finished with the book?"

"Yes, I suppose I am," Mrs. Anthony said, and hastened out of the small building without saying anything more, as if Birdy were contagious, the package left on the counter addressed to a Butkus Literary Agency in New York. *Somebody's Girl* winging its way to the big city, only to wing its way back, coolly rejected by the jaded mentalities of people accustomed both to calamity on a grander, grizzlier scale (serial killers and baby rapers and fist fuckers), and to prose more polished, metaphors more elegant, insights more profound. Mrs. A.'s spidery handwriting made Birdy feel tender, in spite of a niggling hurt that she hadn't been the first editor to be consulted, that her opinions mattered so little to Mrs. Anthony—when she'd come to care so much for the girl. Of course, she also felt relieved not to have to endure any more of the blatant omissions that ruined Mrs. Anthony's story. *Nobody's Girl*, it should have been titled. Nobody knew and nobody said—and nobody ever would.

Later that night, Birdy woke up distressed, suddenly certain about what she'd been talking herself out of all fall: that Mark had told his mother about their relationship. There was no other explanation for her coolness. Now, at three A.M., as Birdy lay in her bed watching the clouds fly scarily across the sky, she was convinced that Mrs. Anthony had not only seen the photograph and picture frame Birdy had given Mark, but had extracted some abashed confession from her only son about his sexual escapades of the last few months. Mrs. Anthony could very well phone the school and tell Hal Halfon to fire Birdy. Though it was true Birdy didn't particularly like Pinetop High, or Pinetop itself, and though she'd been desperate to move away, she didn't think she could bear the humiliation of losing her job, of having her colleagues tossing this gossip like a gaudy beach ball among themselves. Delighting in her demise.

In the morning she grabbed up the last of Mrs. Anthony's mementos, the box of Teresa's school papers, the photos and articles and suede wallet, and drove to the Anthonys' little house in the onion field. Outside the front door, the stack of logs seemed no smaller than it had six months earlier, as if those big ancestral cottonwoods would never run out. It had been cottonwood leaves Mark saw from his tire swing fifteen years ago, cottonwood leaves shimmering like coins under the sunlight as his sister pushed him.

Mrs. Anthony had been awake for hours, it appeared, her breakfast dishes washed, her coffeepot cleaned, the butterfly toaster cozy in place. The door to Teresa's root cellar bedroom sealed shut. Her own clothes pressed, unassailably formal, as usual. The kitchen smelled of pumpkin meat; an orange head rested on the refrigerator, leering down at the scene like a gargoyle. Birdy set Teresa's belongings on the table, glad to be free of them. Mrs. Anthony did not offer her either drink or seat; Birdy stood in that spotless primeval kitchen and simply asked, "What's wrong?"

"You have abused your position," Mrs. Anthony said, standing perfectly straight, her hands clasped at her crotch, her hair a sanguine blaze around her face. "A teacher simply does not . . ." She would not name what a teacher simply did not do. Birdy sighed. What had she expected, after all? The tidiness of the woman's shadowy kitchen struck Birdy as obscene: what use was it, all this order and arrangement and proper dress?

"It's sick," Mrs. Anthony decided.

Birdy felt her teeth grind, her face grow hot. "At least it's honest," she said. "Better to be honest with feelings than lying about them."

"And what does that mean?" asked Mrs. Anthony, perfectly composed. One of her eyes twitched, like a witch.

Where to begin? The untruths flew about in Birdy's mind like a tickertape blizzard. She started at what might have been the beginning. "Mark told me about Teresa, that she wasn't your natural daughter."

Mrs. Anthony's eye continued to twitch. "I loved Teresa as much as a mother could love a daughter. I loved that girl. That's not a lie, Ms. Stone. For more than five years, she was my girl. You show me the lie in that." Upset, she could not prevent her southern accent from shining through. Instead of *lie*, she said *la*.

Birdy successfully fought her urge to point out the domino effect Teresa's puberty suggested: the seduction of Mr. Anthony, his jealousy of the rightful boyfriend, one suicide, a murder, another suicide. She did not accuse Mrs. Anthony of abusing *her* position as author of her daughter's story, although she could have. Mrs. Anthony had not pursued the truth, had not told it when she knew it. Even if no one ever uncovered the precise answer to what happened to Teresa, oughtn't someone to raise the right questions? Surely she could see that: there were documents and evidence and, if that weren't enough, sheer instinct, the human cognition of narrative, fallible cause and mortal effect. There was passion and sex and deceit and jealousy and violence. Jesús had said it wasn't a murder mystery, and Birdy understood that he was right; it was a tragedy, just like every story. All the other genres were subsumed by that one, left stunned in the dust.

Standing across from Birdy, the woman looked held together by twine, thinly bound from toe to head like a netted creature. For Mrs. Anthony, the events would remain a mystery. Never to be resolved. Consulting the experts, the psychics and therapists and policemen and textbooks and tutors, spilling it night after night on the pages of her memoir, finally wrapping it up and sending it away—all for naught. Still it would persist, a hole in the universe, an ache in the body, the killing conviction of something gone irreparably, unbearably wrong. She would not recover. She would not heal.

"But why didn't you tell me she wasn't your daughter?" she asked, softly.

"I'm sick of hearing that, Ms. Stone, just sick to death of it, that's what everyone said when she died, that I shouldn't take it so hard—after all, that girl was *not my daughter*. Her real mama left her, just left her, like a, like a *dog* trailing after the moving van, running and running till its poor legs are worn out, and then when she died nobody batted an eyebrow."

"You can't bat an eyebrow," Birdy murmured without thinking, touching her own. She was preoccupied by the dog image.

"You know what I mean!" Isadora Anthony suddenly screamed. Birdy stepped back, put her hand to the cool deep sink behind her. "You know exactly what I mean!" Her face, for the first time since Birdy had met her, lost its fear and sternness and squeezed into fury, her hands grabbing ineffectually at the air in front of her like crabs, as if she wanted to throttle Birdy, those small hands she'd used at her antiquated typewriter, those fingers worn down like nubbed instruments by scrubbing and scrubbing her house. "You teachers who think you're so smart but you know just what I mean and you pretend you don't! You sit there feeling better than me with all your right words and your ugly questions, but *you know what I mean!*"

"I—"

"I'll tell you something else you didn't find out, I'll tell you another secret, Ms. Stone, and then you won't have to dig it up yourself. My husband was leaving me back in 1984, he'd already filled out all the papers for divorce, hired himself a lawyer. He didn't even live in this house by the time he died. I'm sure you could go snooping around and discover that, too, if you wanted. He lived over at the motel, at the Alpine Inn, you can go check the guest register there. Don't think I don't know you've been checking. He was leaving us. He was drinking too much, and hollering at all of us, taking out his anger when he was drunk, especially on Teresa, especially her. He kept saying she was ungrateful. He'd stand right here and say the most awful things to her, to that child. She was just a girl, and he hated her. I can't understand how a person could hate the way he could. But he did."

Birdy waited, reeling, attaching herself spuriously to Mrs. Anthony's accent, which grew stronger as she went along. *Law-ya,* she'd said. Now that she was talking, now that the dam had burst, what else would she let loose? And would Birdy really be up to the onslaught?

"But I didn't hate her. That girl was my life. That girl was my life. That girl," Mrs. Anthony paused to breathe, a shudder of damp air passing into the open duct of her mouth, "was *me.*" Her face was wet, trembling, wrung and dripping as a rag. She shook as if possessed by seizure, caught in a paroxysm of candor. "You cannot have my son, Ms. Stone," she said. "You simply cannot. I won't stand for it, I won't." She covered her eyes as if her sobbing could be hidden by her palms.

Birdy could do nothing but stare, leaning against the sink.

Circulation in her fingers had ceased as she pressed her weight against them. A bird twittered nervously outside, once, then again. Eventually, as if in exchange, she offered her own jugular to Isadora Anthony. "Mark's a special boy," she said unsteadily. "I care for him."

Mrs. Anthony lowered her hands, leaving a streak of her own tears on her lapels. She sagged as if her spine had dissolved, as if the net had been let loose, her rage spent.

"That's right," she said, her voice tired and flat. "That is exactly right, he is." *Eggs-ackly*, she said. *Eggs-ackly riot.*

🌹 *13*

Winter came so quickly the mushrooms froze, their hoods gone overnight from spongy to brittle, like porcelain. Birdy stomped around her scrappy yard, kicking them to bits. From her metal roof slid collapsed folds of snow, thudding like bodies as they hit the ground. Above her, Ajax and Ballard were dusted, their points and crannies suddenly appearing newly three-dimensional, as if she were seeing them through one of those old toys, the Viewmaster. In the undisturbed sparkling white surface of the driveway, Birdy lost herself as she peered not at but through the blinding silver, into oblivion.

The tree leaves as well as the window signs on Main Street had turned brilliant blaze orange: WELCOME HUNTERS. There were bargains on beer and ammo. Birdy's neighbors, the owners of motorcycles, had made the seasonal trade for snowmobiles. The noise in the morning was the same, revving engines, *vrroom, vrroom*—made flat and unresonant by the smothering snow—and the exit from the house was the same, a blue-smoked charge toward work, the machine and its helmeted rider vanishing down the street. The chickens, mercifully, did not crow. Perhaps their annual fate was to be turned to stew.

Pinetop winter had finally come to Birdy as something customary, recognizable. She knew now what to expect from her town, her trailer, her own assembly of bones.

Her black cat continued to have what the vet had euphemistically named loose bowels. The animal had survived for too long on scraps and tainted food, spoiled prey and garbage, and her system could not adjust to the richness of simple cat chow. She could not adapt to not starving, and so continued to have diarrhea, regularly, in Birdy's kitchen. Was this too high a price to pay? Birdy wondered, as she wiped up the mess every morning. Otherwise, the cat seemed happy enough. The vet had told Birdy, who'd never owned pets, that abandoned animals often made the best companions, grateful, as they were, for whatever refuge they could worm their way into. This pleased Birdy, that her new pet would have no cause for disappointment, no expectations that wouldn't be overmet.

"What's her name?" the receptionist asked as Birdy paid.

"She hasn't got one," Birdy said, afraid to choose one. "Kitty," she called her, when she came home from work, listening for the little thump the animal's weight made as it hit the floor.

At school, her students were slogging through *Romeo and Juliet.* Every day, Birdy wondered when her pal, Hal, was going to storm the room and object to the bawdiness—all these prickings and deflowerings. Surely the Christians or Mormons were going to protest? She hadn't read the play recently; she found herself impatient with it, the inevitable double suicide oppressing her pleasure in the first acts: yadda, yadda, yadda, she thought, get on with it.

In the middle of a lecture on revenge, Birdy paused, forgetting instantly what had seemed necessary to say. Words fled, due somehow to the sight of the fingers on the hands of the three girls in the front row. Brown, white, brown, they wore cheap rings, each of them, on their third fingers. Their arms were teenage arms, smooth as birch limbs, one girl's too thin, one too fat, one just right. But not right at all. Three foreheads, three faces, the palest girl lacking makeup so that she looked ill, the darkest Chicana with shaved eyebrows and black lipstick, and their legs beneath their desks, wrapped twice 'round themselves in the way only teenage girls can do, as if double-bolted, securing chastity.

"Anyhoo," Birdy said transitionally, blinking to clear the webby distraction. "What'd *you* guys think?"

Her juniors, as usual, wanted to dispute the intelligence and veracity of the characters' actions.

"Yo, Miz Stone," said checkered Ivan Greene, "why doesn't this Friar guy get off his butt and go tell Romeo what gives?"

Poppy Wilder thought it was so sad that Juliet had to die *twice*. Little Katie Steele, far too small to be a junior, just didn't get why the two lovers couldn't go off together, why there couldn't be a happy ending.

"If there's a happy ending," said Ms. Stone, bearer of bad news, "then there's no play. Where's the story if it ends happily, everybody making nice, Capulets and Montagues hugging one another at the wedding? To learn something, people have to undergo a tragedy. *Tragedy*," she repeated, her tongue stepping over the syllables as if on a pointed trident.

"Okay. Doy," said Ivan. "They can *die*, but they don't have to be so *dumb*."

Birdy was tempted to argue: yes, they had to be just that dumb, everyone had to be just exactly that dumb. Welcome to the human race. But she gave up on the lessons of suffering—they'd learn soon enough, wouldn't they, her juniors?—and moved to metaphors—what was all this night-and-day stuff, this light and dark? In the lounge, later, she found Hugh Gross. This year, they shared a planning period.

"My students think *Romeo and Juliet* sucks," she told him, popping her Fresca.

His stroboscopic face flew into nervousness, *sucks* not being a part of his working vocabulary.

"It's funny," Birdy said, dropping into the chair across the table from him, "but when I used to read that play, I identified with the lovers. This time, though, I felt so bad for the nurse. Juliet's wet nurse, remember her?"

"Oh, very well." Hugh now put concern in his eyes, lacing his fingers before him, neglecting his coffee, which sat on top of an old maroon Pinetop High yearbook. "We staged *Romeo and Juliet* a few years ago, before you got here. Abridged," he added meaningfully.

Censored, Birdy thought, then continued. "The nurse is the real tragic figure, you know, Juliet's advocate through and through, sticks by her even when the real mother and father cast her out. Remember? She basically raised Juliet, nursed her, literally nursed her, jokes with her when her mother is such a wet blanket, then ends up delivering the messages between Juliet and Romeo, standing up for true love, supplying the ladder, all that, and then," Birdy paused. Hugh now wore an interested expression, but maybe he meant only politeness, the face he adopted to pamper a raving whiner.

"Go on," he said gently.

"Well, she just does all that work of actually caring about the girl, and then she doesn't even get a speech in the end. She finds the body—it's heartbreaking—but then the real

272

parents come in and push her out of the way. Steal the scene from her—after they were ready to disown Juliet just an act earlier." There seemed to be a lump in her throat.

"Criminal," Hugh exclaimed. "*I* always identified with Friar Lorenzo, poor fellow."

"The students think he should have gotten to Romeo more quickly with that message about Juliet's fake death."

"He probably should have," Hugh admitted. "He was foolish to trust an aide."

The two of them continued sitting, thinking about the play, assigning themselves not the juicy impassioned roles, but the aged second stringers, the wrinkled peons. Maybe Hugh Gross would be Birdy's new friend. His empathetic inventory soothed her; she could probably forgive his need to belt out "Climb Every Mountain" every June. And he seemed to like her, but then, he seemed to like everyone.

"What was Mr. John's first name?" Birdy asked, suddenly thinking of this obvious question.

"Hampus," Hugh said, "Hampus John. A Swedish name. His folks both died in the second town fire, 1965."

"No wonder he was so geeked up about fires."

"Yes, there was the one he set, a few years later, but no one died in that one."

"He told me no human beans."

"Did he?" Hugh smiled. "He must have been thinking of his parents. They were painters. Their place exploded, all those old cans of paint."

"Artists?"

"No, no. No, no, no. House painters. Sign painters. Very poor, both stone deaf."

"Really?"

"Yes, so they didn't hear the alarm or the volunteer fire department siren. Hampus, Mr. John, escaped, of course, and that was how everyone learned that he could hear. For a while there had been some question as to whether he was actually retarded, or merely impaired by his parents' deafness, or possibly deaf himself. The only sure thing was that he was unaccustomed to normal interactions."

"Nobody tested him for these things?"

Mr. Gross shrugged. "We're a small town, and it was a long time ago. And it's awfully hard to diagnose a problem when there are so many variables."

True enough, true enough. Birdy wondered if her colleague were chastising her for something, instructing her in some subtle point of etiquette or wisdom. She supposed she could have liked Hampus John, if she'd known him as a child, if his mysteriously skewed life were one she wished to understand, if she'd traced for a long time the angles of the slants, the maze they made of him. Perhaps that could be said of anyone. "Where do you think he is?" she asked, honestly curious for the first time.

Hugh shook his head. "It's anybody's guess. A dog found a foot yesterday in the woods, but it turned out to be a bear's." He put on his teacher's voice, speculating about how similar the human foot was to the bear's, except that bears had no big toes. When he noticed Birdy's expression, he went back to Mr. John. "Did you hear about the missing Anasazi rug? Apparently he took it with him."

"They should check the ruins," she said. "He might have gone there." The museum exhibit had been the one thing Mr. John seemed perfectly adept at comprehending, that and his esteem for Luziana, and of course the seductive allure of nicotine.

"Somebody surely thought of looking there," Hugh said. "Maybe that's where the bear. . . . You can't help but expect the worst, can you? His capabilities are so diminished . . ." Birdy pictured Mr. John's lumbering form, bearlike himself, clodding along in his workboots, his khaki jumpsuit, the

Indian blanket someone wanted to take from him, flakes of snow caught in his prickly scrub-brush hair, his pink-rimmed creamy eyes. This drama of his couldn't turn out well. Such things never did.

"I remembered something," Hugh said, lifting his coffee cup stickily from the yearbook, which had come from the shelf across the room. "Maybe you won't be interested . . ." He opened the creaking volume and turned its glossy pages, locating what he was looking for, and swung the book so that Birdy could see. "Teresa Anthony," he said simply.

The photo showed her on stage meant to look Oriental, some parasols and rice screens dangling about, Teresa in her Yum Yum outfit, a smaller figure than Birdy had fancied, her arms open, her mouth open, as if she were offering herself to the audience. How difficult it was to read an open mouth, Birdy thought. She willed her way into the image, felt herself on the stage singing sincerely, flinging her arms open to her town, sending her sound into the voluminous atmosphere. "Hey," the voice said. Or maybe "Help."

In Teresa's suede wallet Birdy had found predictable things, a photo of a boy, no doubt torn from this same yearbook, a packet of blank hall passes, the lyrics to a sentimental love song or poem Birdy didn't recognize, and the receipt from a dress shop. That receipt, for $22, had been dated July Fourth, 1984. That was the suicide note, Birdy thought.

"Do you think she killed herself?" she now asked Hugh.

He nodded sadly. "I do. Pinetop has had more than its share of suicides. Maybe it just seems like a lot because we're a small town. Edith Pack's husband killed himself, did you know that?"

Birdy shook her head. "Homer? The photographer? I saw all his pictures at the museum." She recalled his idyllic tinting, pink cheeks and blue sky. "I wouldn't have guessed . . ."

"He had cancer, and rather than wait for it to get him, he

took the bull by the horns. A drug overdose, assisted by suffocation. I've heard that's what the Hemlock Society endorses. Edith was forced to help, at least there was a rumor to that effect, if you can feature such a thing." He shuddered, closing his eyes.

In fact, it was not difficult to imagine Edith Pack displaying hidden reserves of fortitude. The woman might, after all was said and done, turn out to make a good role model. "When was this?"

"Quite a long time ago, fifteen years at least. Just before she became secretary here. You know, the museum was almost entirely her doing. She put all of their money into it, it's what Homer intended as a legacy."

"That's why she doesn't like Mrs. Anthony," Birdy said deductively. "Remember when I asked her about the Anthonys, and she told me Isadora Anthony should have been making lemonade?"

"Well," said Hugh, grimacing in the alarming way he had. "Some can."

"Some can," Birdy agreed.

"Are you cold?" he asked, when she shivered.

"It's always cold in here," Birdy said, although that wasn't why she quaked.

"It is cold, isn't it?" Hugh agreed. "Let me turn up the thermostat for you, Birdy."

THE PHONE rang one morning just as she was sealing her kitty in her kitchen for the day. The three necessary pans, in ascending size, she'd laid before the sink: food, water, sand. She'd bundled herself against the wind, muffler, hat, coat, and gloves, and could barely hear through the woolen layers her father's distant voice.

"Birdy," he said, "this is your father."

His identifying himself gave Birdy a two-pronged twinge: familiar exasperation as well as bemused affection. He'd never been comfortable talking on the telephone, even less so on the long-distance meter, and this distress was evidently unchanged. "Everything is fine, now," he went on, "but there's been an accident." He then proceeded to tell her that Becca's baby, nearly seven months in utero, had died inside her. Birdy sank into a chair, her various winter garments and purse and sack lunch and backpack forgotten around her.

"Oh no," she uttered, tears unsummoned in her eyes, blurring the room into simple shapes and colors, silver square, white fan, red and green and yellow cylinders. Her father was silent. "Should I come home?" she asked him.

"Well . . ." he said.

"I'll phone her. Can I phone her? Where is she?"

"She's home. She's had a hard time of things. She had to deliver the . . ." he broke off, his voice doing something Birdy had never heard it do before. It kindled a like break in her own throat. "She had to go through delivery," he said.

"Oh, Dad."

All that day, Birdy felt she lived as a member of her family once more, putting her father and sister among her more charitable thoughts for the first time in a very long time. Her father's focusing on the delivery of the dead child betrayed his new intimacy with childbirth and its course; he had witnessed his twins' births where his first children, Birdy and Becca, had been born during a time when men's role in the process was waiting, sequestered in a distant bland room, armed with cigars. "Do you need any money?" her father had asked, before hanging up this morning. The question came from his old stockpile of lines, as if he had slipped into a position he occupied fifteen years earlier, half her lifetime ago, ready to advance her allowance. He seemed to be using this latent aspect of his character and its part in Birdy's life to cover the new person he was, shelter it, disguise it. Perhaps he feared her scorn, feared she would trample his tenderness. As always, he was telling her, he could support her financially—just don't bank on that other warm fuzzy business.

When she phoned Becca that evening, she thought of their mother, who had always been able to keep the girls straight, over the phone and in her memory. Their two voices had never confused her; their escapades remained individual. Her specific attention to the tiny details of their lives Birdy had appreciated, by and large, where Becca had grown to resent it, had found it cloying. Their father's habit of treating the girls as a unit, interchangeable, dimly perceived, suited Becca. She thrived under his general, topical concern, while Birdy mourned her mother's particular eye and ear, the person to whom she never had to identify herself when she phoned. "Hi," she would say, one single utterance and her mother would promptly answer, "Hello, my Bird."

Maybe Becca missed their mother now, too. Birdy was dying to simply say, "Hi Becca," and proceed from there. But she'd forgotten her sister's number, and when she found it and dialed, no one answered. Their answering machine was not in operation; what message, after all, would seem suitable? Birdy imagined them all, her nephews, her stepbrothers, her father and stepmother and sister and brother-in-law—her family—sitting in church, heads bowed in a line as they occupied a long pew. She knew they weren't at church, didn't, any of them, attend church, but that was how she saw them tonight, grieving in a dark cathedral over their lost little girl.

In the kitchen, with her sick kitty, she lit the novena candles Mrs. Morales had given her last summer, Saints Jude and Dymphna, hopelessness and nerves, and stared into the steady yellow flames as if into the soothing eyes of some larger force, beacons from another world, one with a method beyond her temporal understanding.

MARK MADE no plans to return home until Thanksgiving. This seemed correct to Birdy—he'd been a long time under his mother's watchful eye. He wanted weaning.

On Thanksgiving morning, snow began falling, this time the festive variety that signaled Christmas, holidays, gifts. It was fresh and thick, blanketing the trees and hills, hiding all the ugliness of what had disintegrated or been dumped during the autumn. Birdy busied herself planning the Thanksgiving meal she would share with Mark; he would come in the evening, having eaten a noon feast with his mother. He could eat all day long, ham and pie and pudding and yams, banquet after banquet, without bursting, without complaint, the appetite of a ravenous growing boy. In her house, Birdy worked, happily whistling, stuffing the small bird, peeling four potatoes, making a pan of rolls, listening to music Jesús had left for her, a tape of Barbra Streisand. At school, the new Spanish teacher had a wooden leg. He also had a pregnant wife and three other children. It wasn't that he wasn't friendly, it was just that he wasn't Birdy's friend, the way Jesús was. A flash of longing came over her; what she wouldn't give to hear that slug bug quacking outside her door, to lounge in the perfect warmth of his mother's home watching the biggest television in town. She liked to think Jesús missed her as much as she did him, but she had her doubts. Those foul postcards he'd promised never materialized. Moreover, his returning to Pinetop would mean failure, and Birdy didn't suppose it was seemly to wish his romance to go sour.

She put him out of her head, willed herself to think of other things. She was cooking, sipping at a tiny decorative glass of brandy, Mark was coming. "See you on Turkey day!" he'd said, signing off their last phone conversation. She'd changed the bedsheets and laundered her silk pajamas. She wore no underwear. In the single letter she'd received from him since her visit in October, he'd told her he now understood why she'd said his name was ironic.

Ironic, Birdy thought. A fellow reeking haddock.

The world, today, seemed insulated and small, muffled pleasantly, a village in a fairy-tale forest, her trailer a lighted box of warmth. They would make love in the eager, exuberant way Mark made love, his body as fit and elegantly clumsy as a young animal's. He would insist on his being in love with her, and she would insist that he wasn't, laughing. He would sleep heavily in her arms, utterly dead in slumber right beside her for an hour or so before she made him go home to his mother. This was how she liked him best: her angel, beside her, asleep. Birdy hadn't realized how much she missed him until she'd begun anticipating his arrival. Now she knew.

"Here," she said to the cat, tossing its way the turkey's liver. If the animal were going to get sick anyway, why not on a sumptuous bloody organ?

But then twilight settled, like the snow, deeper and deeper, and Mark did not come. When he didn't, Birdy knew he never would again. The certainty descended coldly, a fatal fact. Get real, she told herself, considering the brandy in its now-sticky snifter, tossing it back like something medicinal. His deserting her was inevitable, she'd understood that, hadn't she, deep down in her tragic heart? All the important things ended, that's what literature had been teaching Birdy for years. Hadn't she been paying attention? Didn't the rules apply to her, too?

But how had loving her student become an important thing? How had he even known she would respond to his touch, those many months ago, when he'd bravely laid his hand over hers? What a forward move, for such a backward boy, she his superior, he a mere pupil. And now here he was making a similarly forward move, leaving her. How dare he perform so mature a deed?

The bird's button had long ago popped, the rolls browned, the potatoes gone soft, then scorched. If she'd lit the candles, they would have been puddles of warm wax by now. The brandy bottle was empty. Full darkness had fallen, and then been followed by yet more snow. It wasn't hard to imagine disappearing beneath its thick cold claim. When Birdy left the kitchen unsteadily, abandoning the ruined meal, the cat wailed, scratched on the door separating her from her human, baldly appealing to be permitted to follow. Idly, Birdy wondered if Isadora Anthony felt like a victor, harboring her spoils. She knew her own loss of Mark would soon occupy her with a loser's repertoire—sorrow, anger, shame—but it was too fresh to quite defeat her now. She was loopy from drink, and trace elements of hope still circulated, love's mute optimistic residue. Losing love would leave a cavity, a dark little private hole, one that would make all simple pleasures and necessities nearly impossible. Aching bite of apple, milky chill of French vanilla, and the tongue's blind probing, unable to leave unwell-enough alone.

Flushed, she turned over other thoughts, patient with them. She wondered if Mrs. Anthony had mentioned her in her book, for instance, thanked her for all her help. She had been of some help, she believed, feeling forgiving of the woman at this moment, Mrs. Anthony with her primly wrapped manuscript. Hadn't it been Birdy who excised those misplaced modifiers and conflicting points of view, those hackneyed phrases and stale images, helped Mrs. A. find new ways of saying the same old things: a heart was broken, a world was falling apart, a person felt like dying?

So what if a few of the salient facts had gone unmentioned?

Birdy allowed as she no longer cared to know if Teresa were pregnant with somebody's baby, nor did it matter if there had been a faint remnant of the girl's skin on the cigarette lighter in the father's wrecked car. It didn't make any difference who was sleeping with whom at the Alpine Inn. She no longer wondered if all of Pinetop High had been sitting in the cliff dwelling, audience to a final performance, looking over their beer cans and joints at the little town in the distance where they'd been born, where the garish fireworks symbolizing their independence lit the night, while one of their own sailed over the edge, right before their eyes, to her theatrical end. Perhaps the girl had chosen to walk barefoot and in a brand new dress, open-mouthed, off that cliff because it had seemed she was stepping into the stars, or perhaps because it had seemed the only thing possible to do with a life like hers: end it. And maybe she was right.

How Birdy's own mother would have wept, knowing what Birdy was thinking. To kill oneself was to perpetrate the most heinous of crimes against a mother. You might as well plunge a knife directly in her heart. But Birdy's mother wasn't around to suffer; Birdy's car sat in the drive, and the cliff wasn't very far. Gravity, as far as she knew, still prevailed. And look at this loungewear, seductive and pretty.

"Stop your whining!" she suddenly yelled at the cat, struggling up from hot bleariness. Where was the groveling gratitude she'd been promised by the vet? Too easily Birdy could envision her own rage, her own desire to scoop up the animal and hurl her out into the cold. "Stop!" She stomped her foot, shaking the whole teetering house. Immediately the desperate noise ceased.

Mark wasn't going to call her tonight, nor was her sister, still busy with her grief, withstanding it without Birdy's assistance. Neither could she count upon her father. Her stomach rumbled with emptiness but now she did not trust herself to eat: what if she choked, drunk and alone here in her house? Who would take her in his arms and supply the lifesaving squeeze, dislodge what would otherwise surely kill her?

Who would bother with her sorry self? Birdy took a quick inventory, faces scrolling dizzily before her as if on that microfiche machine at the newspaper office until she hit upon Luziana's, and there was stopped, caught by surprise. A strange alarm instantly began forming, it felt like frost, spreading from her toes to her head, tingling icily. It had been a long time since she'd thought of Luziana. Luziana had come to her house last summer and Birdy had not even bothered to open the door, had hidden away from the girl and her nameless baby. Mark had been there, so that was one excuse, and then there was the everpresent mystery of dead Teresa Anthony, which was another. But what had Luziana wanted, back then? Never mind the dead girl, what had the *living* girl needed from Birdy?

It was very late when she threw open her little trailer door, welcoming the polar clarity as it washed around her. Tencha had strung some red Christmas lights around her salon, which blinked gaudily, as if announcing a house of ill repute. Over her pajamas Birdy had tied her coat, on her feet pulled socks and boots, then stepped into the silent holiday aftermath, instantly sober. Few houses remained lit, everyone sleeping heavily from a big meal, the odor of wood smoke lingering.

She made her way toward the Rillos house, slipping in her slick-soled boots, silk cuffs swishing interestingly. She tried to feel confident she'd find the place sated and tucked in as all the rest—flesh-toned Cadillacs on the front yard, infant peaceful in her crib. Still, a conviction seized Birdy like an ice-hardening body of water. She had been marshaling the wrong evidence, had, for the last six months traced a perfectly profitless life in lieu of an essential one. There'd been the girl in the book, a total fiction, and then the genuine article, just down the street.

"You are a fathead," she told herself as she rushed along. That was her mother's word, fathead, and it comforted Birdy to have it sitting in her mouth. How in the world could Birdy have lost sight of Luziana?

There was only one car in the Rillos yard now, covered with a flawless sparkling blanket of snow, and not one footprint leading to or from the porch. Maybe they had all driven away in the other Caddy, left Pinetop just like everyone else who mattered to Birdy. Maybe Birdy was too late.

She stepped over a short fence, stumbling upon a row of those plastic milk jugs, frozen solid, and this noise set off the dogs in the yard behind, their yelps so blunted by the snow they sounded as if they were being strangled. Birdy cursed, "Fuck, fuck, fuck," making her way along the side of the house, hand scraping the brick, to the window that she hoped was Luziana's. Its lacy curtains were drawn, but a sliver of light burned through the scalloped edges. Birdy rapped quietly on the glass, waiting, wondering what she'd do if Mr. Rillos, wild-haired and crazed, appeared brandishing the shotgun he probably kept for just such occasions.

But the curtains shifted gauzily and there was Luziana's vaguely expectant, stunning face, staring right into hers like an answer, like a reflection in a mirror. They blinked at each other; Birdy did not think she could stand to see Luziana drop that curtain closed between them. She could not endure another rejection.

"Hey Miz Stone." Luziana's warm breath fogged the glass. For a second Birdy thought she could feel the moisture, as if she'd spoken herself, so near were they to each other. This was the first person she'd seen or spoken to today; it mattered a great deal that Luziana was here, alive, well, and in possession of Birdy's name. "Come around," the girl went on, motioning with her hand, "and I'll let you in."

Birdy was tired. Thanksgiving had passed, lapsing into the day after. The feasting weekend would be a long one, and on Monday all the students would be hopelessly distracted; Christmas was coming, they were still seventeen. Snow fell, on and on, like a bag of loosed feathers, like a shaggy dog joke. Tomorrow, the town's mountains would sport another new look, their crevices and pits emphatic black granite next to dazzling white, gruffly imposing, immortally, inhumanly beautiful. As she stomped her feet on the back stoop, listening for the door to open, Birdy cast herself back to last spring. In her mind's eye, she could clearly see Luziana as she'd been then, when her baby lived inside her, when she still attended school, sitting in her melancholy pose, lifting the massive, overwhelming anthology, her skinny arm a mere flower stem, weak under the weight of all the sad stories.

ABOUT THE AUTHOR

ANTONYA NELSON was born and raised in Wichita, Kansas. She has published three collections of short stories—*The Expendables, In the Land of Men,* and *Family Terrorists*—and a novel, *Talking in Bed.* Her short fiction has been published in *The New Yorker, Story, Esquire, Redbook, Mademoiselle,* and other publications. She teaches in the creative writing programs at New Mexico State University and Warren Wilson College. She divides her time between Las Cruces, New Mexico, and Telluride, Colorado, with her husband, the writer Robert Boswell, and their children.